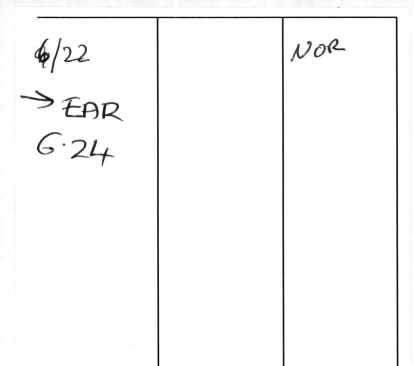

6/22

→ EAR

6.24

NOR

This book should be returned/renewed by the latest date shown above. Overdue items incur charges which prevent self-service renewals. Please contact the library.

Wandsworth Libraries
24 hour Renewal Hotline
01159 293388
www.wandsworth.gov.uk

Wandsworth

DOMESTIC BLISS AND OTHER DISASTERS

by

Jane Ions

Bluemoose

Copyright © Jane Ions 2021

First published in 2021 by
Bluemoose Books Ltd
25 Sackville Street
Hebden Bridge
West Yorkshire
HX7 7DJ

www.bluemoosebooks.com

British Library Cataloguing-in-Publication data
A catalogue record for this book is available from the British Library

Paperback 978-1-910422-72-4

Printed and bound in the UK by Short Run Press

Joyce Anderson née Eggleston 1921–2010

Thank you so much, Mum, for giving us a sense
of humour, and showing us how to use it.

XXXX

Chapter 1 – June

I have two very close friends who I've known for most of my life and I don't get on with either of them. Despite the long years during which we have remained friends, if they and I were stuck in a lift together for thirty-six hours, I am not confident that all three of us would emerge without wounds.

I'm comfortable with this, because a combative togetherness is what we have grown to expect from each other. We don't always see eye to eye, we are more likely to see eye to the back of the other's head, but up until now we have observed the three basic rules which determine whether a friendship will survive. We make an effort to meet up, we don't punish each other by being too successful and, very occasionally, we're honest with each other.

So when Jen told me what she was planning to do, I thought she was crazy, and said so. I said I didn't think she'd be daft enough to agree to it. I tried to make her reconsider, but now it's too late, she's done it.

She is leaving. She has sold the house she loves, and she has left her job at the doctor's surgery which has given us so many curious insights into human nature over the years. She has said goodbye to her treasured garden and her favourite coffee shop, and to me, her closest friend. Why? So that she can move three hundred miles north to be her daughter's child-minder.

When Jen first told me of this plan, I wanted to save her from this surge of self-annihilating maternal instinct. I felt that she was sacrificing herself on an altar to her grandchildren. The plan reminded me of a nature programme I watched years

1

ago. It featured a spider who carried her eggs around on her back until they hatched, and then she lay down and allowed her infants to eat her alive to save them the trouble of looking for food elsewhere. I shouted at the television, 'Get up! Get up and shake them off!' But her infants were chewing at her ears, so she didn't hear me.

Obviously, I needed to be more subtle with Jen. I couldn't suggest to her that she shake her grandchildren off. So I just asked her whether she thought she was doing the right thing by giving everything up to become her grandchildren's child-minder. In my experience, *Are you sure you're doing the right thing?* is a very unsettling question. It engenders a sense of dread. I'm always quite happy with my decisions until someone asks me whether I've made the right ones. Then in an instant my resolve is shaken, I think I've made the wrong decisions, and I'm doomed if I don't change course.

So I asked Jen whether she thought she was making the right decision to move north to provide childcare for her grandchildren, and then I followed that up by saying it sounded like banishment into servitude to me. I said, far be it from me to interfere in a family decision, but I thought this family decision was completely wrong-headed. I said going into exile to be an unpaid child-minder was a terrible idea from her point of view, and she should be fighting it, not embracing it.

Jen understood that my reasons for wanting her to stay put were purely selfish. She knows as well as I do that a friendship built up over more than twenty years is not easily replaced, however dysfunctional it might have turned out to be. It takes years to know someone well enough to tell them they're an idiot. So instead of telling me to butt out and shut up and mind my own business, she said more tactfully that I might be putting a rather negative spin on things. She said it would be wonderful to see more of her grandchildren, of course it would. This could only be a good thing, surely?

I told her that the problem here is not that she will see more of her grandchildren, the problem is that she will see no-one *but* her grandchildren, and how could that possibly be a good thing? I reminded her that she is still young, only fifty. Her own youngest has only just left home. These should be her Prosecco years, not more years of baby formula and disposable nappies and whoops-never-mind-I-didn't-like-that-necklace-anyway. She should be letting her hair down, not tying her hair back to keep it out of the zinc ointment and whatever else might be going on close by.

Jen said she took my point, but she was in a difficult position. Her daughter Emily had suggested the move, telling her that the twins missed her and loved her so much and wanted her to look after them when their mummy and daddy were at work. Emily said she knew how devoted Jen was to her grandchildren, and it would be wonderful if she moved north and they could all be together. Jen didn't think she could then say to her daughter, 'Actually Emily, I think I'll pass on that one if you don't mind.' And so the plan has rolled on to fruition. And now she's gone.

Just before Jen left, but after she was committed to the move, she had a little panic about moving out of the city and living in the country, on the edge of a small town. She said it's probably irrational, but fields make her nervous. She was anxious because for the first time in her life she will not be able to hear the soothing background noise of a big city when she falls asleep at night. She'll miss the planes overhead, the thrum of traffic, car doors slamming shut, intermittent sirens, and voices calling to each other across the street. She said without her metropolitan lullaby it would be too quiet in the country, and too dark at night. She would find it impossible to sleep, tossing and turning in the peace and quiet, missing the orange glow of city lights and having to make do with moonlight. It was as if an umbilical cord she had relied on all her life would suddenly be cut, and she would be set adrift, diminished and diminishing. Uncorked. She would be so far away, with no friends and just her family for company, contemplating the severed end of her umbilical cord and losing substance.

I said I would visit her, and told her she could come back and stay with me whenever she liked. Her chin began to wobble, and it wobbled in a way that was not consistent with great anticipatory joy at being an on-tap grandma.

For her sake if not my own, I tried to think of some positives. I said I'd heard there were roads in the north you could drive on for over an hour without stopping, and there are hills up there with actual points on the top, and you can buy a nice little house and garden without mortgaging your DNA. There's space up there and clean air to breathe, and proper Yorkshire pudding. I said, no matter how far north, I'd come and see her, once she claimed some territory and secured her borders.

She said she would be on the wrong side of the country for proper Yorkshire pudding, but she was looking forward to getting her teeth into some Cumberland sausage. She is going to view a nice little house, perfectly adequate, a fraction of the price of her house down here, and after selling up she now has money in the bank which she plans to be very vague about when talking to her family. She quite liked the idea of living a more simple life, without clutter and surplus possessions to tie her down. I asked her where she would put her collection of thirty-eight china cruet sets. She said she has already sold them on eBay to someone who should have known better, and she hopes they like fannying around with a duster.

So, she left yesterday, we embraced on the pavement and she got into her little Polo and headed off towards the M25. I can hardly believe it, after all the confidences we have shared over the years during our more harmonious exchanges. I am the only other person in the world who knows what her husband used to shout during sex. You have to know someone really well before they tell you that kind of thing. It's not something you would share with a work colleague. If someone tells you that kind of detail about their life you know you are a trusted friend.

Anyway, it's academic now because the poor chap died of a heart attack during a surprise quickie before *Match of the Day*. He managed to shout out, apparently, but Jen said as last words go, his weren't very profound. She certainly couldn't put 'Goal!' on his tombstone.And now Jen has sold up and gone, and left me with her confidences and her pot plants. There's twenty of them in my front garden huddled together in pots of various sizes. They look as if they are hatching a plot to trot off after her.

It will be a while before I see Jen again, so I won't be sitting down with her to talk about Dan. Dan has come home from university with debts and no means to support himself. He is at a loose end. He is ranging about the house picking things up and putting them down again and staring out of the window and asking me what I do all day. It would be great to have him around the house again, if he wasn't giving every impression of having stumbled into the wrong life.

Dan told me last week that his latest plan is to make a living from performance art. I don't like to undermine him but, to be brutally honest, I can't work up any enthusiasm for this performance art career plan. Maybe I lack vision, or faith in miracles, but performance art seems to me to be a precarious career choice, compared to say, training as an accountant. I'm not saying Dan should abandon performance art and train as an accountant, but I had hoped that he might settle on something that would combine both strengths. Although I admit there aren't many performing accountants making a go of it out there.

If I had suspected for a while that he was planning to make a living as a performance artist I would have had time to get into the brace position. But he sprang this idea on me before I could think of a smooth and well-formed response, so my initial response leapt out, ill-formed and covered in verbal spikes. I used words like 'idiotic' and 'stupid' and 'completely mad', words that you should try to avoid in these situations. And now Dan's gone off in a huff. Thinking about it more calmly and with the benefit of hindsight, I should never have said that I have been putting on premenstrual performances for years and no-one has ever paid me a penny.

In truth though, your children should learn to give you warning when they intend to make sudden announcements about their future, then you would have time to buttress yourself against involuntary shrieking. If you had advance warning of them telling you 'I'm going to ride a unicycle around the equator to raise money for orphaned parrots', you might be able to say, 'That's an interesting idea, let's take a moment to consider it', instead of saying, 'What? Like hell you are! Stuff the bloody parrots!'

It's being caught off guard that's the problem; it can make us sound so unsympathetic. It's the element of surprise we can't cope with, not just the idiotic proposal itself. Years ago, Laura came home from school and said to me, 'Mum, I've told Sarah we'll look after her pet rats when she's on holiday.' I think we were both surprised by my response.

Anyway, Dan has gone off to contemplate my lack of sympathy for his life, leaving me to think about my unsympathetic maternal responses to his plans. Maybe I wasn't very sympathetic but... a career in performance art? Give me strength. Better still, give me his university tuition fees back, if this is where it's got us.

Also, I could do with talking to Jen about Laura. There's something going seriously wrong there. We were so pleased, Jen and I, when Laura got married last year, but now she's had a baby and she keeps ringing me up and asking me why I didn't warn her about what a massive commitment it is to have a child. She says she didn't realise what she was taking on and I should have made it clear to her, warned her. I don't know how much clearer I could have made it, I've done my maternal best for her for twenty-six years – you would have thought she'd got the message that having children isn't exactly a rest cure. Apparently, I should have sat Laura down and explained to her that her life would never be the same again.

Jen and I used to have a bit of a rueful laugh about the belief entertained by most expectant parents that that they will be able to have children and carry on their lives unchanged afterwards. From our perspective, it seemed akin to thinking you could invite a rhinoceros into your home and hardly notice it. But now Jen's left, it doesn't seem quite so amusing.

***

Dan and I had a little heart to heart discussion this morning, or perhaps it was more of a spleen to spleen. He told me, *apropos* of my wake-up-and-smell-the-coffee career advice the other day, that I trample over his dreams. I told him I was having a few nightmares that he might be responsible for. He said the trouble with me was that I had lost my creative energy, my joie de vivre, my sense that anything is possible if you just have the passion to make it happen. He said his driving force was Carpe Diem.

I thanked Dan for pointing out what the trouble with me was, and at the same time I warned him that it was entirely possible to Carpe the wrong Diem. That's the trouble with all these little life-affirming slogans painted on wooden boards in gift shops. The last one of those I saw was in 'Coffee and Toffee' with Jen, and it said, 'All You Need is Love.' She looked at it and said to me, 'Well, that's a lie for a start.' And it is.

Anyway, I had the feeling this morning that Dan was building up to telling me something, so I was readying myself for another hare-brained scheme, but still, when it came it was a shock. He began by saying he needed some independent living space, and at first I thought, oh – he's going to move out, he has somewhere to go, maybe a friend with a spare room. He'd have to pay rent of course, so that would mean getting a proper job. We could be moving in the right direction here, I thought.

But that wasn't it. He wasn't planning to move out and get a proper job, he was planning to construct an extension to our house from recycled materials and live there independently, apart from meal times, which he would share with us. I said, after collecting my thoughts which were bouncing erratically around the room, 'But Dan, you have no experience of building anything. You can't build a shelter just like that, with no experience.'

Apparently, I'm wrong. More than half the world builds rooms and whole houses without any formal training at all. None. Dan explained to me that if mankind had needed an NVQ in Building and Construction to build a shelter, we would only just be moving out of caves. He said the Ancient Egyptians had built the pyramids without an NVQ between them.

I tried to be reasonable. I said I took my hat off to the Ancient Egyptians. I said credit where credit's due, the pyramids are stunning. They are all beautifully proportioned, and every single one of them is the right way up. But things were different then, there were no health and safety regulations, people didn't want windows, and the flat roof hadn't been invented. And then I changed tack because I thought I might be talking rubbish, and I reminded Dan that he always hated his Meccano set. He was always losing the little screws and wanting to use nails.

Dan said this would be nothing like building with Meccano, he would be using recycled materials, crates and plastic bottles and the kind of stuff you see at recycling banks. It would be intimately eco-friendly.

So I said – again too spontaneously – 'My God, Dan, you can't be serious! You might as well go down to the recycling bank and carve out some sort of burrow for yourself and live there like a derelict Hobbit. *Carpe diem*? You need to *carpe* some common sense.'

He said I was mocking his ambition, and I had no faith in his ability to make something beautiful out of rubbish. I told him a building made of rubbish would very likely look like rubbish. Sad, but true. He said it would be the best showcase for his performance art, and I said it would knock £50,000 off the value of our house. There was no meeting of minds. His

8

mind was in the sky, my mind was on the ground. He didn't mind, and I did.

Jen texted me just after dinner, to say How r u doing?

I texted her back, Fine. I've fallen out with Dan over career plans.

But it's good to spork, she texted. She had obviously had a tiring day. Glad you're ok. I'm feeling low. Grandchildren wonderful but v young. Maybe I need a man? Think I do. Lonely here.

Chapter 2 – July

I spoke to Bill last night about Dan's rubbish extension. Bill is Dan's father, and I like him to be fully briefed on all his son's eccentricities. I don't believe in shielding him from his children's bizarre decisions just because he's a very busy man. I tell him as soon as I see him if either of his children plan to do something particularly stupid. So I outlined Dan's plan to build a one-bed studio out of waste products to the side of our house, and Bill said, 'Why not let him do it? If he's adding an annexe made of plastic milk bottles to the side of our house, he won't have time to hang around the pub hoping someone will buy him a drink. Much better to have him working out how to construct a bachelor pad out of the contents of our recycling bins. If it falls down around him, at least it's not likely to be very heavy; he should survive it.'

I thought about it and decided there might be something in that argument. If Dan is building a rubbish annexe, then he's not doing anything worse, and this should be a cause for celebration.

So, I have given Dan the go-ahead to throw rubbish at our house, and he and I are friends again. He asked me this lunchtime if I would collect all our used plastic bottles because he will need them for his window installations. His construction will be called 'Aspire'. It will speak to his generation and say, *Re-Cycle and Build your Life!* Unfortunately though, when it speaks to my generation it will say, *There's a Pile of Crap Stuck to the Side of your House!*

I got my hair done this afternoon. Highlights and a trim. Abbi usually does it, but she was off today because she has accidentally poked herself in the eye with her contact lens, so Denise did it. She looked about the same age as Dan, and we got chatting while she was wasting yards of tin foil putting highlights in my hair.

I asked her if she was living at home still, or if she had a place of her own. She said she was living at home with her parents. I said that's nice, but apparently it's not. She said her parents complain about her all the time. Oh dear, I said, why is that? Thing is, she said, she has to put her earphones in as soon as she gets home from work, so she doesn't have to listen to her mum and dad talking, and she spends as much time as she can in her bedroom on Facebook and Instagram. Well, I said, clutching at straws in what seemed to be a pretty bleak landscape, I expect you all watch a bit of telly together in the evenings? No, she said, she doesn't watch telly hardly at all. Sometimes she takes her dinner upstairs into her room and eats it there.

I looked at her in the mirror and thought she must be a little ray of absolute sunshine to live with, and I felt better about Dan at least talking to me about his plan to live in a pile of rubbish at the side of the house.

When Denise was finished with my hair she asked me if I would like tea or coffee, so sweetly that her mother would have swooned to hear it. I declined politely, because I wasn't quite sure what she might do to it, given that I was the same generation as her parents. So off she went for half an hour, leaving me with my hair all packed away in neat parcels of tin foil, reading a copy of *Hello!* like an extra-terrestrial searching for some meaning to life on Earth.

I rushed off to meet my friend Judith in Marks and Spencer's café after my hair. Judith and I were at school together, I've known her longer than Jen, but we have just started meeting up more regularly again. Judith has three adult children, and they

11

are all, every one, doing extremely well. I try not to let her talk about her children if possible. There's one at Oxford University and one at Cambridge University and another one shitting gold bars somewhere in America. You'd think she'd have the decency not to mention them, but no, as soon as the toasted tea cakes arrived she told me that the one at Cambridge is going to do a PhD in something very clever, Neurofuckingology I think she said, and then she waited for me to be very impressed. She wanted me to say, 'Wow! Neurofuckingology? How amazing! That's so clever! Wow!' But instead I said, 'Shall I pick up a pot of jam to go with these teacakes?'

Judith doesn't give up easily. She ignored the jam query and told me that when her daughter gets this PhD, she'll have a very lucrative future in plastic polymers. I told her to try not to get upset about it, it would probably turn out all right in the end.

Honestly, it does me no good to meet up with Judith. I'm a nice person when we sit down together but, by the time we leave, I'm not. I don't bear her any ill-will, I just wish she didn't exist. We're meeting up again in a fortnight.

Bill's mother is coming to us tomorrow for lunch, so there will be conversation then of a different kind. My mother-in-law usually comes with an agenda of topics she'd like to talk about, and once she's gone through the list she starts again at the beginning. Last time she came, Bill excused himself when she'd gone full circle and begun again, saying this was where he came in.

***

Bill's mother, Ella, comes to us most Sundays for lunch. When she came in today she said that we seemed to have a small shanty town springing up to the side of our house, and what was the problem exactly? I said not to worry, it was a project Dan was involved in. She said good, she was glad he was making himself useful, and the sooner he got the whole lot cleared away, the better.

Dan opened his mouth to say something, but I caught his eye and gave him a look which meant, 'Don't stir this pot Daniel, your grandmother will never approve of any plan to build with recycled packaging materials, however eco-friendly you tell her this is.' It was necessarily a complex look, but Dan understood my meaning, and he didn't say anything. Instead we covered the usual topics over lunch, including all the old favourites. We discussed how difficult it is to get good help in the garden, how lucky you are to have good help in the house, how there is no-one around to help you in the bank, and so on and so forth.

Problems with her high street bank are exercising Ella particularly at the moment. She said she used to go in there and have a chat with the bank tellers, and they all knew her name, and they helped her out if she made a mistake when she had to fill in forms. Her visits were a pleasant experience. But now when she goes to the bank and is confronted with all those machines lining the walls, the atmosphere is hostile. She says she may as well be in an episode of Dr Who. She daren't interact with the machines in case they start flashing and shouting 'Exterminate!' and waving little stalks at her. Dan loved the idea and said if the cash machines did that he would look for a job in a bank.

After lunch Ella likes to reminisce. She asked us if we could remember Lily Cooper, originally from Bolton, who used to keep a horse in the field behind her house in the country. Ella had urgent news concerning Lily, so she pressed us to remember her. We did our best. We racked our brains to remember Lily Cooper. You must remember her, said Ella, you were so fond of her horse. We tried to remember her horse, we tried to recall our fondness for the horse, we tried to visualise the field, the horse, the woman, the horse in the field, the woman on the horse, Bolton, women in general – but we drew a blank.

We confessed, and said we just couldn't remember Lily Cooper, or her horse, or our love for her horse. But tell us about her anyway, we said, it might jog our memory.

'Well', said Ella, 'she's dead. Died last Tuesday of a stroke.'

Oh. We looked at each other. That's that then. We can't remember her – and now she's dead. There was a general sense of relief. 'How's the horse?' said Daniel.

I got up to make the coffee, and when I brought it in on a tray, Daniel had gone out somewhere, to see someone about something. Bill thought he would take his coffee upstairs because he had to do some preparation for a meeting tomorrow, if we two ladies didn't mind. Go ahead, I said, your mum and I will chat over coffee. No problem.

So Ella and I drank our coffee, and I heard about her dizzy spells and her constipation and all the kind of stuff that men can't be trusted with. We puzzled over that little rash that won't go away. Ella said it was a shame the rash was on her bottom, because she thought it would benefit from being exposed to some fresh air. After about half an hour Ella asked me if I remembered Jill Robertson. I said – is she dead? She said no, she's having the outside of her house painted buttermilk yellow.

Oh good. Better news for Jill.

Daniel rang me when Bill was taking his mother home. He doesn't usually ring when he's out so I was expecting trouble. 'Mum,' he said, 'I'm bringing a friend round. She's going to help me with Aspire, but she hasn't eaten for a few days so I've asked her round for the rest of that roast.'

'Why hasn't she eaten for a few days?' I asked him. He said he didn't know, he hadn't asked her, and anyway, it was none of our business. I said I thought it was our business if she was going to turn up and eat the rest of our roast.

Anyway, Daniel arrived with Gentle Rain at about ten o'clock, just as Bill and I were going to watch the News.

***

Yes, Dan's friend is called Gentle Rain. She has long blonde hair and a sweet smile and she came in and said softly, 'Hello

Daniel's mum, I'm Gentle Rain'. I'd had a glass or so of wine by then and I said, 'Hello Gentle Rain, pleased to meet you. I'm Big Roast Dinner'. Bill laughed but Daniel didn't.

Anyway, both Dan and Gentle Rain tucked in to what was left of the roast, despite Gentle Rain having qualms about eating meat. I had to reassure her that the lamb had been organically farmed and ethically reared and had frolicked all summer long among buttercups and daisies and died of an excess of happiness and a longing to swim in gravy and mint sauce. I don't know whether I convinced her, but her appetite did. She ate everything on her plate.

They slept out under the stars last night in sleeping bags at the side of the house. I said I didn't think that was a very good idea, but Dan said it was.

***

Jen rang me this morning. She said she had caught a stomach bug from Tiffany, one of the twins, but she was looking after Sammy, the other twin, because he was sickening for it now and he couldn't go to Tumble Tots.

I said, 'For heaven's sake Jen, you can't be expected to look after Sammy if you're not well yourself. They're asking too much of you.'

But she changed the subject in that rather annoying way she sometimes does, and said, 'How's Dan?'

So I told her we were letting him build an extension made of rubbish on the side of the house and he was planning to live in it. I said we weren't happy about it but we were hoping it would stop him spending his time in the pub.

I think after that we both reckoned we were quits in the stupidly indulgent stakes, so I asked her whether she still thought she might need a man.

Jen said she did. She said she was lonely, to be honest, despite settling into the bosom of her family. Her family's bosom was lumpy and uncomfortable, it was incompatible with rest and lacking in a civilised wine o'clock routine. Her daughter and son-in-law were frantically busy all the time, her grandchildren were too young to be any use to her. She needed an adult to hang out with in a middle-aged sort of, seen-it-all-before sort of, more-wine-don't-mind-if-I-do sort of way. Preferably a man, of course, preferably rich, well groomed, good fun, short finger nails – and please, no stock of boring stories he simply has to tell. Not that. She has done her stint on that front with her last husband. She has served her time, and these are new days. So, Jen asked me, what could I suggest?

I said join a class. She said what sort of class? I said anything but embroidery or knitting woollen animals – what about art? She said she couldn't draw for toffee. I said perfect, she needs the tuition. She said what if the art class is full of women of a certain age looking for rich men with short fingernails? I said join a French class, there are far more men than women in French classes. She said, really? Is that so? I said yes, everyone knows that, it's something to do with the effect of testosterone on the vocal cords.

Anyway, I think she's got the message. And what is absolutely certain is that she's not going to find a man when she's wiping her grandchildren's bottoms. Jen has wiped her fair share of bottoms, she has had three children of her own. She needs to live a little.

And speaking of going out and living a little, I have a smear test this week.

***

Smear test. You'd think they could give it a better name than that. They weren't trying very hard, when they named that test. Smear test, for goodness sake. It doesn't even sound respectable. It might as well be a grot test or a blot test. Or a smudge test, or a smut test or a scum test. Personally, I'd draw the line at being told I had to turn up at the GPs' surgery for a scum test. If someone offered me a scum test I'd reject it on principle, so why am I trotting along meekly for a smear test? We should rearrange the letters a bit, and see if we can come up with something better. I had a go this morning. If we left out the 'm' and rearranged the letters it would be an arse test, but in terms of aesthetics we're no further forward.

Anyway, the GP was lovely, just a young girl. Not a great sense of humour. She got down to business briskly and efficiently, snapping on her rubber gloves and inserting the vagitron where it needs to be, cranking it open to have a good look around. It's difficult to say anything sensible when you're lying flat on your back while someone peers up your vagina, but you do feel that a little bit of light conversation might help dispel the awkwardness. So, in a desperate bid for levity, I asked her if she ever worried about being pulled in. She looked up and said, 'I'm sorry?'

Obviously, she's not the frivolous type. God knows what she's written in my notes.

I had a bit of shopping to do afterwards, as Dan and Gentle Rain would be wanting something to eat this evening, after a hard day on the rubbish tip. She's a sweet girl, but I don't think Gentle Rain is her real name. I don't think that's the name on her birth certificate. She must have given herself that name. Difficult for me to understand, after the years I have struggled with my own daft name, why anyone would deliberately choose to give themselves such a curious name.

For twenty-two years I was very happy to be Sally Bailey. It was a nice bouncy name, I liked it. Then I married William Forth and from one day to the next I became Sally Forth and sounded like a call to arms. I'm used to it now, of course, but it took a few years. If I'm honest, I think it might have altered my personality slightly. You can't hang back with a name like Sally Forth, that would make you an oxymoron.

On my way back to the car with my shopping a young woman wearing a tabard and carrying a clipboard leapt out at me from a doorway next to H&M and asked me if I'd like to sponsor a cat. I thought I'd misheard her at first, I had to ask, 'Did you say sponsor a cat?' 'Yes', she said, so I asked her – 'Sponsor a cat to do what?' 'Nothing,' she said, 'you wouldn't be sponsoring it to do anything.'

I couldn't quite get my head around it at first. I told her that when I was a girl, cats just got on with being cats, they didn't require sponsorship. I don't mind sponsoring a cat to climb Everest or swim the Channel, but sponsoring a cat to be a cat seems a bit ridiculous.

The young woman put her hand on my arm. She said if I had five minutes she would tell me about the work they were doing with traumatised cats, and she began by asking me if I had ever had a cat. I suddenly felt very weary, so I gave her fifty pence and told her I had six cats at home and I had to go because they would be missing me terribly. No-one deserves a lecture on traumatised cats after a smear test.

When I got home Laura's car was parked across the drive, so I had to park on the road. Oh dear, unannounced visits from Laura never bode well. She must have something to tell me, and it's unlikely to be something I want to hear.

I've had a bit of a session with Laura. She's a young mother. Her baby, Harry, is only four months old and she's struggling with it a bit. I didn't like to tell her that I'm an older mother with children in their twenties and I'm struggling with it a bit too. So we discussed her struggles as if I didn't have any.

It turns out that it's the commitment of motherhood that is continuing to bother her. Her baby is ruling every aspect of her life. When she wakes up, when she sleeps, when she eats, when she goes to the toilet, when she goes out, when she goes home, when she sees her friends – if she sees her friends.

She asked me if I knew how long it had taken her to get ready to drive the ten miles from her house to mine this afternoon? I said I could imagine it took a bit of organising. She said it did, and it was so difficult now for her just to leave the house. There was so much kit to assemble first – bottles, nappies, creams, wipes, carry cot, change of clothes, favourite toys, (all for the baby, none for her), endless straps to tighten and adjust, fasten and unfasten.

I sympathised. I said I could remember how difficult it was to leave the house with a baby in tow.

But it's so much worse now, said Laura, than it was for me. There's much more equipment now, and more stuff to assemble and take with you when you go out. Most of it hadn't been invented back then, when I squatted down behind a bush to give birth to Laura.

I said yes, that's probably true. Back in the day when I was a young mum and wet nurses were two a penny, we just wrapped the baby in a rabbit skin, threw a firkin of ale into the cart, and hitched it up to the oxen. We were ready to set off for the nearest witch-burning in no time. It was a breeze.

Anyway, sadly, that observation didn't help, so I tried to cheer Laura up by telling her that in fact, for most of the time you have children, they're adults, and then you can leave the house no problem. In fact, coming back to the house is more likely to be a problem, because that's when you have to deal with what they've done to it while you've been away. And on that subject, I suggested she might like to cast her eye over the rubbish metropolis clinging to the side of our house that her brother was responsible for.

At least this took her mind off her own concerns. She said what on earth was I thinking of letting Dan make such a mess? Why didn't I tell him to clear it all away? The neighbours must hate me. She couldn't believe Dan was actually thinking he could live in a pile of rubbish. She would never, ever, allow little Harry to do anything like that to her house. I had to take a firm stand.

I promised her I would. I said I would definitely stand firm. I was trying to calm her down. She was overwrought, poor thing, a combination of not enough sleep and too many hormones and the discovery that her whole life had been hijacked by someone who hadn't even learned to sit up yet. I gave her a soothing cup of tea, but she continued to fret.

What did I mean, she asked me, when I said that most of the time you have children, they're adults? Surely, once a child reaches the age of eighteen, they are responsible for themselves and your responsibility as a parent ends? She certainly wasn't planning to fuss over little Harry once he reached his eighteenth birthday. Once he reached eighteen years old, her job would be finished, and she would be her own woman again, and he would be responsible for himself. Then she asked me if I could make her a couple of chocolate cakes and bring them over next week, and look after Harry for a few hours while she had her hair cut.

I love her more than life itself, but it was such a relief when she packed up little Harry and all his accessories, and went home.

Jen texted me this evening. She said – Trying out tart class tomorrow night. Inside info –-Apparently there are men! Some unattached!! Some young enough to have own feet!! How u?

I texted her back – Session with Laura. Motherhood getting her down a bit.

Jen texted – After 4 months?

Me – Just a wobble. Art class? Men with teeth?! Keep me posted. Wear red dress, Scoop neck. Gives you lots of sex apple xx

Such a strange dream last night. I was running up and down a beach next to the sea. I had the children with me. They were growing at the rate of about ten years a minute. Seconds after making sand castles they were teenagers, and then they were looking at a glass boat on the shore. They started shouting against the wind, 'Mum! Dad! We're going to sea in this boat!' 'No!' I said, trying to make myself heard, 'No! It's made of glass!' 'That's okay', they shouted back. 'It'll be fine.' 'It won't!' I was yelling now but they couldn't hear me, 'It won't! It's made of glass! It'll break!' But they jumped in, and paddled out to sea.

Then I saw the oars lying on the sand. They were at sea in a glass boat without oars. 'You've left your oars!' I called after them, frantic. 'You can't steer the boat!' They cupped their hands to their mouths and shouted across the waves to me, 'Don't worry Mum! We don't need oars!' I picked up the oars and crashed into the sea after them, and the water woke me up.

I sat up in bed. My heart was pounding, and I was too hot. Bill woke up, 'Bad dream?' he said.

'Yes,' I said, 'I dreamt Dan and Laura went to sea in a glass boat.'

'Glass boat?' Bill said. 'God. Isn't that bloody typical?' And he turned over and went back to sleep.

I went to sleep too. But it took me a little while.

So I was tired going into school today to help with the lunchtime clubs and do my teaching assistant stint in the afternoon. It's the end of term in less than a week, and the kids are going bonkers. Fortunately, lots of them have decided to take the day off. I saw Tom Jenner, Head of English, and he said he had a full-time supply slot in the English department next term if I was interested.

No fear, I said, I was having time out. Almost twenty years of new initiatives at the beginning of each term was quite enough for the moment, thank you, and if I had to spend another five minutes discussing *To Kill a Mockingbird* I would catch the wretched bird and wring its neck and eat it with chips.

Tom knows I love schools and I can't keep away altogether, but I told him last year I'm not coming back to full-time teaching any time soon, supply or otherwise. There's no other job which requires you to argue with someone about whether or not they need to go to the toilet, and it takes its toll.

So, I went along to the maths department just to help Lee with his sums and generally keep him out of the teacher's hair.

Today we were given what the teacher assured us was a game to play. We were matching numbers with shapes, and it was billed as loads of fun. I got started, and tried to interest Lee in some triangles, but he regarded them with frank loathing. I tried to convince him that this was actually just a game, a bit of fun, and not really maths at all. But Lee pitied me for being the gullible fool that I was. Work which disguises itself as fun is an abomination in Lee's view, he has no respect for it. He said I could play with triangles if I wanted, but personally, he thought triangles were shite.

When I got home, Dan came in from the recycling emporium and said he'd cook dinner. I said, great, and asked him if he would wash his hands first. He said we would be eating in the south wing of Aspire, which was now finished, and I should wear something nice. Gentle Rain was dressing up.

'Right,' I said. 'So how formal is this?'

Dan said it wasn't 'formal', obviously, but a lot of effort was going in to building Aspire, so I should make a corresponding effort on this inaugural social occasion, and wear something appropriate. I said I thought a boiler suit would probably be about right, but Dan said I could do better than that.

I asked Dan what he was planning to wear, and he said he would wear his best jeans, and his 'Fuck Me Sideways' T-shirt. So I knew I'd have to make an effort.

Dan made a vegetable and lentil stew which was approved of by GR. No ingredient ever had legs or a beating heart, so nothing had suffered to provide our meal. It was absolutely safe to eat, if you ignored the fact that the lentils had taken a pounding.

Bill wondered if we should put some ham to it, we had some in the fridge.

I said no, if you're invited out for a meal you don't go trying to improve your hosts' efforts with left-overs you've brought from your fridge at home. He reminded me that we were just stepping outside to eat in a lean-to rubbish burrow resting against the side of our house. I said yes, but even so... Anyway, we took some wine, because we didn't think we'd get through the evening without it.

Aspire seems to be made mainly of crates, plastic sheeting lined with cardboard, and plastic drinks bottles. I didn't look too closely.

I wore my pink acrylic jumper which washes like a rag, and a pair of black jeans. Gentle Rain wore a green silky dress which had one or two tiny holes in it, apparently they were cigarette ash burns. I asked her if she smoked, and she said no, not since her Conversion. I didn't ask, Conversion to What? No sense in looking for trouble.

We ate our stew and Bill made a few enquiries about the prospect of Dan looking for gainful employment, which Dan didn't seem to understand. Gentle Rain talked to me about fulfilment through artistic expression and I offered to sew up the holes in her dress. Dan talked to Bill about the dangers of being consumed by a consumer society. Bill replied with details of Marks and Spencer's retail management graduate programme. We were at a summit meeting in a bunker with no interpreters. We couldn't understand each other, and then it got dark and we couldn't see each other. So we called it a day, and went back into the house carrying our plates and put them in the dishwasher. Dan and GR went off to the pub to meet some friends.

I poured myself the last of the red wine and said to Bill, 'Hang on, why are we letting Dan throw rubbish at our house to keep him out of the pub, if he's going to the pub anyway?'

'Ah yes', said Bill, 'but he's going at ten o'clock, not six o'clock. And he's living at home, instead of in some sort of squat drinking cheap lager and smoking weed with people who never brush their teeth. The rubbish is worth it,' he said. 'It's a small price to pay. It would be different if Dan was old enough to be a proper adult.'

I said, 'Dan's reached his twenties – how old does he have to be before he's a proper adult?'

Bill said that he saw Dan as somewhere between a child and an adult, still halfway between a boy and a man. An emerging adult. He thought there should be a name for people in this transitional stage, people who won't grow any taller, but who still expect that life will be fair, and that you should always just be yourself, and that Christmas will be fun, and that one day you will win the lottery. 'Daft' would fit the bill.

***

I was beginning to feel quite relaxed about the rubbish annexe, until Susan Forster from next door started banging on my front door late this afternoon to tell me about the rat. She said she'd seen a rat running out of the pile of crates and towards her house. I said – 'A rat Susan? Are you sure it wasn't a squirrel?'

'Of course I'm sure it wasn't a squirrel!' she said. 'Since when did squirrels have long, pencil-thin tails?'

I couldn't remember when squirrels had long pencil-thin tails, so I had to concede that it could have been a rat. Anyway, Susan needed calming down a bit so I asked her in for coffee and a chat to see if I could defuse things. She sat down at my kitchen table and described the rat in some detail, its pointy nose, its whiskers, its long tail. By about five-thirty I was sick of hearing about it, so I gave her a glass of red wine, and miraculously she started to think it might have been a small cat.

I said – 'Funnily enough Susan, I've seen a small brownish cat running about recently which I thought at first was a rat.' That cheered Susan up so much I began to feel bad about it being a bare-faced lie. We got quite merry together in the kitchen once I produced the wine. Susan is much better company after a unit or two of alcohol, or maybe I expect less, but the chemistry works in the right direction. Susan said she hadn't had such a nice glass of red wine since the night after the Brexit vote, and

I said I hadn't had such a nice glass of red wine since squirrels had long pencil-thin tails. We did laugh.

After Susan left, I decided to give Dan and GR a public health lecture on rat infestations the next time I see them.

I thought about Jen when I was filling the dishwasher after dinner. I should have heard from her about the art class. I started to worry about suggesting she wore her red scoop-necked dress for her first art class outing. Maybe I should have advised against it? Jen has a very generous bosom and there might be a lot of bending over at an art class. She might have felt a bit uncomfortable with such a low neckline. I imagined her sitting at her easel, all in red with her magnificent cleavage on display. Oh well – too late now. She'd have looked wonderful, and she would have somewhere to put her paintbrush when she wasn't using it.

***

Jen rang this morning. Very upset. Her art class has been a big disappointment. There were only two men – one was there with his wife, and the other was a train spotter who only painted steam trains and said 'Choo choo' instead of hello and goodbye and told her that his marriage had gone off the rails and hit the buffers.

I hadn't heard Jen so upset for a long time. I think the trauma of the move must have caught up with her, and the whole 'Choo choo' business had unnerved her. She said her marriage hadn't been any great shakes, but she was an optimist. She wanted to have another crack at a relationship before her face melted and her bum slipped all the way down her legs to the back of her knees.

'Look Jen,' I said, 'the answer is staring us in the face here – you have to join an online dating agency.'

She said she didn't know how to do that, and she would feel embarrassed to ask her family, it was just impossible, she wasn't that good on the computer, and her lap top was rubbish. She was close to tears.

I told her I'd help. I said I would find out about it and get her started on a dating website.

She said 'How? How will you find out? You're not that good on the computer either.' She reminded me of the time when I did an online shop and bought six kilos of mushrooms.

I told her to forget the mushrooms. Everyone is allowed one online shopping fiasco and it usually involves mushrooms. Anyway, I said, I would get some advice. I have two young adults hanging around the house, and I could ask them for help. They have to be good for something, and they're bound to know about dating websites. I told her they might even help to write her dating profile.

Jen said she would write her own dating profile, if it came to it, thank you very much. But in the meantime, maybe I could make a few discreet enquiries about dating websites, without giving too much away? Of course, I said. I promised her I'd make some sensitive enquiries and let her know what I managed to suss out.

So, when Dan and GR turned up this evening I told them that Jen was desperate for a man and her only chance of finding one was a dating agency, and I had promised to help because I thought she was going mad with frustration looking after her grandchildren. I said I would need some assistance from them.

Yeah, they said, no problem, they could help with that. Probably tomorrow, because they had to go out soon to see a man about some more crates and possibly some small bales of hay.

I told them about Susan Forster seeing the rat. Gentle Rain got very excited and wanted to put food down for it. She said she'd heard that rats were very intelligent and made excellent pets. A friend of hers doing psychology at university had trained a rat to play *God Save the Queen* on a primitive keyboard. I had to stop her there and say I don't care whether you can train rats to play *Swan Lake* on a primitive nose flute, you must not encourage them onto the premises with food.

GR looked at bit puzzled at my anti-rodent rhetoric, and Dan made the mistake of accusing me of being hysterical. It was a mistake, because nothing is more designed to make me hysterical than someone accusing me of being hysterical. I told Dan that in all the circumstances I was nowhere near hysterical enough. I said if he wanted to see me in proper hysterics he should entice performing rats into my garden and then stick around because he wouldn't be disappointed. Then I told them both that they must not keep food in Aspire, or whatever they were choosing to call it, unless the food was sealed in an air tight container inaccessible to a rat, with or without training in picking locks.

They looked aggrieved, and said they kept Aspire practically as clean as an operating theatre. They wondered if Susan might have been mistaken about the rat sighting. I told them it had taken a very nice glass of red to have any effect on Susan's eyesight, and I didn't want to have to make a habit of it.

They got the message, and they promised they would have loads of advice on dating agencies for Jen in a day or two, if she could just hang on that long.

Chapter 3 – August

Must pin Dan and GR down to a proper discussion about dating sites. Jen texted me to tell me she was writing her dating profile, and wondering whether she should mention her A-levels. I asked her whether her A-levels were especially good. Jen said yes, they were good, and she thought her two Bs and a C should make people sit up and take notice.

I'm not sure, to be honest, about mentioning her A-levels in her dating profile. Does it matter, after thirty years, what your A-levels were? Do you care? Does anybody? Can't you just invent your A-level results after a thirty year period, and give yourself the A-levels you should have had, instead of the ones you actually got? Those of us who sat some A-levels way back when, know the grades we should have got, and are fed up with the miserable grades we were actually awarded. If we'd just had a little more luck on the day we sat the exams, or if we'd worked just a bit harder, our results would have been much better. Hell, I got three Cs but I would never admit to that now. It was a travesty of justice. The last time the subject of my A-levels came up I gave myself three Bs, and if anyone were to ask me again I would give myself at least one A. I'm done with those three Cs. It won't be long before I have a PhD from Oxford University.

Apparently, Jen has heard of a dating site called Tender, and she thought that sounded rather nice – what did I think?

I said Tender sounded lovely. I told her it sounds sweet and caring, as if it was run by a committee of retired domestic science teachers who have known you since you were just little and want the best for you. I told Jen I thought she'd be in good hands there.

I managed to catch Dan and GR this afternoon before they rushed off somewhere to do something stupid, and I asked them about Tender. They said it's not Tender, it's Tinder. They said tell Jen not to use Tinder if there is any possibility of her having self-esteem issues. Right, I said, and while we were on the subject, I asked them about writing dating profiles. Specifically, I asked if Jen should mention her A-levels in her profile? Dan said, 'Jesus, Mum, she's not writing a CV.'

I texted Jen back and suggested she hang fire on Tender, because it's not Tender, it's Tinder, and that's probably not the best site for her. I didn't say anything about her A-levels. I didn't want to put a downer on everything, and I thought it probably wouldn't do any harm to give her two Bs and a C a mention. I asked her whether she was planning to say anything about what she liked doing in her spare time. A bit of background information would say something about her, and indicate where there might be some common ground with a potential partner. She could say she likes going for long walks, or reading, or going to the cinema, or pulling the heads off daisies. That kind of thing.

Jen rang me minutes after that text, and asked if I thought she should mention her recent knitting obsession. She told me she has started knitting fruit and vegetables – carrots, bananas and so forth. She knits them and stuffs them with kapok. She's been doing it for her grandchildren apparently, and she's really enjoying it.

I said – to be absolutely honest, Jen, I wouldn't mention your obsession for knitting vegetables on a dating web site, and she agreed that on reflection it probably wasn't the right vibe. She said it was a shame, because she had just knitted a whole family of broccoli sprigs, and the kids loved them, and they all ate their broccoli now, and she'd like to share that with someone.

I wanted to move her on from the knitted veg, which would be a passion killer in a sailors' brothel, so I asked her whether she had a nice photograph of herself she could use for her profile picture. She said she had given this some thought, and she was planning to be honest when she described herself, and to use a candid photograph. She said she thought she might say somewhere that she didn't want to make the same mistake as Anne of Cleves, who had allowed Henry to see a very flattering portrait of herself before they met for the first time, because look at the trouble that had caused. She was sure people would understand the reference, and it would chime with the mention of her history A-level.

I asked her whether she meant the same Anne of Cleves who was briefly betrothed to King Henry VIII? Because if so, things had moved on a bit since then and it wasn't a good idea to sound as if she had grown up at the Tudor Court. She might get away with a mention of Duran Duran but she shouldn't sound too familiar with medieval dating practices.

Jen asked me whether I was hinting that she should give the impression that she was younger than her age? I said no, not younger exactly, I just thought she should aim to give a generally youthful impression. There's more to youth than chronological age, I said. And anyway, she shouldn't be making excuses for her age, she should be celebrating it. So, best not to mention it at all, I said.

Jen said she wasn't sure what I was talking about but she had to hang up. She was knitting a celeriac without a proper pattern and it was starting to look like Jabba the Hutt. She would have to go.

***

Dan and Gentle Rain explained to me how Tinder works this morning, and I got a bit of a sinking feeling. I wondered if I should have encouraged Jen to try a French class instead of on-line dating. She could have been parleying with a monsieur *très agréable* by now, instead of waiting to be swiped off a digital cliff.

But Dan and GR said I was taking the online dating thing much too seriously. Dan said that was the problem with my generation, we took all the wrong kind of stuff seriously. He said he took his art seriously, and his relationship with Gentle Rain seriously, and his concern for the future of the planet seriously. And then, because he was feeling chatty and he had a minute, he told me what I took seriously. He said he thought I was too preoccupied with the state of the house and the garden, and whether the grass needed cutting and who was going to wash my car, and the whereabouts of my Boots Advantage Card.

'Is that a fact?' I said, when he had quite finished. And he said yes, that was his general impression.

I thanked him for his accumulated wisdom of twenty-one years and said how sorry I was that it had come too late to save me from wasting most of my life. Dan agreed it was a real bummer.

My phone bleated to tell me I had received a text. Dan and GR hung around to see what it was. I think they are quite intrigued that anyone out there thinks it's worth texting me. I read the message and told them what it was about, to demonstrate that I, too, had important business to attend to. I told them it was from Jen, and she was offering to knit vegetables for Laura's Harry. She urgently wanted to know whether Laura wants her to knit carrots, or leeks, but she wasn't offering to knit broccoli, because she had just knitted a whole floret and she fancied a change.

Dan said I'd better get on to that straight away. He and Gentle Rain would see me later, once the pressure was off.

So off they went, each carrying a large bin liner full of something ridiculous, and I rang Laura to discuss Jen's generous offer. As soon as Laura answered the phone and heard it was me, she asked what I was doing this afternoon.

Obviously, she had no interest in my plans for the afternoon. She was interested in whether I could drop everything and come over to help out.

So when I said I wasn't doing anything in particular this afternoon, she said, 'Great! Mum, can you drop everything and come over to help out? I need you to look after Harry while I go into town to meet Shaz and Maz.'

'No problem,' I said. 'I'll come over straight after lunch, be with you by 1.30.'

'Great,' she said. 'Fantastic.'

She was going to ring off, but I said, 'Hang on, Laura, I need to ask you something. Jen has offered to knit a vegetable family for Harry – do you think he would prefer carrots, or leeks?'

'God, I don't know,' she said. 'Can it wait? I'm a bit rushed at the moment, and it's not exactly a priority.'

So I said, 'This isn't a difficult decision, Laura.'

She said she was sorry, but she had other things on her mind.

I thought this was a good time to remind Laura that Jen has never forgotten her birthday once in twenty years, since we first knew Jen when Laura was six. If someone has remembered your birthday for almost the whole of your life, you owe them respect. And on top of all that, Jen is now offering to knit vegetables for Harry. The least Laura could do would be to express a preference for which vegetable.

Laura said, okay, okay. Jen could knit Harry some sprouts.

'Sprouts?' I said. 'Sprouts aren't on offer. You can have carrots or leeks.'

'Carrots then,' she said, 'would be great.'

'Good choice' I said. 'It'll teach Harry to recognise a carrot. And carrots are a more important vegetable than sprouts, for children of Harry's age. Sprouts are more of an adult vegetable. Excellent.'

And then, when I had finished talking absolute tosh, I had my lunch and got ready to rush over there for one thirty. Harry was so good, despite having been very grizzly all morning. He slept the whole time Laura was out. Laura was furious when she came back, she said he'd be awake all evening.

***

Bloody hell! Dan and GR are talking about getting married! They came into the kitchen this afternoon and announced their intention to get married. I said (regrettably), 'Shit! You can't do that – you're much too young. Nobody gets married at twenty-one these days!'

They told me that they knew for a fact that I was only just twenty-two when I got married back in the day, and if it was a good idea then, it's a good idea now.

Yes but, I said, there were exceptional circumstances in our case. Bill and I expected to meet with a lot of parental opposition on both sides to our plans to marry so young. As it happened though, both sets of parents were preoccupied with other things, and they just didn't have time to think much about our plans. They were happy enough for us to get married if we did all the organising, and didn't bother them with the details, or expect them to stay long after the ceremony. Bill and I got married because everyone was too busy to tell us not to. I told Dan and Gentle Rain that they were lucky, by comparison, that I was able to give them both my full attention and my dire warnings.

They ignored my warnings, and said they thought it was fantastic the way Bill and I had got married so young. So romantic. It's exactly what they want to do. They said they would organise the whole thing. It would be wonderful, they would ask all their friends to celebrate with them. It needn't cost much, and they wanted to pay for it themselves. In fact, they would insist on paying for it themselves, because they wanted to own their own wedding, it was important to them.

I took a deep breath. What you need to know, I explained to them, is that now, twenty-seven years on from my cheapskate nuptials, weddings are horrendously expensive. Hardly anybody owns their own wedding these days. The bank is more likely to own your wedding than you are. Now people spend tens of thousands of pounds on weddings – routinely. You really can't get married for under about twelve thousand pounds these days. Even then the bride has to wear a paper wedding dress and have only one, very thin bridesmaid. After the ceremony everyone must drink a toast to the bride and groom with Ribena and listen to a very short, economical speech made by a second best man. You needn't abandon the idea of wedding favours, but they must be IOUs. No, it doesn't make any financial sense for you to make a sincere and lasting commitment, I told them. You can't afford it.

But – they said – they were in love! They wanted to make this formal commitment to be together, always. They said they thought it would be rather beautiful, even wonderful. They looked at each other, and held hands, and said they were a little in awe of taking this step, but they knew it was right for them, and it would be so sad not to do it.

'Sad?' I said. 'No. Not really. You'll get over it, don't worry. It'll pass. Have a bottle of wine and watch *Star Wars* and you'll be fine. You'll feel the Force and think– bloody hell, that was a lucky escape. We nearly got married when the sensible thing is just to live together. Good Sense Strikes Back. Beam me up Scotty. Unlock the escape hatch.'

They looked at me as if I'd gone mad. They said they didn't understand me. They had given this a lot of thought, and they had chosen marriage. What did it matter how old they were? They thought it was very middle-aged and depressing of me to be so hung up on the expense. And anyway, they were going to have a recycled wedding, so I needn't worry about the cost.

'What?' I said. 'A recycled wedding? How would that work? Are you going to use somebody else's wedding after they've finished with it?'

No, they said, don't be ridiculous. GR would buy a wedding dress from an Oxfam shop for a fraction of the price of a new one, they would get married in a registry office, and catch the bus back here with the guests. Everyone would bring a picnic, and they could have the reception in our back garden amongst flowers that were actually growing in the earth. The wedding breakfast would be shared out and, as with the loaves and the fishes, everyone would have enough to eat and fall in love with thy neighbour, especially after all the water had been turned into wine. Any food left over could be handed out to the poor at the garden gate, and the poor would mumble grateful thanks and be cured. All halos would be collected in at the end of the day and polished, before being auctioned off for charity the following week. And lo, there would be rejoicing! And everything would be splendid and hunky dory.

'Wait,' I said. 'Wait.' I was panicking now. 'The thing is, you've only known each other a couple of weeks. That isn't long enough. You have to know each other long enough to really dislike each other. Trust me, you need to give yourselves a chance to find out what you can't stand about each other. Then you will have the basis of a good working relationship. Don't rush into marriage,' I said, 'and then gnash your teeth for all eternity.'

They said there was no reason to postpone a wedding, now that they had a place of their own.

I said – 'You're not referring to that pile of rubbish out there, I hope? Because there is no way that could be considered a permanent address. I love you both,' I said, 'I really do, but this is a half-baked plan. Put it back in the oven and check on it in five years.'

***

I haven't seen much of Dan and GR these last few days. A consignment of bubble wrap arrived in the garden yesterday and disappeared into Aspire. I hope they aren't making a wedding dress out of it. The kitchen scissors have disappeared.

Jen has emailed me her dating site profile for my comments. It begins with the words, '*Although I am well past the first flush of youth, (and may be having some interesting alternative flushes), I am very active and definitely not dead yet!'*

I didn't read any further because I thought that opening sentence needs work. I emailed Jen back to say, *'Jen – Thanks for suggested profile, will read it carefully and get back to you asap. Had an initial thought though – maybe not a good idea to open with a boast that you still have a pulse? I haven't read all the way through but I'd suggest an alternative first sentence. Something which doesn't give the impression that you are chuffed your heart is still beating. Also, drop the ref to hot flushes.'*

That should give her something to think about for a while.

Looking through the post this morning I came across a letter addressed to The Hon. V. F. Venning, 38b, The Chestnuts, etc. I turned it over and it had a small coat of arms embossed on the back. It didn't look like junk mail, the paper was good quality and it didn't seem to be advertising anything. As far as I am aware, there is no 38b along The Chestnuts, we are 38 and we have 37 and 39 on the other side of the road, behind the trees. I wondered whether to open it, but it's not addressed to me.

I've been thinking about it, and wondering whether 38b The Chestnuts could possibly refer to the heap of junk at the side of our house, and whether Gentle Rain could be The Hon. V. F. Venning?

I turned this possibility over in my mind and considered its implications. If Gentle Rain is The Hon. V. F. Venning she might be the daughter of a Viscount. Her family might have great wealth and lands, an ancestral home, stables, a village of tied cottages for faithful retainers, a villa in Cap Ferrat, and an account at Harrods which need never be paid. I looked again at the envelope and held it up to the light, and tried to see through it. I held the envelope this way and that, but it was impenetrable to light. That's the thing about aristocrats, they aren't satisfied with cheap paper. I looked again at the embossed coat of arms on the back of the envelope. I don't know anything about heraldry, but I tried to make out the heraldic forms emblazoned on the shield. There was an animal of some sort in the top left-hand quadrant, possibly a recumbent penguin, or a *penguin couchant* I think is the correct term. At the bottom right there seemed to be a banana, or possibly a dildo, although they aren't recognised heraldic forms as far as I know. I squinted at it, but it was impossible to say what was going on really, without being a medieval knight.

So – if it turns out that Gentle Rain comes from a rich noble family with estates and a penguin farm and a dildo factory and an endless supply of vellum stationery, will this make any difference to the way I feel about her, and the way I feel about her relationship with Dan?

Not really.

OH NO! I thought, I've just put them off getting married! What an idiot! What a fool I've been! I should have left well alone. I'll try and backtrack, it might not be too late. I looked out of the window to see if I could see them coming up the road.

My phone was lying on the window sill; it chirruped to tell me it had swallowed something. It was an email from Jen. The strap line said, *How about this?* And when I opened it there was another dating profile attempt, *Hello! My name is Jen. I am a fun-loving mature woman who is always 'on the go'. When I'm not looking after my grandchildren I go walking and cycling. I only sit down when my varicose vein is absolutely killing me!*

I replied, *Jen – do you have a dating death wish? Keep your varicose vein under wraps, if it isn't already. More later.*

A bit of an abrupt response, but I had other things on my mind. I picked up the envelope addressed to The Hon. V. F. Venning for another look, and boiled the kettle for coffee. I accidentally wafted the envelope through the steam, and back again. I held the envelope in the steam for a few seconds, thinking, am I really the kind of person who steams open other people's mail? But the envelope showed no sign of coming open, so maybe I'm not. The seal held. That's the thing about aristocrats, they aren't satisfied with cheap glue.

I made my coffee, and drank it staring out of the window. I wondered if I should buy a few cushions to put in Aspire.

**

God almighty. Laura's arrived home. With four suitcases, a buggy and a carry cot.

'Laura? What's up?' I said as she was unloading everything from her car into the hall. Even with a baby in tow, there was more stuff coming out of her car than would be needed for a couple of hours, or even a week. 'What's the matter, Laura?'

She said that she and Ben weren't getting on. She was absolutely fed up and was coming home for a while.

What a nightmare! I tried to stay calm but my blood pressure went up with every bag she brought in from her car. 'Laura,' I said, 'just leave the rest of the stuff in the car for now and come and have a sandwich and tell me about it. Surely things can't be as bad as all that.'

She sat down at the kitchen table with Harry asleep on her lap, and I gave her a box of paper hankies. 'What's the problem?' I asked her.

I glanced at the cooker clock which said 11.15. While Laura blew her nose, I wondered what my chances were of getting this girl sorted out, her car re-packed, and her and the baby back on the road heading for home in under three hours. I'd arranged to meet Judith in M&S café at 3.30, and I just couldn't stand it if I had to meet up with her and confess that Laura's marriage was on the rocks. Judith would hand me her phone to show me photos of her daughter deliriously happy with her fiancé. I would have to dip her phone in my tea, and then take it out and stamp on it to give me any hope of feeling better.

It took about seven paper hankies to get the full story from Laura, but eventually she told me, although she was uncharacteristically coy about it all. It turns out that Ben is making unreasonable demands on her 'in the bedroom department'.

I think I'm a reasonably good judge of character, and I like Ben. I had always imagined he would be rather splendid in the bedroom department, so this was it bit of a surprise. Well, I thought, we've come this far, so I'm going to have to ask. So I said – 'What's Ben wanting you to do, Laura, in the bedroom department? Is it something like dressing up, for example? Or is he wanting to chase you around the house naked, or does it involve strawberry jam? Or some other preserve? What kinds of demands are these, exactly, that he's making in the bedroom department? I need to know what we're dealing with, if I'm going to be any help.' (I thought – if it's dressing up, I have a Marie Antoinette costume at the back of my wardrobe that I wore for Jen's 'French Revolution' themed fortieth. That might come in useful.)

But it wasn't dressing up. That wasn't the problem. In fact, the problem wasn't *what* he wanted, it was how often he wanted it.

'Look Laura,' I said, 'you don't leave home over a 'how often' discussion. 'How often' isn't a leaving home issue – it's a thrashing things out issue.' I put my marriage guidance hat on and explained that, in a marriage, it's important to know when to leave home and when to stand your ground and put your boxing gloves on and fight. I told her she had miscalculated, and left home when she should be back there with her husband, battling things out in the ring.

Then I began to worry that I had accidentally put my boxing match promoter's hat on, because I seemed to be putting a rather adversarial spin on things.

So I suggested to Laura that she rang Ben and told him she would be home tomorrow, but she was staying here tonight because she was a bit tired and upset, and wasn't up to the drive home. I said, tell him everything will be fine in the morning, and not to worry. And then after the call, we could relax, and have a chat.

I had to ring Judith to cancel our tea date in M&S café. I told her I couldn't manage to meet up this week because unfortunately something absolutely wonderful had happened. I'd tell her all about it when we catch up next time. So, with any luck she'll think I've had an amazing stroke of good fortune, and she'll be eaten up with curiosity and envy and be out of sorts for the rest of the day and snap at her husband when he gets home. And I have a full week to invent something sufficiently wonderful to fit that bill.

Laura calmed down gradually and was recovered enough to eat a good meal with us all at dinner time. She began to think that she may just be a bit premenstrual. She said she always thinks Ben is doing something wrong when she's premenstrual. But despite this, it infuriates her if Ben looks at the calendar when she accuses him of something, to see whether he needs to take the accusation seriously. And I can sympathise with her there.

I was very pleased after dinner when Laura and Daniel managed to have an exchange of words, sibling to sibling, which almost amounted to a conversation. It was very touching, and I held my breath as it extended into its second minute. Ninety seconds is a recent record, but they broke through that threshold, and better than that, there were definite signs of affection for each other. It was nearly three minutes before they each told the other to piss off. I was so pleased. I still feel a warm glow, and I've told myself that as their mother I must have done something right.

***

Bill opened the bedroom curtains this morning and said there seems to be a cupola arising from the centre of Aspire.

I said, what's a cupola? He said it's a dome. He said as far as he could tell it was fashioned from bubble wrap and bamboo struts and it was emerging from the roof of the structure below. I'll look at it later when I feel strong enough. At least it isn't something organic, so it shouldn't spread to the rest of the house.

Laura has gone home. She's been back a few days. I haven't asked, and she hasn't said anything, so I'm assuming things are settling down between her and Ben. If I ask her how things are, she'll start to think about it, and she might decide things are not going well. Laura is at her best when she is not dwelling on things. She tends to underestimate how happy she is to prevent fate proving her wrong. A couple of hours in John Lewis is what she needs now. I'll suggest it. Thirty minutes of retail therapy in JL's household department is worth hours of relationship counselling.

Dan and Gentle Rain spent last night in the house, and came down for breakfast around ten. I showed them the letter addressed to The Hon V.F. Venning, and asked them if they had any idea who this was. Dan obviously had no idea. Gentle Rain claimed not to know either. She wrote 'Not known at this address' on the envelope and said she would drop it in a post box later.

I'm convinced GR is The Hon V.F. Venning. She has very nice table manners, and I discovered when I was doing a crossword the other day that she knows the words to 'Jerusalem'. So she didn't go to a state school.

I asked them both how the wedding plans were going and they said that actually, our conversation the other day had made them reconsider. Things were on hold at the moment.

'Oh,' I said, 'don't take any notice of silly me. What do I know? Make your own minds up.'

This was in such sharp contrast to my advice the last time we spoke that I started to tell them about my idea for quilted toilet roll confetti to head off any requests for an explanation of my U turn. But they weren't listening. They had moved on from wedding plans. Instead they wanted to give me some advice to pass on to Jen about dating web sites. And it was actually very interesting. They told me that Jen will have to know how to interpret internet dating site profiles, and they gave me some useful pointers to pass on to her. Then they asked me to come outside and admire their latest addition to Aspire.

We went out, and they showed me the bubble wrap dome. It was as if a giant breast had been delivered to the roof of Aspire, carefully packaged, and lay waiting to be unwrapped. I was about to say so when they told me it was a dome to echo the great domes of classical architecture, like Hadrian's Pantheon in Rome, and the Duomo in Florence. I decided not to mention its similarity to a giant bubble-wrapped breast. They said they were going to look for gold and silver aluminium foil today to decorate it, and make it catch the light. Wonderful, I said. Great. Fantastic idea. Perfect. It will look stunning. And off they went.

Susan from next door yoo-hooed me from the other side of the garden fence, so I went over to talk to her. She nodded in the direction of Aspire and said, 'What the hell is that boob-shaped thing on top of the heap?'

We both considered it for a few seconds, and then I told her it was a dome to echo the great domes of classical architecture, and I asked her whether she had ever been to Florence. She said she hadn't, but she was pretty sure she wouldn't see one of those in Florence. Then she asked me how long I envisaged this creation being there, blighting the neighbourhood. Was it just a summer thing? Or would it survive the winter? She said her son had popped in to see her yesterday and told her she should make a formal complaint.

I told Susan that for the moment I was thinking of it as a temporary art installation, and that its transience was part of its charm. She said, 'Does that mean it's going in a skip anytime soon?'

It was a bit early in the day to talk her round with a glass of red wine, so I tried to appeal to her better nature. 'The thing is, Susan,' I said, 'this project is very important to Dan, and although it's not ideal to have a growing pile of junk accumu-lating outside your house, he's been so much happier since he started working on it, and we'd like to let him run with it for a while.' I was going to add that if Dan isn't happy, then it's difficult for me to be happy, but something about the set of Susan's facial expression told me to hold back on such frivolous nonsense.

Susan has been our neighbour for years, but we aren't close, except in proximity. We have a relationship because we live next door to each other, and it's based on mutual incomprehension and a strained willingness to tolerate each other's oddities. Susan doesn't have a fanciful nature, she is not given to whimsy or introspective musing. She plants her daffodils in rows six inches apart, and she never forgets to put her bins out for collection. Generally speaking, these aren't the actions of a poet. So I promised her that Aspire would be for the skip very soon, and she said the sooner the better.

I must pass on to Jen the advice Dan and GR gave me on on-line dating profiles earlier today. I'm sending her this email. *Jen, there's something you need to know about the way people describe themselves on dating websites. 'Curvy' means fat. 'I'm known for my plain speaking' means people say I'm rude. 'Fun-loving' means I have an alcohol problem. 'Keen cyclist' means I have a bike. 'I like to keep fit' means I walk to the pub, 'but I don't overdo it' means I get a taxi back. 'Mature' means old. 'Discerning' means snob. 'Good sense of humour' means I laugh at my own jokes. 'Bubbly' means not very bright. 'Solvent' means you'll be paying for everything. 'Thoughtful' means don't expect much conversation.*

Jen has replied, saying, *Re your cautionary list. Is it OK to say 'I enjoy travelling'?*

I've responded. *'I enjoy travelling' means I like being on holiday. But say it if you want.*

***

I confessed to Bill last night that Gentle Rain was probably from an aristocratic family with a country seat and stables and a coat of arms, and she wanted to marry Dan, but I had poured cold

43

water on the idea, and now the wedding was off, and I had ruined his life, but I was trying to rekindle their plans for early nuptials so that we could join the ranks of the aristocracy as hangers-on.

Bill was surprised. He knew Dan had a girlfriend but hadn't realised there was this much to it. He suggested we chill out a bit and hold off on any immediate plans to join the aristocracy, no need to rush out and buy ermine cloaks just yet. I said if we were going to buy ermine cloaks we should do it now, and get some wear out of them before we need them for ceremonial occasions. Bill said yes, he could see where I was coming from, but if the marriage didn't come off we might look a bit over-dressed when we are out and about on a Saturday morning, even in Marks and Spencer's Food Hall, even in Waitrose. I said I was going to Marks and Spencer's later today to meet Judith, and I would take notice of the dress code.

I was at our usual table in M&S a bit before two, so I was in position with my coffee and a flapjack when Judith arrived. She gave me a wave, bought her coffee and something to eat and made her way over. She plonked her tray down on the table and stood with her arms out saying, 'Before I sit down, d'you notice anything?'

Oh God, I thought – she's lost some weight. Quite a bit by the look of things, she must be at least a stone slimmer than me now, and we're the same height.

'Well?' she said, arms outstretched, waiting to be admired.

I shook my head and looked puzzled. Then I said, 'Oh hang on, have you had your hair cut?'

'No!' She said. 'It's nothing to do with my hair! Look at me! I've lost nearly a stone! In the last month! What do you think of that? It's been so easy. I'm having to buy new clothes. Imagine! And I feel so much fitter. And guess what? Someone told me I look ten years younger!'

God. She is such a depressing woman. I said, 'That's wonderful Judith, really wonderful,' and ate my flapjack. She sat down and picked at some fruit in a little plastic pot.

44

Then, flushed with the success of losing some weight, Judith asked me if I knew how many calories there were in my flapjack. I said yes, I did, I knew exactly how many, to the last half dozen. She was disappointed because she wanted to tell me I had just eaten my whole daily allowance of calories, and most of tomorrow's. And then she changed tack, and reminded me that when we spoke on the phone last, I had said I had marvellous news. So – was I going to spill the beans? She could hardly wait! She was so excited!

I took a bite of my flapjack, and nodded to give myself time to think of some marvellous news. Then I said yes, I did have marvellous news concerning Laura's son Harry. He has an IQ of 160.

Judith said – 'A hundred and sixty! But he's only 4 months old!'

And I said, 'Yes! That's the marvellous part. Amazing, isn't it?'

Judith said she hadn't realised it was even possible to test a child's IQ at that age. I said yes, it isn't generally known, but you can test a child's IQ at any age. Well, said Judith, how amazing – she said she must remember to mention that to her daughter's fiancé, he's an eminent child psychologist, and he knows all about this kind of stuff.

I bought another flapjack and ate it. I find it stops me wailing out loud.

We went our separate ways soon after three. I was exhausted and needed to lie down. Judith is so wearing, and I dislike her intensely. We are meeting up again in a fortnight.

Home by 3.30. The kitchen had been completely taken over by Dan and GR Enterprises. Dan was washing piles of aluminium foil in the sink, and drying pieces of it on my tea towel. GR was cutting the pieces into star shapes and ironing them flat between sheets of newspaper on my ironing board.

I said – quite forgetting that I might be speaking to a member of the aristocracy – 'What the hell are you two doing?' Although it was perfectly obvious what they were doing; I had taken it in

45

at a glance. They explained they were preparing the star shapes to decorate the dome, because when they were in position they would catch the light and look wonderful, particularly in the morning and the evening when the sun was low in the sky. The dome would be magical and shimmering, tinged with crimson and rose, turning from silver, yea, even unto gold.

I tried to rejoice, but I couldn't. Instead I gnashed my teeth and told them to clear up all their mess when they'd finished, or there would be trouble. It was the best I could do.

**

I was rummaging in the freezer this morning, pulling out pieces of meat which had been in there so long they could be cuts of woolly mammoth, when the phone rang. I heard Laura's voice on a bad line saying, 'Hello? Hello? Can you hear me?'

It was difficult to tell, but I thought she sounded agitated. 'What is it, Laura? What's happened?'

She couldn't hear me. 'Hello? Hello?' she said again.

My heart started to race. What now? Had she left little Harry in the Post Office? Did she want me to look after Harry for two years while she joined a circus? Please, not more problems in the bedroom department.

'Laura,' I said. 'Can you hear me?'

Then the line cleared of static and I heard her say. 'Oh! It's you. Sorry – I thought I'd rung Maz. Catch you later!' and she rang off.

I sat down and collected myself because I was all over the place. When my heart rate was back to normal I rang Jen for a steadying chat, and news of her dating site profile. Things had gone a bit quiet on that front, and I thought an update might calm me down.

Poor Jen. She is not having a good time at the moment. She told me she had gone on-line and bought some kapok to stuff her knitted vegetables. She had ordered a 20 kilo bag which was very reasonably priced. Kapok, of course, is a very lightweight stuffing material for cushions and soft toys and the like, so when it arrived the 20 kilo bag was as big as the internal dimensions of her living room. She said she dragged it inside, and now her sofa and her television have disappeared behind it. She said her little living room was now occupied by a massive blancmange, and she was squashed against her walls looking for enough space to exist.

I said maybe you can return it? She said she could try, but she would have to do that on-line, and the bag of kapok had settled on top of her computer, and she didn't know when she would see it again. She said her little knitted vegetables only use about a cupful of kapok each, how many would she have to knit to make any impression on this thing?

I was curious, and asked her whether her ball of kapok looked anything like the pulsating life form discovered by Professor Quatermass in the film *The Quatermass Experiment*, the life form which engulfed and ate human beings? Very like, she said, only hers was a lot more inconvenient.

I suggested that she start to knit a huge elephant straight away, and then she could decant all the kapok into it, and give it to her grandchildren.

Jen asked me what she was supposed to do in the meantime? There wasn't enough room for both her and the kapok in her lounge. Well, I said – climb on top of it, and live on it. It should be very comfortable.

She said she would have to go, because she has a date this afternoon. Coffee at three thirty with a man she met in the library.

I said – 'A man? A man you met in the library? Not through a dating website? But – he hasn't been properly vetted! What do you know about this man?'

She said she knew he had had both his hips replaced. How much of a threat could he be?

I said, 'Don't do something stupid and ask him back to your place.'

She said, 'Ask him back to my place? There's barely room for me in my place. And even if I did, he's not going to get up to much with two hip replacements, sitting on top of a ball of kapok.'

But I wasn't reassured. I said, 'Jen, listen to me – he might have universal joints in both hips and be at his best on a ball of kapok.'

And then she told me to get lost, because she had other fish to fry.

I made myself a cup of coffee and mulled it over. Jen has a date. There was an emotion I couldn't identify writhing around in my unconscious. It bobbed to the surface and I took a good look at it. I was jealous.

How ridiculous. Jealousy is such a juvenile emotion. I haven't felt properly jealous since I was fourteen, and a girl called Barbara Wallbrook in my class at school broke her leg. She broke it falling on ice, and then she had six weeks off school lying around watching television.

She came back to school with an enormous plaster cast on her leg, and hobbled around pathetically on crutches and was loved by all the dinner ladies as if she was Tiny Tim. Her parents bought her a consolatory kitten, and she was taken to school and back home again by taxi.

Anyway, that was a long time ago, and I've forgotten all about it now. The taxi's registration number was ATN 107.

***

Didn't sleep well last night. Strange flashing lights were casting weird shapes onto the ceiling of our bedroom. I got up and looked out of the window. The dome on top of Aspire was flashing on and off. It was two o'clock in the morning, and the flashing dome was keeping me awake. I didn't want to knock on the bedroom window, or open it and shout out to tell Dan and GR to switch the flashing dome off, because it would wake Bill and he has a big day tomorrow. So I stood and watched it for a while.

Actually, it was quite beautiful. The dome was pulsing rather than flashing, gently pulsing, growing brighter and then fading in turn, as if Aspire was trying to communicate with a Mother Ship somewhere out there in space, calling for it to come and scoop it up, and take it away. I looked out into the night sky, to see if I could make out a Mother Ship with an enormous pair of bubble-wrapped breasts heading in our direction, answering the call to suckle Aspire. But there was nothing. Then I thought I heard a faint humming, a thrumming, or maybe a moaning or a droning, and wondered if for some reason Dan and Gentle Rain were humming to themselves or to each other. You never really know with young people, and I certainly don't.

Maybe Aspire was going to take off? Maybe it would lift off before my very eyes and levitate outside my bedroom window just long enough for Dan and Gentle Rain to wave, before shooting off at warp speed into the heavens. Susan from next door would be pleased. It would be problem solved as far as she was concerned. She would say to me, 'So you finally decided to get rid of it?' And I would say, 'Actually Susan, it took off and flew into orbit at three o'clock this morning.' And she would say, 'Oh good. No need for a skip then.'

I went back to bed and closed my eyes and forced myself to go to sleep by imagining I'm making a coffee and walnut cake. I'm usually asleep before I have to make the icing.

Dan was in the kitchen when I came down in the morning. He didn't look as if he had slept, and he was on his own. 'You're up early,' I said, and I knew something was wrong.

'I've split up with Gentle Rain,' he said. 'She's gone.'

'Oh dear,' I said. 'That's a shame. Why? You were getting along so well. You were talking about getting married. What happened?'

'You won't believe this,' he said, 'but it turns out she's fantastically rich, and her family all have titles and estates. They own huge amounts of land and property. She's only here over the summer because she's bored with cruising around the Med in

49

her dad's yacht. She lied about everything. I can't believe she's done this to me. I had to end it.'

I looked at his face, crumpling with pain as he wrestled with the infamy of GR's wealth and good fortune, and the heart-breaking realisation that she normally spends the summer cruising around the Med in the family yacht. I took a deep breath, and called upon my shallow reserves of maternal tact. 'Daniel,' I said, 'have you gone completely mad? Are you telling me you've split up with Gentle Rain because she's very rich? Couldn't this be a good thing? Why split up with Gentle Rain because she's rich when you thought she was poor? She's still the same girl, surely?'

'But she's not,' he said. 'She told me her parents were Celtic troubadours farming llamas on the Isle of Theneu off the west coast of Scotland, and she didn't see any television until she was sixteen. She said her whole family was desperately poor but very creative, and she was educated by a hermit guy. Turns out she went to a seriously posh boarding school from the age of eight and she's never even seen a llama.'

This sounded like win-win to me, to be honest. An occasion to merit wild rejoicing. But I couldn't talk him round. I tried, but it was no good. He said GR had strung him along, fed him lies, made him think she was someone she wasn't, invented a ridiculous fictional past for herself which she thought he would be stupid enough not to question, and now he felt duped, and he wouldn't be able to believe anything else she ever told him.

I said – 'But on the plus side Dan – the yacht in the Mediterranean sounds rather nice.'

He was shocked, and said he couldn't believe how materialistic and shallow I had become. Actually, I've always been materialistic and shallow, but I sensed he wouldn't be reassured to know there had been no recent deterioration.

'Oh well,' I said. 'You've still got her phone number. You might feel like getting in touch again once you get a bit of perspective on things.'

'Yeah,' he said. 'Maybe.' Then he asked me if there really was an Isle of Theneu off the west coast of Scotland. I said I hadn't heard of one. So he picked up his phone and deleted her number.

Young men are a bit inclined to take themselves too seriously. I'll wait a while before I tell him I have her number in my phone but, I have to admit, at the moment a reconciliation doesn't look likely.

I made him some bacon and eggs, and asked him what he would do today. He said he was going to have an hour's kip, and then he was going to look for pine cones, and then he thought he might go to see Baz. Baz was working for a local landscape gardener, and he was a good mate, and there might be a job going.

My heart sank slightly at the mention of Baz. I like Baz, he's a nice lad. I taught him English when he was in year ten, or rather, he was present in the room when I was teaching English to a year ten class, which is not the same thing. Somehow Dan and Baz together combine to make some other kind of entity which is a lot less manageable than either of them separately. When they were younger they amounted to more together than the sum of their parts, but not in a way you would particularly want to celebrate.

***

Laura on the phone this morning. Said she was ringing to tell me that little Harry had moved.

'Moved?' I said. 'Moved where? Moved out?'

She said she had put him down on a cushion on the floor to change his nappy, then nipped upstairs to get the zinc ointment, and when she came down he had moved across the floor. She said she got such a shock. Apparently, he was a whole metre away from where she had put him down.

I said, 'Well, he's a big boy and he's quite lively and vigorous, he must just have rolled over.'

She said I didn't understand. Now that she knows he can move around, her life will have to change. She can't rely on him staying in the same place ever again.

I had to explain to her that the thing about children is that you can't rely on them staying in the same place. If they did, and you could move them around like chess pieces, parenting would be easy, and Dan would be in Sainsbury's having a Management Trainee badge pinned to his shirt, instead of wherever he actually is at the moment.

Laura said she had thought it would be at least another month before Harry started to roll over. And I said, maybe he's advanced for his age? He might have a very high IQ.

Anyway, whatever it is, said Laura, she would have to watch him very carefully from now on, now that he can move around. She was just letting me know, to keep me up to date.

'Thanks love,' I said. 'Much appreciated.'

Actually, I am quite well updated on the whole children moving around thing. I have known for a while it can be problematic.

I thought about it while I emptied the dishwasher from last night, and imagined how it might be to have some knowledge and control of your children's whereabouts. I imagined a large map-table in a Second World War bunker. I saw it surrounded by women in uniform with headphones and microphones and long sticks with flat ends for tracking their children's movements across the map. I imagined these women nudging little wooden figures around the map-table, and heard them saying into their microphones – 'Suitable girlfriend dead ahead. Forward full steam!' Or – 'Sighting of unsuitable drinking buddy! Take immediate avoiding action!' I saw myself nudging a little wooden model of Dan across the map with the flat end of my stick, saying, 'Approaching Sainsbury's Management Training Programme undercover and with stealth. Switch off radio transmissions.' And – 'Lost contact with suitable girlfriend!

Panic stations! All hands on deck!' And finally, 'Vodka bottle and drinking straw now clearly visible. Dive! Dive!'

My phone chirruped on the window ledge. Something was stuck in its throat. It was a text from Jen – Are you going to bother asking me about my date? Do you care? Have you forgotten I exist? What the hell's the matter with you?

I gave her a ring and made my excuses, I told her Dan and Gentle Rain had split up, and things were a bit difficult.

Jen has no sympathy. 'But they're *children*,' she said. 'What does it matter at that age? It's normal, it's natural, it's part of growing up. Who cares if they've split up? Dan'll have another girlfriend in five minutes. Five minutes! I'm almost fifty, and this whole thing is starting to get pretty serious. Forget about them, I need you to worry about me.'

'Right,' I said. 'So tell me, how was your date with the man from the library?'

'Terrible,' she said. 'It was terrible. He moaned the whole time. Moaned about his former wife, moaned about his kids, moaned about his hips, said he wasn't impressed with the café, complained to the waitress that the coffee was cold and the flapjack was soggy. He didn't ask a single question about me, other than he wanted to know where I'd parked the car. Then he told me I'd parked it in the wrong place.'

I said that's awful. I asked her if she had made her excuses and left.

She told me no. She didn't make any excuses. She told him straight that he was giving every indication of being a miserable bore and that wasn't the kind of person she was looking for, so sadly, she was going to have to say goodbye. He took offence apparently, and said she hadn't given him much of a chance. So she'd said, okay, he had five minutes to change her mind, because she didn't have time to mess around.

I admired her direct, no-nonsense approach, but I sensed this date was pretty well doomed.

She said she thought at first that he was going to rescue the situation. After she had delivered her five minute ultimatum he made a promising start and said, 'Enough about me, what about you?' And then he'd asked her how long she had been on her own.

She told him she had been on her own for two years, and he cut her off at that point and said – 'Two years? Just two years? That's nothing! I've been on my own for ten years since my wife took off with our mortgage advisor. The first two years are a piece of cake compared to the next eight, believe me. I don't think there's much you can tell me about being on your own after a break-up.'

And as it turned out there was absolutely nothing she could tell him about anything at all, because she upped and left and she hopes she never sees him again.

'Sorry to hear that, Jen,' I said. 'That's not the best start to your dating career.'

She agreed, and then she told me she's had it with libraries. What she needs to join now is a rambling group. That's where the action is. What's the point of living in the north if she doesn't get out into the glorious countryside? She could be walking around with rugged northern men strong enough to carry her over mountain streams, or to carry her across nasty muddy patches, or to carry her down the mountain if she twisted a delicate feminine ankle. If she plays her cards right her feet need never touch the ground. She's going to find a rambling group, and fall into the arms of a strong rambling man.

Chapter 4 – September

I was woken up last night at 2.30 am by a general collapsing noise and stifled laughter. Dan and Baz had been out somewhere and had ended up back here well after midnight. Baz had tried to open the cupola on top of Aspire, thinking it was hinged. They told me all about it at lunchtime today. Apparently, it was a real laugh. Apparently, I would have pissed myself. Baz said they had had a few, and they thought they would just doss down in the Ass Pile, and he had tried to open the plastic tit on the top to let a bit of air in. He said he thought it was a skylight, so he pushed on one end, and the whole pile of crap nearly fell down.

I marvelled at how – in so short a time – the dome to echo the great domes of classical architecture had become the plastic tit on the top. With Baz on the scene, Aspire was beginning to lose some of its mystique. I wondered if it had a future without Gentle Rain's devotion. Perhaps Dan will lose his enthusiasm for it.

I said, 'Maybe it's time to think about taking it all down?'

Baz said, 'Take it down? No. It just needs sorting out. I've got friends living in half that much space. It's got shed-loads of potential. For a pile of crap.'

Then they both went outside to assess the damage caused by last night's attempt to ventilate the pile of crap. Baz is in favour of strengthening the construction with material which has not been recycled. This will flout the eco ethic of Aspire, but without Gentle Rain's influence I think a flouting is very much on the cards. Baz is much more interested in the potential of

Aspire to offer accommodation than to offer hope for the future of the planet.

I flicked through my BettaBrush catalogue this afternoon, impressed by the ingenuity of the items on display. I wondered whether I could buy a brush specifically designed for brushing all my other brushes, but there didn't seem to be a special brush-brushing brush. However, I did spot a fascinating gadget for removing wax from the ears. It looked a bit like an electric toothbrush with a right-angled bend in it. You stick it in your ear and switch it on. It scoops all the wax from your ear, and when it's finished a small scented candle pops out the other end.

Marvellous. But it was the advertising slogan, 'Make yourself a better listener!' that made me think about Jen, and her date yesterday, and how unsuccessful it had been.

I can understand perfectly Jen's irritation with the complaining man in the café, and his very poor attempt to be an entertaining date. But really, this common scenario could be so easily avoided. Social conversations of this sort would not fail so completely if we all had proper tuition in how to conduct them. Conversation skills should be on the curriculum at school, and the first general lesson we should learn is that talking is not conversing, and complaining is not entertaining, and if you open your mouth to make noises at another person you have a duty not to unwittingly anaesthetise them. The second lesson would be how to recognise when the person you are talking to is becoming dangerously bored.

We are told how to recognise the signs of someone having had a stroke, or having a heart attack, but we are not warned about the signs of someone suffering from terminal boredom. We should be taught how to spot the signs – but we aren't. So, in the event of anyone reading this now or at any time in the future, here are those tell-tale signs.

If you are talking to someone and you notice their eyes starting to roll back into their sockets, this should alert you to something amiss with your line of patter. If after another minute you see your companion's head drop forward onto their chest, and you detect in them a complete lack of muscle tone and see them lurch to the side and appear to have died, then you must stop describing the layout of your holiday bungalow.

Even if you have not mentioned the flange on the kitchen cupboard drawers, even if you have not fully described the moulding on the architraves around the doors – you must, *must* stop. Resist the temptation to describe how you cut and glued the tiles to the floor. Lives are at stake, and time is short.

Quick! Administer a series of reviving questions about your companion's own experience, and give them therapeutic injections of intelligent interest in their replies. Gradually their posture will appear more normal, and they will be able to lift their head, and look about them. They will be dazed at first, but soon they will be able to focus their gaze, and contemplate a future for themselves.

In Jen's case her male companion did not correctly interpret her body language. Jen's body language was crying out, 'Help! Help! I'm too bored to take a breath! My heart can't be bothered to beat!' and he thought it was saying, 'Please! Tell me more about these minor annoyances that you find so intensely irritating!'

Big mistake.

Relationship over.

I am never bored with what Dan has to say. I sometimes wish I was. He came home late this afternoon with two carrier bags full of something and tipped one of them out on the kitchen floor. About fifty pine cones spilled in all directions. 'Pine cones,' he said. 'And some earwigs.'

I asked him what the pine cones were for. He said Gentle Rain – Victoria – thought they would look good sewn onto thread and hung like a screen at the door of Aspire.

I said I thought that was a lovely idea, but Dan said he didn't think he could be bothered with it now.

I know Daniel well and I thought there might be a bit of a funk coming on, so I decided a little pep talk might be a good idea. 'Dan,' I said, 'I hope you're not going to neglect Aspire now, because if it falls into disrepair it will quickly become the pile of rubbish it actually is.'

He looked at the pine cones and nudged one with his foot. He told me he missed Gentle Rain. I said, give her a ring. He said he didn't have her number. I said I've got her number in my phone. He took his phone out of his pocket and I went to get mine from the windowsill.

Then his phone rang, and he answered. 'Baz!' he said. 'Yeah, all right. Yeah. All right. Yeah. Right. Yeah yeah. Right. Bye.' He rang off, and said he was going out.

I looked through the BettaBrush catalogue after he left. I was looking for a gadget, long and thin, black with a white tip, which you could wave about in the air and use to change things for the better.

***

Susan from next door rang me at quarter to eight this morning. Bill had just pulled out of the drive and the phone rang. Susan said, 'Is that you Sally?'

I said, 'Yes, Susan, it's me.'

And she said, 'Your lad is asleep on my lawn.'

I said, 'Dan? Dan is asleep on your lawn?'

'Yes,' she said, 'fast asleep. And he's got someone with him. I think you'd better come round.'

I checked Dan's room on my way out to see if by some miracle Susan was mistaken and he was actually in his bed, but he wasn't. I ran downstairs and out of the house, through my front gate and into Susan's and down along the side of her house. She was standing on her lawn with her arms folded, staring down at two figures recumbent on the grass. They were Dan and Baz. 'What do you make of this?' she asked me.

'Sorry Susan,' I said, 'I'll wake them up and take them away.'

Susan wasn't satisfied. 'But what are they doing here?' she said. 'Why are they asleep on my lawn? Can't they sleep in their own beds?'

I made a stab at an explanation, 'Maybe it was dark when they got back here last night, and they wandered into the wrong garden?'

'Wandered into the wrong garden? They've got no business wandering into the wrong garden. They can't go wandering into people's gardens in the middle of the night for a kip, Sally. It's not right.'

'Yes, I know,' I said. 'It's inexcusable. They'll come and apologise properly, just as soon as they get freshened up a bit. I promise.'

'Freshened up a bit?' she said. 'Sobered up, more like.'

I went over to Dan and bent down and shook his shoulder. 'Dan,' I said. 'What on earth are you doing here, on Susan's lawn?'

He didn't open his eyes, but he said, 'Can I have ten more minutes?'

'Ten more minutes!' Susan said. 'I'll give him ten more minutes!'

Dan woke up, rolled over and woke Baz up, and they both shambled to their feet, and dusted themselves down. Dan was appropriately shamefaced, and apologised to Susan for being in the wrong garden. But Baz was in excellent spirits, and seemed unaware that Susan was not his willing B&B hostess. He told Susan he had slept well, and complimented her on her really comfortable grass, and wondered whether a high moss content had made it nice and springy. He said the contours had been good for his back and he looked very pleased with the whole experience.

Susan was momentarily nonplussed and Baz took this as encouragement. He leant against a plum tree and wanted to hang around for a bit and chat about the merits of Susan's al fresco accommodation, and possibly to enquire about bacon and eggs with a view to awarding her five stars for her excellent hospitality. But before he could get going I shepherded him and Dan out of Susan's garden and back into ours. When she regained the power of speech Susan would not be in the mood for pleasantries.

Soon the three of us were assembled in our kitchen, and I asked both Dan and Baz what on earth they were playing at, dossing down in our neighbour's garden overnight?

Baz explained that they had had a few last night, and they were looking for the Ass Pile, but they couldn't find it, so they thought they'd just go to sleep and find it in the morning.

I said, 'Do you think there is any possibility that you two might be drinking too much when you go out of an evening?' I said I was only asking because this morning I'd found them asleep alongside next door's flower beds, and that does make you wonder.

They were genuinely puzzled. No, they said. No, they didn't think the problem was too much to drink, definitely not. They'd had a few last night, but they weren't drunk. Dan said he thought he had been very tired, but definitely not drunk. Baz said he had been very tired too, but sober as a judge. Then he went to the loo, had a drink of water, and took Dan off to find work with the landscape gardening firm. Apparently, there is a huge pile of decorative stones to shift.

After they had left, I noticed Dan's phone lying on the kitchen table. He had forgotten to take it with him. I looked at it for a little while, and thought how odd it was that this phone, this lump of plastic, knows so much more about my own son than I do. This phone had nothing to do with his birth, it has never made Dan a meal, nor has it washed so much as a pair of his socks. But it sits there smugly on the table, knowing all sorts of things about my own flesh and blood that I don't know.

A few dishonourable thoughts went through my head. Thoughts which did me no credit at all. I thought about looking through his texts and messages, maybe seeing if there had been any communication with Gentle Rain, and so on. I allowed myself to think these thoughts, and bounce them around a bit, toying with them, trying them on for size, seeing if any of them fit. Once or twice my hand reached out for his phone and then withdrew. I was wrestling with my conscience, I suppose. Generally, my conscience is pretty easily overcome in a straight fight, usually I can get it in a headlock and knee it in the balls and throw it aside effortlessly and proceed without it. But something was holding me back. So I picked up Dan's phone delicately between finger and thumb as if it might bite, and I put it on the window ledge next to mine, out of harm's way.

I had almost forgotten it was there, until a couple of hours later when I was putting shopping away and Dan's phone rang. I picked it up and answered it. 'Hello,' I said. 'Can I help you? This is Dan's phone but I'm looking after it for him today.'

'Hello Sally,' said a girl's voice. 'It's Gentle Rain.'

I said, 'Hello! Hello Gentle Rain! It's lovely to hear from you!' I asked her how she was. I said I missed seeing her around. I asked her how she was again. I smiled at her down the phone, in case she could see me.

She said she thought I might be annoyed with her for not being honest with Dan about her title, and her wealth, and her family's yacht in the Mediterranean.

I said 'No, no! No, no, no, no! I'm not annoyed – not at all.' And I went on to say that I thought the whole honesty thing was over-rated, by and large. I told her I didn't bother with it much.

She asked how Dan was. I said, 'Well – I had to tick him off this morning for spending last night asleep in next door's garden, but, you know, apart from that, he's okay.'

She asked if I thought he would take a call from her.

'Of course he will,' I said, 'why wouldn't he? He'll be glad to hear from you.' I said – 'Shall I ask him to give you a ring when he gets home?'

She said, 'Yes please, I'd really like to hear from him.'

'Great,' I said, 'I'll do that. I'll ask him as soon as I see him.'

***

I heard Dan come in after Bill and I had gone to bed last night. He woke me up when he came in at about 12.30. He sounded quite sober, I could tell by the way he managed to get his key in the lock first time.

So I was awake, and I wasn't able to get back to sleep, and then I started to fret in that middle-of-the-night way that we all do. It's obviously a chemical thing that happens in the brain after we've been lying horizontal in bed for a few hours. Some sort of depressing sludge collects in the lobes of the brain and starts to get us down. Maybe when we're up and about it drains away harmlessly and is digested by our gut. I realise this isn't mainstream thinking, but that's what it feels like. Anyway, after about twenty minutes of turning my head this way and that on the pillow in a bid to dislodge the sludge, it became clear to me that the whole sorry episode of my life was a disaster. Both Laura and Dan had problems I couldn't help them with. My closest friend had moved away. I was eating too much chocolate. I was getting older. I'd be fifty before you know it. The MOT on my car might have expired four months ago. I had probably missed my last dental appointment. My memory was getting worse. I was eating too much chocolate. Dan might go to prison for fly tipping. The planet is doomed.

After almost an hour of this mental turmoil I was friendless, ancient, toothless, gorged on chocolate, unable to remember how to drive my car, in prison and facing Armageddon. Then it occurred to me for the very first time that my husband was called Bill and my son-in-law was called Ben and my whole life felt absurd.

I was only minutes away from getting out of bed to slit my throat with my leg razor, when I fell asleep. It was nearly broad daylight.

So I slept in. Bill and Dan had both left when I got out of bed at 8.40. There were two notes on the kitchen table when I got downstairs, one from Bill saying, 'A lie-in will do you good' and one from Dan saying, 'Can you wash my red T-shirt?'

I felt a little better after a strong cup of coffee.

I was in school this afternoon, doing my learning support stint, encouraging Lee to draw a diagram of a rift valley in his geography lesson. We had the rift valley more or less on the page, traced onto a double page spread in Lee's exercise book. We were just about to do some labelling when a bug with legs on it fell from Lee's head into our crayon ravine. Lee pushed the bug around with the tip of his brown pencil and said, 'What's that?'

I said, 'I think it's a head louse.'

He recoiled, and said, 'Fuck, Miss! Have you got head lice?'

I said, 'Well one of us has, Lee.' I was going to add, 'And my money's on you,' but I didn't. I took him along the corridor via Reception to the sick bay, and sat him down under an Anglepoise lamp to inspect his head. Lucy from Reception came with us, because she knows how to spot head lice, and they can be quite difficult to see. As it happened, we didn't have any trouble at all spotting head lice on Lee's head – they practically marched up in formation and introduced themselves. Lucy took over from me at that point, she knows the procedure, and Lee was more than happy to have head lice once he understood it was not compatible with being in school.

So I left school a little early, seeing as my pupil had been taken away to be fumigated. My head felt itchy on the way home, but I told myself that it had to be psychosomatic. I've been a teacher for long enough to know that head lice don't have wings, and they don't jump from one head to another like grasshoppers.

I was home in time to rehearse how I might suggest to Dan that he should return Gentle Rain's call of yesterday. And it did need some rehearsal. If I said to Dan, 'Gentle Rain rang yesterday and she'd like you to give her a call and I told her you would,' he would say he would think about it. Obviously, I couldn't just tell him to return her call because he would say no. Neither could I say it would be a good idea to return her call because he'd say it wouldn't be a good idea. I could suggest that it might be a *nice* idea to return her call. 'Nice' could have more traction than 'good', but he might sense moral blackmail.

I was peeling potatoes around six-thirty when the kitchen door opened behind me and I heard someone say, 'Hiya! Dan said it would be okay just to come in.'

I turned around and saw a girl I vaguely recognised brushing her feet on the doormat. She looked brisk and energetic — I could tell by the way she was brushing her feet that she was not a dreamer. She looked up and smiled, 'You've got a really nice kitchen,' she told me, 'I like those wipe clean units much better than wood. And I bet those are real granite worktops.'

'Thank you,' I said. 'We used to have wooden units but I like wipe clean better. The tops aren't real granite, though.'

'Are they not?' She was very surprised. 'They're really good fakes then. Best I've ever seen.'

She was stroking the front of a wipe clean unit and smiling at me. She seemed familiar but I couldn't quite place her. I was going to ask her who she was but we seemed to have got beyond basic introductions. I wondered if I should just cut to the chase and adopt her.

'Dan'll be in in a minute,' she said cheerfully. 'He's just doing something to the heap at the side.'

The heap at the side. Sounds as if this girl knows her onions. Dan came in seconds later and put a flask and an empty sandwich box down on my really good fake granite worktop. 'Mum,' he said, 'I'm going to have a shower then me and Sophie

64

are going out for a bit. Have a seat, Sophie,' he said, and she sat down at the kitchen table.

Dan went upstairs and Sophie said, 'It's funny me being here when you used to teach me English, isn't it?'

I said, 'Yes, it is a bit.'

She said, 'I was crap at English.'

'Oh,' I said, 'I'm sure you weren't that bad.'

'Well you said I was,' she told me.

Thankfully Dan wasn't long in the shower. I managed to have a quick word with him before he went out, while Sophie was busy texting her mum. 'Dan,' I said, 'can you find time just to give Gentle Rain a quick ring? She rang yesterday asking if you would get in touch.'

Sophie looked up. 'Gentle Rain?' she said, 'Is that somebody's name? I suppose they can't help it, but it sounds a bit daft.'

'Yeah,' said Daniel. 'Pretty bloody silly.'

And they went out.

***

Bill and I had a long chat last night. At least fifteen minutes. I told him I was concerned about both Dan and Laura. I said Dan's behaviour was frankly bizarre, and I hadn't heard from Laura for a while, so God knows what's happening there. Last I heard she thought her husband was a sex maniac.

Bill listened very attentively and then said he thought I should join an evening class. He thought he remembered me saying I would join a French evening class after I took a break from teaching. Forget about the kids, he said, they're grown up now and they'll make their own decisions and live their own lives. They're doing fine. But he thought I might need to do something just for myself, and an evening class might be a good start. It would give me an interest. Something to occupy me.

I'd had a glass of wine by then. I find that just one glass can make me very resistant to the idea that I might need to be given an interest to keep me occupied. The grapes made me truculent.

Maybe they were an awkward vintage. I said I didn't want to learn fucking French.

'Well,' said Bill, 'what about writing? You've always enjoyed scribbling. What about joining a writing group? There's dozens of them now. You'd enjoy that, wouldn't you?'

'Scribbling?' I said. 'Scribbling? What does that mean – scribbling? Maybe if I'm only capable of scribbling I should look for a scribbling group? Perhaps I'll find a little group of chimpanzees looking for another member to join them in some scribbling? That would be fun.'

Bill said he hadn't meant to say scribbling. He meant to say writing. Totally unintentional slip of the tongue. Not what he meant at all.

So I relented, and told Bill that he did have a point. I do need to think of other things, and stop worrying about Dan and Laura. Nothing they do makes sense to me. Everything they say makes me wonder if they're sane. But Bill's right. I should stop worrying about them, it's a waste of time. I may as well worry about Saturn having too many rings, which it has of course, but there's nothing I can do about it.

And since that conversation with Bill, I've been thinking it over. Maybe joining a French class would be a good idea? I'd love to be able to speak French, as it happens. But the trouble is, I don't want to go to the bother of learning French. That's it in a nut shell, really. In a petite noisette. It's a problem, and I don't know how to get around it. It's the reason I don't speak French. It makes me mad to think about it. I could be fluent in French if I made the effort. It's infuriating, but I just don't want to work that hard. I'd like to learn French by plugging myself into the mains and drinking Burgundy.

I've had several stabs at learning French over the years, with tapes and then CDs. I'm familiar with the bleak, circular conversations you have to listen to and take part in. The people in these language-learning hinterlands have such strange obsessions. One CD scenario I remember from years ago featured a Frenchman who was fixated on buying a warm hat for his grandmother. He went on and on about this stupid hat and how big it had to be and what colour. He was constantly asking for my opinion on the wretched thing – as if I cared – I'd never even met his grandmother. I abandoned the *Learn French the Easy Way by choosing Hats for Old Farts* language course just three lessons into a possible twenty, so I still don't know what his grandmother has on her head. She was outrageously demanding, so I imagine the poor bloke is probably still looking for a hat that suits her. I hope she saves him the trouble by choking on a verb and dying a horribly irregular death.

No, I've been thinking about what I'm going to do to give myself a bit of an interest, and instead of learning French I'm going to do some entertaining. I'm going to become a social hub, and host a dinner party. A proper dinner party for eight people. I'll bring the dining room out of mothballs, buy some pretty serviettes, and root around for some matching knives and forks.

Tomorrow, I'll start looking through recipe books.

***

It's ages since I've tried a new recipe. I seem to be rotating the same four dishes over and over again. It's odd nobody's noticed. My recipe books have been undisturbed on the shelves for years. They were a bit shocked this afternoon at being suddenly pulled off the shelves and consulted. They shed pages in alarm and several pages stuck together with fright and refused to be pulled apart. They thought they had gone into a quiet retirement, and never expected to yield up a new recipe ever again. They were fast asleep when I made a grab for them and started pointing at their pages and criticising what they had to offer. I spent about half an hour looking through recipes and dismissed them all for one reason or another. I don't like recipes with too many ingredients, and I never cook anything I can't pronounce, or have to soak first.

Jen texted me while I was wondering whether bulgur wheat has anything to do with Bulgaria. She asked if I was busy. I texted back, Not especially, and so she rang. She said she was going on a ramble in a couple of days, and she would be rambling mostly with men. She has joined an advanced rambling group, because that was the group with the men in it, and she was wondering what to wear to go rambling about with men. She said she had worked with men and drunk with men and danced with men and gone to bed with men, but she had never rambled with men, and she had no idea what to wear.

I said she would need some stout shoes, or possibly proper walking boots. She said she wouldn't be seen dead in stout shoes, but she had some comfortable trainers, and some leggings, and a rather nice wool jumper which came down to just above her knees, and she thought she would wear a sky blue bandana. I said that sounded about right, that was what ramblers wore, and the bandana was a good touch. I told her once you have a sky blue bandana on your head, you can ramble about for miles.

Then I told her about my plan to do some entertaining. I said I was going to host a dinner party for eight people and it would be fun.

'Bloody hell,' she said. 'Eight people? Have you invited anybody yet?'

I said no.

'Thank God,' she said, 'there's still time – you can scrap the whole idea.'

'But,' I said, 'I like the whole idea.'

She asked me how long it was since I'd hosted any sort of dinner party? She asked me if I had forgotten the panic, the stress, the sauces that won't thicken, the essential ingredient you forget to buy, the rice which congeals to a glutinous brick, the potatoes which boil dry, the slimy chocolate mousse, the tube of KY jelly accidentally left lying on the kitchen bench that you just don't see until halfway through the evening when someone picks it up and says, 'I hope we're allowed some cream with this!'

'God, Jen,' I said. 'What sort of nightmarish dinner parties have you experienced? They sound like hell on earth. I'm not planning to have that sort of dinner party.'

She said no-one plans to have that sort of dinner party. However, if something is going to go tits up in your kitchen, it will wait until you have eight people coming round for a meal. She pleaded with me to forget the whole idea. She said after five years she is still recovering from the last dinner party she ever gave, which went wrong from the moment the guests arrived early to the moment they all left with food poisoning.

I said don't worry Jen, I can handle it.

She said I was a brave woman. She said rather me than her. She was very glad that her new flat mate, a ball of kapok the size of a bull elephant, had moved in and made it impossible for her to have anyone around for a meal.

***

I have now constructed a shopping list to cope with the demands of this dinner party. It runs to pages. It has headings and sub headings, and it is colour coded. To call it a shopping list is to underestimate it. It is a purchasing document. It will take two days in the shops to meet its demands.

Everyone I have invited can come. Two of Bill's work colleagues and their partners, and Pam and Dave, Judith and Geoff. Bill gets on really well with Geoff, so I will cope with Judith. This should be a good mix overall, but a logistical problem has become apparent. We can't seat ten people around the dining table. Bill said he thought I was inviting six, making eight including us. I said no, I've invited eight people. Bill said he and I would have to sit on a smaller table in the hall just outside the dining room. He said if we left the door open we would be able to hear most of the conversation. I said no, that wouldn't work, and he asked me if I had a better idea.

So, we're going to move the chest of drawers out of the dining room, and use the extra space to accommodate an extension to the dining table which we will construct from an MDF board and some supports. Bill says he can easily knock these up. Once we put a tablecloth over the whole thing, it will look like one long dining table. I asked Bill if he thought he had time for DIY, all things considered. He said it would make a very relaxing alternative to his day job, which at the moment consisted of knocking heads together and stopping people travelling too far up their own arses, which is always a danger in politics.

I've decided to do two roasts. Everybody likes roasts. I'll do a big piece of beef and some home-made Yorkshire puddings, and a piece of pork with home-made apple sauce and sage and onion stuffing, roast potatoes, mashed potatoes, vegetables and two nice meaty gravies, one with pork stock, and one with beef. Keep it simple. Should be a piece of cake. I have two weeks to prepare. Loads of time.

I went off to school this afternoon to see Lee, quite excited by the thought of doing some entertaining, it will be great to have lots of people round, even if one of them is Judith. I was in such a good mood when I got to school and went down to the art department to help with the lunchtime Art Club. But there's nothing like being surrounded by a bunch of kids armed with glue and staples to cure a good mood, and it only took a couple of minutes.

The art department is organising a space exploration themed exhibition, designed to impress parents on Open Day. It was my job to stand on a ladder and suspend a papier mâché astronaut from the ceiling with thin nylon threads. I almost had him in place when his head fell off and made a hole in the command module balanced on the desk below. I had Lee with me, and he made things worse by kicking the head around the room and trying to score goals with it.

The children who had lovingly fashioned the head were understandably squeamish about this, so I took Lee to one side and told him to stop kicking the astronaut in the head. Lee is not an overly sentimental child. He pointed out that the head had started life as a football, and with his help it was now , reverting to type. He said you can buy balls like that for £1. in Tesco's. Then the art teacher weighed in and told Lee to sit down and shut up, or he would be in detention until Tesco's opened a branch on Mars.

Lee sat down but he wasn't happy. He started to rock backwards and forwards on the back legs of his chair. He surveyed the room and looked hostile. He had a carnivorous look in his eye. To distract him and get him back on-side I suggested we made a big round moon, which we could hang from the ceiling alongside the astronaut. I told him we had some silver paint, and he could paint it with one of the massive paint brushes he so admired. It wouldn't take long, I said, and it would look fantastic.

But Lee said that idea was shite. So we decided against it.

I asked him whether he had brought his games kit to school, because he had games next lesson. Lee tried to remember whether he had any games kit with him, and he scratched his head. I thought at first that he might be concentrating, but then it occurred to me that I'd never actually seen him concentrate, so I began to wonder whether he still had head lice.

We went along to the PE department to get him kitted up with something before his lesson started, and on the way over I asked him if he had used the special shampoo to get his head really clean after the head lice infection. He said he had, but it stank, so he wasn't using it again. And anyway, he said, he liked his head lice and he didn't want them all to fuck off.

I got home around four-thirty and Dan came in by himself soon after, carrying a large plastic bag. He's almost always with someone these days, so I don't often get the chance to talk to him alone. I made us both a coffee and sat down with him at the kitchen table. He started to look a bit edgy. I think he suspected I was going to settle in to some sort of cosy mother-and-son chat which might result in me giving him good advice that he didn't want to hear, or me asking him questions he didn't want

71

to answer. Maybe he thought I would try to make eye contact and ask him how he felt about something. He glanced at his watch and said he thought he'd go and have a shower. I said, drink your coffee first, and offered him a biscuit.

'So!' I said – and I smiled in a chummy, here-we-both-are sort of way – 'How's the gardening job going?'

Good, he said, it was good. He liked working outside, he liked working with the other guys. Hard work though, he could do with a shower.

'Is this something you could see yourself doing longer term?' I asked him, casually.

Maybe, he said. But he didn't know yet. He was just going to see how it goes. Too early to say. It was hard work, though, and he was looking forward to a shower.

'I've been meaning to ask you, Dan,' I said, 'Did you return Gentle Rain's call? I told her you would, so I'd feel a bit bad if you didn't. She might think I didn't pass her message on.'

Yeah, he said. She'd texted him and he'd texted her back.

'Oh good,' I said. 'How is she?'

'She's okay,' he said. 'But I'm with Sophie now.'

'Yes of course,' I said. 'What's in the bag?'

He said it was a doormat, Sophie had bought it for Aspire. He hadn't seen it yet. He picked up the bag and opened it, and the mat sprang out of his grip onto the floor. We both looked down to admire it. It lay on the floor inscribed with the message, 'Wot? No Underwear!!'

I said, 'Well, that's very kind of Sophie.'

Dan said it was, but now he was going for a shower. He went upstairs and left most of his coffee. I ate his biscuit.

***

Some days humiliate you almost beyond endurance.

I bumped into Judith this afternoon by chance while I was buying some non-perishables for the dinner party. She suggested we just have coffee together today, instead of waiting for our next scheduled session. We were both in town, we could both do with a break, it seemed like a good idea. So we went to M&S and settled down with our coffee, a flapjack for me and a poncey thing of fruit for her.

I drifted off a bit when she was telling me about a pay rise one of her children had just been given. Then I heard her say, 'Why do you keep scratching your head?'

'Sorry,' I said, 'I didn't realise I was scratching my head.'

'You've been scratching your head all the time I've been talking to you,' she said.

My God, I thought. Bloody hell fire. I've got head lice. I've got Lee's head lice.

I froze and stared at Judith in shock.

'Your head's itchy, isn't it?' she said. 'You've got head lice, haven't you? You must have got them from one of your toe-rags at school.'

'My head's not itchy,' I told her. But it was, it was very itchy. I couldn't scratch it now, not with Judith looking at me like that. So instead of scratching I opened my eyes very wide and then tensed my brow to try to move my scalp back and forward.

'Well there's something wrong with you,' said Judith. 'You look weird.'

'Tell me again about Morticia's pay rise,' I said.

'Morwenna,' she said. 'It's Morwenna's pay rise.' She looked at me suspiciously but she carried on. 'Yes, well, Morwenna was given promotion after she invented cold fusion –look!' she said. 'You're doing it again! You're scratching your head!'

'Judith, I'm going to have to go,' I said.

'Go by all means,' she said. 'Go straight to the chemists and get some of that stuff, what's it called? You know the stuff I mean. For infestations.'

'Catch you later,' I said, gathering up my bags.

She called after me as I made my way out of the café, 'Sally!' I turned and looked. 'I've just remembered! It's called Jeyes Fluid! Put it on your head twice a day!'

I went home via Boots, and by the time Bill got home from work I had some special Nit No More lotion on my head. I thought I'd give my hair a good soak, so I was sitting around while it took effect. Bill came in and said, 'Funny smell?'

'Bill,' I said, 'I've got head lice. You'll have to use some of this lotion too.'

'Oh right,' he said. He looked a bit anxious. 'Am I able to approach you, or should I keep my distance?'

I told him he could approach me but I'd rather he went into the kitchen and put the kettle on.

So he went into the kitchen, and seconds after he put the kettle on Dan came in. I heard Bill say, 'Hi Dan,' and Dan say, 'Hi Dad, how're you doing?'

'I'm fine, son,' said Bill. 'But your mother's got head lice.'

'Oh shit, Dad,' I heard Dan say. 'We'll have to chuck the furniture out.'

'They're not sitting on the furniture, Dan,' said Bill. 'They're sitting on your mum's head.'

'Hiya!'

'Hello Sophie,' I heard Bill say.

'Don't go in there Soph,' said Dan. 'Mum's in there and she's got head lice.'

'Has she?' said Sophie, 'I didn't think teachers could get head lice. I thought they were immune or something. But I suppose she's not a proper teacher now, is she?'

I went upstairs to have a bath and rinse my hair. I thought I could use the nit comb, and weep.

As I was running the bath my mobile rang. I picked it up off the bed. It was Jen, with a rambling-with-men progress report.

'How did the walking go?' I asked her.

'Well it was a complete fucking disaster,' she said.

'Why? What went wrong?'

I turned the bath taps off and sat down on the bed while she told me the story. She said she met up with a bunch of men in a pub. There were two other women in the rambling group, but

74

they didn't look like her, one was made of gristle and bone, and the other was made of sinews and grit. They weren't wearing sky blue bandanas.

They showed her a map the size of a tablecloth, and started pointing to it and talking about it as if it meant something. They unfolded it and refolded it, and pumped it like a set of bellows to get some sense out of it. Then they looked at her footwear and they weren't happy. They asked her how much walking she'd done. She said she'd been walking around for years. They asked her if she had brought a compass. She said did they mean the little twiddly thing for drawing circles. They showed her the route plan on the map and asked her whether she was comfortable with it. She said it looked good to her.

Then they set off. But what they didn't tell her, Jen said, what they hadn't bothered to mention, was that it was all uphill. They went up, and up and up. She said her heart was pounding, her legs were screaming in pain, she couldn't keep up with the others even when they stopped and waited for her, and she had never hated anything as much since she had given birth.

She managed to ask someone when the walk would level out, and they said not for a good bit yet, so she sat down on the ground and grunted for a while and then said she couldn't go any further. Someone had to accompany her back down the hill, but it wasn't one of the men, it was one of the wire women, Myra.

Jen and Myra ended up back down the hill in the pub they had set off from. Myra had a ginger beer and Jen had a gin and tonic. They had a long chat while they were waiting for the others, and they talked about men.

Jen confessed to Myra that she was looking for a man, a male companion, someone to have a bit of fun with. Myra said she had come to the wrong place with the rambling group, because half the men were married and the other half were insufferable. But, she said, her brother was looking for a friendship with someone. He was divorced and a little lonely, a very nice man, a dentist working part time now. She could put Jen in touch.

So, Jen has another date. She's going to meet Myra's brother for coffee, but she's going to keep her expectations to a minimum so she won't be disappointed.

'Sensible,' I told her. 'Although,' I said, 'you could expect him to have his own teeth.'

'No,' she said. 'I'm not even going to expect that. Anyway, how's things with you?'

I said, 'Fine. I've got head lice.'

And she said, 'You always cheer me up, Sally.'

***

Bill has been working on the dining table extension during his very limited leisure time. I've been supplying him with cups of tea. I don't have much of a spatial sense, so I haven't offered to help.

A year or so ago when Jen was still living down the street she rang me and asked if I could come over and help her assemble an Ikea flat-pack. I went down and we pulled it out of the box and started putting it together. After a while, when it was partially assembled, I asked Jen what it was, and she said it was a bookcase.

We took a good look at it then. It was triangular with some spokes radiating outwards and an oblong off to the side. I said maybe we should have looked at the instructions before we started putting it together, but Jen said no-one ever looks at the instructions for flat-pack furniture. We turned it around a few times and tried to stand it upright. I said it was odd that there didn't seem to be any visible shelves in the conventional sense, and I wondered whether we were building a bookcase or something else entirely? Jen said she couldn't think what else it could be, she'd definitely ordered a bookcase. I said no-one in their right mind would order the thing that was taking shape before our eyes, not unless their floors weren't level and they had a large collection of triangular books. Jen agreed, and said it was beginning to unnerve her a bit, but she suggested we should just bash on and get it finished, rather than judging it when it was only half built. That was a common mistake most people made, she said, with flat-pack furniture. Often, it's not until you put the last few pieces in place that you see what it's meant to be.

So we carried on, and I was just putting the finishing touches to the flying buttress arrangement at the back, when Jen said she didn't think her books were the right shape for this thing. I said I thought we must have gone wrong somewhere, because as a rule bookcases don't look like spinning wheels. We tried balancing books on it here and there but they slid off onto the floor. It would have been an excellent bookcase if books were not book shaped, but for book shaped books it was no good at all.

Eventually Jen managed to get two books sitting on it quite nicely, and we left it at that. Neither of us could be bothered to take it all to bits, so it stood in the corner of Jen's living room until she moved house. She decorated it with fairy lights and it looked quite attractive, then she boxed up all her surplus books and took them down to the Oxfam shop.

***

Bill is making a really good job of the dining table extension. It is impressively underpinned with supporting struts, and looks like an offspring of our dining table and the Forth Rail Bridge. He's going to paint the whole thing with a dark oak stain. If he has time.

Ella came for lunch today, Sunday. She was anxious when I told her Bill was in the shed making an extension to the dining table. She tackled Bill about it before lunch and asked him whether he ought to be letting a professional do it, rather than making a mess of it himself. She reminded him that his talents didn't lie in that direction. She said the wooden spatula he made her for Mother's Day when he was ten years old had never worked properly. Bill said the table extension wasn't a difficult job, and he thought he could manage it.

Ella and I sat a while over our pre-prandial glass of sherry after Bill went back to work on the table. She was on edge. There was a noise from the shed and she gripped my arm. 'You're not letting him use power tools in there, are you Sally?' she said.

I told Ella that Bill was fifty-two and his power tools make him feel twenty years younger. I said we had to let him live a little, he spent too much time cooped up in offices trying to be reasonable. I said using power tools unleashed his inner Rambo. He would like to take power tools to work with him to support his arguments but he wasn't allowed. She asked me if we had a first aid box.

Laura called in after lunch, to say hello on her way home from lunch with Ben's parents. Little Harry was asleep in his carrycot, and we had strict instructions not to wake him up, otherwise he would grizzle until bedtime and take ages to go to sleep tonight. Ella was disappointed, and watched him sleep while willing him to wake up. She forgot about her plan to fashion a tourniquet from a tea towel, in case Bill severed a limb using glue.

I made us all a cup of tea. 'Isn't this nice?' I suggested, as Laura settled herself comfortably on the sofa beside her grandma. 'Three generations of womenfolk all together for a cosy chat.'

'Actually,' said Laura, 'there was something I wanted to ask you both. It's a bit personal, so don't feel you have to answer.'

'What's that dear?' said Ella.

I guessed what Laura was going to ask, and I didn't think it was a good idea.

'If this is what I think it is, Laura,' I said, 'I don't think this is a particularly good time.'

'You mean,' said Laura, 'because Grandma might be embarrassed?'

'She might, yes.'

Laura turned to her grandmother. 'Grandma, would you be embarrassed if I asked you how often you and Granddad had sex when you were younger?'

'Not particularly,' said Ella. 'When we were younger? I'm trying to remember. About three times a day? Does that sound about right?'

'Three? Three times a day? Are you sure, Grandma?'

'Well, not every day. But most days. Three or four times. I think I'm right.'

'Three or four? That seems quite a lot.' Laura looked at her grandmother with renewed respect.

'Does it?' said Ella. 'Is there a recommended upper limit now?'

'No,' said Laura. 'I don't think so.'

'Oh good,' said Ella. 'Things change so much, don't they, from one generation to the next. We used to think bacon fat was good for you, but I don't think they do now, do they? Yes, three or four times would be about right. And my advice would be, don't slacken off in your seventies and eighties, because it's even more important then.' Ella looked again at little Harry. 'Now then, I notice you're not swaddling. That's something that must have changed. In our day we used to wrap them up so tight they looked like little rows of plump cigarettes.'

And the conversation moved on.

When Bill was taking Ella home, and as I was helping Laura get her things together for her trip back, she suddenly sat down on the sofa and said, 'Mum, I think I might need some counselling.'

'Okay,' I said, 'shall I do it now? Or do you want me to come round later in the week?'

'Not from you, Mum,' she said. 'From a proper counsellor.'

'Oh.'

'No offence Mum, but you're not a professional.'

I didn't argue, so we continued packing the car and off she went. I watched her car drive off down the road and turn the corner at the bottom and then, in a bid to stay sane, I picked up my phone and gave Jen a ring. I was planning to discuss my thwarted counsellor status, but Jen got in first. She said she had had her date with the dentist and he was wonderful. She said he was really interested in what she had to say, he laughed at her jokes, he made jokes that were actually very funny, he read books and wanted to talk about them, and he wasn't like a man at all. He was like some other being that she hadn't realised until now walked the planet. She said it was early days, but she already knew he was the one she was looking for.

I said, 'He sounds great, when are you seeing him again?'

She said as soon as possible as far as she's concerned. In fact, she was waiting for him to ring, so did I have anything else I wanted to say?

'No,' I said, 'not particularly.'

'How are you, anyway?' she said, before she hung up. 'Weren't you planning to do something mad? A parachute jump or something? A sponsored tightrope walk? A naked swim with sharks?'

'You mean the dinner party?'

'That's it,' she said. 'The dinner party. Let me know when it's all over. You might need counselling.'

Chapter 5 – October

The day of the dinner party dawned sunny and unseasonably warm. Maybe not the best day for roasts, but with two large joints of meat in the fridge there was no possibility of switching to anything else.

I started on the meal about three o'clock, and contemplated my two roasts and all the separate trimmings menu. I could see now that this wasn't a good plan, so I jettisoned half of it, put the beef in the freezer and concentrated instead on the pork. I remembered that I had quite a good 'ham braised in cider' recipe, so on the spur of the moment I thought I'd use that.

I didn't have any cider, so I braised it in Coca-Cola. I didn't have Bramley apples so I used pears, and I didn't have red onions so I used leeks. I had no button mushrooms so I substituted sliced parsnips. I didn't have butternut squash so I used sweet potato, and of course, I was using pork not ham, but essentially it was exactly the same recipe. It was simmering nicely on the stove when the guests arrived.

There was a slightly tricky moment early on when everyone had been given a drink and we were all standing around in the living room, chatting. Judith said to Bill that I had been telling her about little Harry's IQ, and he must have been delighted to hear it was over 160. This was, of course, news to Bill, and I wondered how he would cope with it. But in his line of work, Bill is very used to appearing to know about things that are completely new to him, so he just said, 'Yes, marvellous isn't it?'

Judith pressed on, saying she had been so surprised to hear that it's even possible to test a child's IQ at only four months old. She looked around, inviting the others to share in her surprise. Bill asked her amiably whether she's ever had her own IQ tested. She said no, she hadn't. Bill offered to do it for her there and then, if she was interested. He said he had all the kit in the shed and it would only take ten minutes if she didn't mind wearing brain tongs and being wired up to the Clevertron machine. Judith said no thanks, maybe some other time, and they laughed, and the conversation moved on.

We sat down to eat. The first and second courses went smoothly enough. Everyone skilfully avoided political topics, and the conversation was lively and genial, but unfortunately it turned to drains and drain rods in time for the pudding. Geoff thought he had a blockage somewhere between the garage and the house and was seeking advice. My advice would have been not to talk about it while I was dishing up sherry trifle, but Judith had other ideas about how to achieve this end.

'Did I ever tell you,' she said, to distract the assembled company from contemplating the build-up of fatty deposits in drains, 'what happened the last time I met Sally for coffee?'

Geoff's flow, or lack of flow, had been interrupted, and people were turning to look expectantly at Judith. 'It was such a scream,' she said, 'I was talking to her in Marks and Spencer's café the other day, and I noticed she was scratching her—'

I couldn't possibly allow her to continue. I really did not want my head lice to be a topic of conversation over pudding. So I kicked out in Judith's direction under the table to try and shut her up, and at the same time I offered her a large scoop of trifle. My foot caught one of Bill's underpinning struts, and displaced it, and our end of the table began to lurch to one side. I reached out to steady the table, and took the opportunity to throw the generous portion of trifle at Judith. Bill dived underneath the table to shore it up, and Judith was shocked to incoherence by the serving of trifle now resting in her lap.

'What?' she said, 'What's this? How? How did—? Did you—?'

I stood up and went around the bottom of the table to scoop the trifle out of her lap and put it in a bowl. It occurred to me just to set the bowl down in front of her and invite her to eat it. After all, it hadn't been in anyone else's lap, and it was only in hers for a few seconds. But instead I took her off into the kitchen to sponge her down, and give her some pointers about acceptable dinner time conversation.

'Bloody hell, Judith!' I said, when we were both standing beside the kitchen sink. 'I didn't invite you round to tell everyone I had head lice! I don't know these people particularly well. My head lice would probably be the only thing they remember about me.'

'What's the big deal?' she said. 'Everyone gets head lice at some time or another. What the hell are you so touchy about? Christ sakes, you didn't have to throw trifle at me. Look at the state of my dress!'

'Your dress is fine', I said, dabbing at her with the dishcloth. 'It was very good trifle.'

'You did that deliberately, didn't you? You threw trifle at me to shut me up.'

'Of course I did. It was the only sane thing to do. I couldn't let you start entertaining everyone with tales of my head lice infestation! Over dinner? Give me a break, Judith!'

'I don't know what's got into you,' she said, as if I was being unreasonable. 'You're over-reacting. Big time. Stop rubbing my dress with that dishcloth, you're making it worse. I think you might need help Sally, I've thought it for a while.'

'What I need', I said, 'is for you to shut up about my head lice, because if you mention that again I'll tip the whole fucking trifle over your head, so help me God.'

'Everything all right?' Bill stood in the doorway.

'Absolutely fine Bill, thank you', I said. 'We'll be in in a minute.'

Bill left, and I threw the dishcloth in the direction of the sink.

'I think you're mad,' said Judith. 'Dangerously mad.'

I picked up a spoon and pointed it at her. 'Can we agree that you will not make any further reference to my head lice?'

'All right, all right. If it's going to cause this much trouble. Bloody hell. You're deranged. Back away and put the spoon down.'

I put the spoon down where I could see it and made sure the handle was turned towards me. 'Let's go back then,' I said.

She wasn't happy, but she didn't resist. We went back into the dining room and Judith sat quietly picking at some fruit salad. The conversation around the table had turned to holiday destinations. Pam was describing a yurt in which she had Dave had spent a pleasant week living like medieval serfs, when –

'Hiya!'

'Oh hello, Sophie,' I said. 'We've eaten most of the food, I'm afraid, but there might be enough for you and Dan if you have a rummage around in the kitchen.'

'Thanks!' she said, and she turned towards the kitchen. 'Oh!' she remembered something, and turned back, 'I've been meaning to ask you Mrs Forth, did you ever get rid of your head lice?'

***

So, I'm a bit off entertaining as a means to give myself an interest. I think I'll look elsewhere.

This time, I thought, I will approach identifying an interest more scientifically. I have been haphazard in my search for recreational pursuits. So, this morning I decided to make a list of all my interests and prioritise them. Then I would narrow down to one or two interests from the top of my list, in terms of how practical they would be to pursue. Some might be expensive, and others might be too time-consuming. I found paper and pencil, and sat down, ready to let my interests spill out onto the page.

I thought as hard as I could and bit my pencil and looked out of the window. Finally, after about five vacant minutes I wrote 'Milk' 'Bread' 'Fish' 'Eggs' 'Toilet paper', and went shopping.

I was so pleased to be in school this afternoon with the Learning Support Team. There were people here who could remember me in the days when I could still call myself a teacher. Back then, what I was doing seemed to matter. Back then, nobody expected me to have time for interests, or similar flummery. Proper teachers don't have time to be interested in anything.

Lee and I were in a maths lesson this afternoon, and soon it was obvious that like me, he wasn't having a particularly good day. Lee has never struck me as a numbers person. I'd like to say he's more of a words person, but he's not. He doesn't think in pictures either, so he's not a good visualiser. Sadly, he's not much of a team player, so he doesn't do well at sport, or any activity that requires a degree of co-operation on his part. Lee's talents are well disguised. No-one has any idea what they are. No-one on Earth. They are written in a code that no teaching qualification has been able to crack, and I know if I were to tell Lee this, he would regard it as the greatest achievement of his school career. This is why he is such a challenge for the education system. And likewise, of course, the education system is a challenge for Lee. The two are mutually incompatible. Lee understands this and has accepted it. However, School won't accept it, and this is why we have a problem.

All this situation needs to make it worse than it already is, is a requirement for Lee to understand vectors, and that's what we had this afternoon.

The vectors arrived, ten of them bristling on the page, lined up in a worksheet, ready to frustrate. Question one was all right, and questions two and three were okay, but question four was tricky. Lee is not a fan of working things out. He either knows the answer, in which case everything is fine, or he doesn't know the answer, in which case everything is shite.

So when we got to question four, everything was shite and he'd had enough of maths. He became restless and snapped his pencil in half. I knew how he felt, because I wanted to snap my pencil in half this morning when I couldn't work out what my interests were.

However, Mr Parks, Lee's maths teacher, made the mistake of chastising Lee for breaking his pencil. Worse still, he then went on to ask Lee how he would feel if all his pencils at home were snapped in half by one of his teachers. Lee said he wouldn't give a fucking shit and got us both thrown out of the lesson.

We went along to what is trendily called the 'Chill-Out' room, which is where staff can take pupils to calm down after they have become outraged by the necessity to attend school. There were one or two other renegades sitting around in there, throwing balls of paper and snapping pencils. A young and inexperienced member of staff was trying to make a bracing appeal to their better nature. 'Come on guys,' I heard him say, 'I'm sure you could be doing something much more interesting than throwing balls of paper around the room.'

I looked at the guys. They would take some convincing.

I took Lee off to one corner of the chill-out room for a little chat. I thought I should speak to him about his tendency to use bad language, which was getting him into a lot of trouble.

'Lee,' I said, 'you know, you wouldn't get into so much trouble at school if you didn't use such a lot of bad language.'

'What do you mean?' he said, bewildered.

'Do you think you could stop swearing so much in school, Lee?' I said. 'Because if you could, I think you would get on with your teachers better.'

'Swearing?' He looked puzzled. 'Like calling a teacher a knob head?'

'That's more of an insult,' I said. 'I was thinking of words like 'fuck', for example. You shouldn't use that word in school.'

'Is fuck swearing?' he asked me.

'Yes it is, Lee It's swearing.'

'Fuck,' he said. 'I didn't know fucking fuck was swearing.'

'And shite,' I said.

'Shite's swearing?'

'Yes it is.'

'Shit,' he said. 'That's shite.'

Anyway. We explored this theme for a while, and I think we made some progress. Clarified things a little. We had a bit of a session on it, looking into which words were all right to use and which words he should avoid. When we finished, he was worried about how he was going to communicate effectively in school with almost half his vocabulary denied him. He thought he wouldn't have enough words left to access his emotional side, and that was a concern. We have more work to do on this, but we've made a good start.

I texted Jen when I got home. She would probably have heard from her dream dentist by now. Any news from the dentist? I asked, coyly.

She texted back – Yes.

So I replied – And?!!

He doesn't want to see me again.

After a minute of staring at my phone and wondering how to reply, I rang her. 'Jen,' I said, 'I'm really sorry to hear that. That's so disappointing. What went wrong?'

'Nothing went wrong,' she said. 'He just said he'd really enjoyed our date, and he was sorry, but he didn't want to take it any further. Maybe he didn't fancy me.'

'He what? Are you sure that was it?' I said. 'How could he not fancy you? You're so nice.'

'Well – maybe, but being nice isn't enough. Obviously. You know how this works, Sally. Mother Theresa was very nice but nobody wanted to see her in a bikini. I fancied him and he didn't fancy me. And we're both too old to mess about. I have to move on.'

'Listen Jen, why don't you come up for the weekend? We could have a nice couple of days visiting old haunts.'

'Actually Sally, I can't. I might be seeing someone else this weekend. Someone I met at Tumble Tots. I've got to know him a bit.'

'Oh,' I said. 'So – a grandparent of a tumble tot?'

'Uncle, actually. He was with his nephew,' she said.

'Right,' I said. 'So, er, how old is this uncle?'

'I have absolutely no idea, Sally,' she said. So I knew he was very young.

***

I noticed a headline from our local paper on a billboard outside the Co-op today. **Grandma Stabs Cheating Husband.**

Why 'Grandma'? Why is it necessary for us to know that this woman is a grandma? There is obviously plenty of other stuff going on in her life, and the fact that she is a grandma is taking a back seat with her just at the moment by the sound of things – so why bring up the fact that she is someone's grandma?

I've noticed that once you become a grandma, you become endlessly fascinating to our local Press. **Grandma Runs Marathon! Grandma in Pub Brawl! Grandma in Naked Wrestling Shock!**

Even when going about their daily business grandmas make headlines. Not long ago, I saw a billboard proclaiming **Grandma Finds Toad in Lettuce!** When a woman does anything of note around here, the first thing the Press must ask when they get wind of it is – 'Is she a grandma?' Once they know she's a grandma, they know they've got a story.

Consider the following:

Grandma In Massive Lottery Win!

Amy Linklater, (a grandma), was delighted this week to win a massive £100,000 on the National Lottery. Our reporter Kath Dodds asked her, 'Do you put this win down to being a grandma, Amy?'

'I don't think so,' said Amy, 'I think I would have won anyway.'

'But surely, being a grandma will affect what you do with the money?'

'I don't think so, no. I think I'll just piss off to the Maldives.'

And next day on the billboards, **Lottery Win Grandma Pisses Off To Maldives!**

Grandads are not so newsworthy, I've noticed. It's less of an issue, when a man does something, whether he is a grandad or not.

I thought about this on the way home with my shopping, and wondered what it could possibly mean.

When I got home from the shops there was a man standing outside our house, looking at Aspire and making notes. He looked official. My heart sank. I thought, it's someone from the Council, someone from the Department of Rubbish Houses coming to declare Aspire a health hazard and slap a demolition order on it.

I said, 'Can I help you?'

'Yes,' he said. 'I was just admiring this structure.'

Admiring it?

He said he had been admiring it in passing for a week or so, and he wondered if he could have a quick look inside Aspire, to see how the dome had been fashioned and attached to the roof. I said by all means, so I showed him inside, then I stood just outside on the 'Wot? No Underwear!!' mat while he had a poke around at the walls and the dome. He pronounced it all very satisfactory, and explained that he was a jack-of-all-trades in our local amateur dramatics group. He wondered whether the person who built Aspire might have any interest in helping them out with set design and construction? He gave me his card. I said I would give it to my son, because – as he had probably guessed – I hadn't built this myself. No, he agreed, he'd have been very surprised if I'd built it!

Grandma in Rubbish Extension Shock!

So, off he went, and as he left, out came Susan from next door. She had obviously been watching this exchange from behind the geraniums in her porch.

'Don't tell me you've got a tenant!' she said.

'No, no,' I said. 'He was just admiring it, actually.'

'Admiring it?' she said, rolling her eyes. 'God love us.'

I wondered what it was that made Susan so relentlessly down-beat, some other aspect of her life must surely be getting her down.

'How's Derek?' I said. 'I haven't seen him for ages.'

'Well you wouldn't,' she said. 'He sits in front of the television, complaining about everything on it, farting and cutting his nails. I think he's depressed. I've tried cheering him up. I told him yesterday that if he doesn't perk up I'll put him out with the recycling, but even that didn't get a smile out of him. He's driving me mad. Since you ask.'

'Oh dear,' I said. 'It's your wedding anniversary around now, isn't it? Are you planning anything?'

'I'm not planning to celebrate, if that's what you mean.'

'That's a shame,' I said. 'Poor Derek. Don't give up on him. You sound about ready for the rhubarb leaf.'

'What rhubarb leaf?' she asked me.

'Well, you know,' I said. 'The rhubarb leaf you might slip into your husband's beef casserole.'

'Why would I do that? Put a rhubarb leaf in his casserole?'

'They're poisonous. It was just a joke, actually, Susan.'

She looked interested. 'How poisonous?'

'I think they're pretty poisonous. You definitely wouldn't want to put one in the casserole.' I looked around her garden over the fence. 'You haven't got any rhubarb anyway.'

'Have you got any rhubarb?'

'No. Listen, Susan, I hope you don't think I was being serious?'

'No, no,' she said. 'I just hadn't heard of it, that's all.'

When I got back into the house I regretted mentioning rhubarb leaves. I'm glad it's not in season.

I was still feeling uneasy about it when Bill came home. I told him about my odd conversation with Susan, and asked him when he'd last seen Derek. He reminded me that we'd seen both Derek and Susan outside the polling station on the day of the Brexit vote. He'd been against, and she'd been for. They didn't seem to be getting on particularly well, but we'd assumed it was because they didn't see eye to eye over Brexit.

I said I remember now. They were at each other's throats over it. And then I said I hoped I hadn't just given Susan any murderous ideas.

'Don't be daft,' said Bill. 'You couldn't be held responsible for committing murder because you talked to someone about rhubarb leaves.'

I drew breath to reply and then,

'Hiya!'

'Sophie!' I said. 'Where did you spring from?'

'I was just upstairs. Dan gave me his key. I was having a snooze, and then on my way downstairs I heard you planning to murder someone.'

Bill and I looked at her in astonishment. It's extraordinary how this girl can just pop up.

'Anyway,' she said. 'I have to go now because I'm doing a night shift. I'll leave the keys for Dan.' She put Dan's keys down on the table and slung her bag over her shoulder. 'Bye! See ya later crocodile!'

When Dan came home I gave him the set designer's card, and said how impressed this chap had been with Aspire, and its dome. Dan seemed very keen to follow it up. He looked the drama society up on the internet, and discovered their next production was a space epic. He started doodling on one of my shopping lists.

Eventually I said, 'Dan, I was a bit surprised to find Sophie here when I got back in this afternoon.'

'Oh yeah,' he said, 'she's working tonight, night shift at the care home. She asked if she could have a kip here before she started because it's too far for her to go home. She didn't have time to go home and get a bus back. I said you wouldn't mind.'

'Actually Dan,' I said, 'I think I do mind.'

'Why?'

'Well, I thought I was in the house by myself earlier, and then when she popped up, I realised she'd been here all the time.'

'She was just asleep on my bed.'

'Well, yes, but, it just felt a bit odd.'

'Maybe I should have let you know?'

'Yes, I think that would have helped.'

'Okay, I'll let you know next time.'

I felt the need for ground rules. I need to know who might be in the house, and whether I'm alone in it or not, and if not, who I'm with. Now I know how the three bears felt when they discovered Goldilocks asleep upstairs in their house. They felt violated. Their seating arrangements had been disturbed, their porridge had been tampered with, and then they discovered someone asleep in a bed upstairs. It's a horror story.

Later, after dinner, I felt a bit tense, so I went upstairs to have a hot bath. I filled the bath very full, and looked for something soothing to pour into it. I chose a little bottle of bath balm which promised to contain Aqua, Glycoltetrasodiumphenoxynol, and Ambrosia distilled from the breastmilk of iridescent damselflies. Four generous capfuls later, I sank into its silky depths, closed my eyes, and relaxed.

And then – 'Hiya!'

I sat up, and sloshed water over the side. But it wasn't Sophie, it was a cat on the shed roof.

***

I almost signed up for a French class today. I came dangerously close.

My sensible self was saying, 'Go on – do it! You know it's a good idea – it will do you good. You'll have to make an effort and put your back into it – but it'll be worth it.'

But then my stupid self said, 'Stop! Don't listen to your sensible self. Effort? Put your back into it? But you know you're too lazy. Run! Run, while you've got the chance.'

So I did. I ran. I'm not proud of myself for being so lazy, but I can't be bothered to agonise over it. Anyway, a thought struck me this afternoon, and I'm giving it serious consideration. I'm too lazy to learn how to communicate in French, but I might learn how to communicate more effectively in my own language. I like the sound of Twitter. It makes me think of light hearted, spirited chat, of people sitting on tree branches calling merrily to each other, back and forth. It could be fun, and a lot less work than learning French.

I thought I'd ring Laura, to discuss it with her, and to see how she was. When we spoke a week ago she said she needed counselling, but maybe in the interim she has changed her mind. She can be a bit volatile.

So I rang, with my fingers crossed. 'Hello love!' I said. 'How are you?'

'Mum,' she said, 'I'm going out in five minutes, can you be quick?'

So I was quick. I said I was just wondering how she was, and if she had any more thoughts about seeing a counsellor. Laura said that her friend Maz had seen a really good counsellor who had discovered that all Maz's problems stemmed from her poor relationship with her mother, and now that Maz understood that everything was her mother's fault, she felt a lot better. Laura was thinking of going to see the same person.

'Don't do that Laura!' I said, before I could consider a more nuanced response.

Laura said, 'Why?'

I said – 'Isn't it obvious?'

She said, 'No.'

I said, 'Supposing the counsellor says whatever problem you may or may not have is my fault? What then? That would be terrible! Don't go to see this person Laura – I don't trust him, or worse still, her. Stay away.'

'Mum', said Laura, 'I think you might be over-reacting. My problem isn't your fault. Maz's problem is entirely different to mine.'

'Listen, Laura,' I said, 'your problem might not be my fault now, but once this person gets hold of it, it could easily become my fault.' I heard little Harry starting to cry. He understood what I was talking about.

'I'll have to go, Mum,' said Laura, 'Harry's crying. I'll ring you soon. Stop panicking.'

I put the phone down, and thought about it. Was I over-reacting? Panicking unnecessarily? I didn't have anything to fear from this counselling person. Very likely to be a woman. There would be no harm in Laura going to see her, surely? So why was I feeling guilty and defensive?

I don't know what Laura's problem is, I don't even know if she has a problem, or whether she just thinks she has. But I'm worried in case whatever problems she may or may not have, real or imagined, they are my fault. I am her mother after all, so I can't be entirely blameless. Suppose this counselling woman decides I didn't breast feed Laura well enough, or long enough? What if she discovers I bottle fed Laura while reading a book and became so engrossed in the book that prolonged suction created a vacuum, and the teat turned inside out with a rubbery plop and disappeared inside the bottle. What kind of damage does that do to a child?

I decided I don't like this counsellor, and don't trust her as far as I could throw her. I wonder who she is? If I can find out who she is I could ring her and say if she turns Laura against me, I will seek her out and murder her to death. Maybe that would convince her that my heart is in the right place, and I'm essentially a kind person and a good mother.

I mulled the whole thing over and worked up a head of steam against the entire counselling profession. I ranged around the kitchen and hallway like a tigress ready to defend her young, pacing back and forth as if I had drunk adrenalin with a slice of lemon.

The front doorbell rang when I was down that end of the hall, and I flung the door open. A man stood on the step.

'What? What do you want?' I demanded to know.

'I wondered if you'd had a chance to look at your BettaBrush catalogue?' he said.

'BettaBrush?' I said, incredulous. 'BettaBrush? God!'

'Maybe I've called at a bad time?' he suggested.

'Do you have a BettaLife catalogue?' I asked him, 'Because if you do, I'd like one of those.'

'Er,' he said. 'I seem to have caught you at a bad moment.'

'Tell you what,' I said, 'I could really do with a brush that will sweep away everything I have ever done wrong. Have you got one of those brushes? Actually, I'll need more than one.'

'Why don't I call back later?' he said. 'I can pop back tomorrow.'

'Good idea,' I said. 'Pop back tomorrow with a pair of glasses that makes everything look better. If you've got some of those, I'd be very interested. Just don't bother me with plughole strainers. Not now.'

'I'll see what I can do,' he said, humouring me, and turned to go.

'Great!' I said, and slammed the door shut.

I leaned against the door, and took some deep breaths. I needed to calm down. I grabbed my coat and my bag and decided to walk down to the Co-op, it's about a mile. I thought, by the time I get there I will have burned off some nervous energy. So I set off, powering down to the Co-op ready to bite the heads off small dogs if they got in my way.

I felt slightly calmer when I arrived, calm enough to look at the newspaper billboard and give it some consideration. **Man Dies. Good Riddance Says Grandma**. I like this grandma. She's my sort of woman. She doesn't take any unnecessary crap from people. I admire that in a grandma. Then I went into the shop and bought some milk and some boxing gloves, and set off back up the hill towards home.

Dan was in when I got home. He made me a cup of coffee and seemed not averse to chatting for a while. I started to feel better, and decided to put my anxieties about Laura slightly to one side just for the moment. Instead, I thought I'd tell Dan about my inclination to join Twitter.

'Dan', I said, 'how's this for an idea? I thought I might open a Twitter account, and start tweeting.'

He looked at me, stunned. 'No', he said. 'You don't want to do that.'

'I thought I did', I said.

'No Mum, honestly, that's a bad idea. Twitter's not for nice older ladies. Mums and such. No. I don't think you'd like it.'

'I thought I might give it a try.'

'No. Why don't you just, like, chat to your friends? You know, over coffee and scones in Marks and Spencer's café, like you do already. You don't want to be on Twitter, Mum, honestly. I don't think there would be any point, really. No-one would be interested in what you had to say. Apart from maybe some weirdos.'

Great.

***

Jen took my mind off Laura this morning. She rang to tell me she was getting her hair coloured this afternoon, and she couldn't decide whether to go lighter or darker. Did I have any thoughts? Some people said darker was actually ageing in the more mature woman. Others said the opposite. She just didn't know what to do.

I said, what effect are you aiming for? Do you want to look younger?

She said of course she wanted to look younger. What woman in her right mind choses a hair colour to make herself look older? She said she wasn't going to look at the colour chart this afternoon and pick out 'Old Crone Grey' with hints of 'Antique Witch' and 'Wispy Granny'.

'Okay,' I said. 'Go darker.'

'Yes, but – that might not look natural.'

'Well, go blonde,' I said.

She said I wasn't being any help. She said this was going to cost her the thick end of sixty quid and she thought I could give it more consideration.

So I said, 'Okay, let's approach this scientifically. What is your actual hair colour?'

She said, 'You mean, my actual natural hair colour? The colour of my actual hair?'

'Yes,' I said. 'What colour is your actual hair, naturally, now?'

'God, I don't know,' she said. 'It's been years since I've seen my natural hair colour. I've no idea what it is now. I don't want to know. I hope I never find out.'

'What colour was it? Do you think it might have been light brown? Originally? I seem to remember you being light brown.'

'Do you?' she said. 'Possibly. Light brown. That rings a bell.'

'In that case, I don't think you should go any darker than light brown.'

'Why?'

'It's to do with skin tone,' I said. 'You have to match your hair with your skin tone.'

'Skin tone?' she said. 'Skin tone's no problem. I can go into Boots and buy any skin tone I want. Once I know what colour my hair is, I'll get the matching skin tone. Don't worry about skin tone. Skin tone is optional.'

'Tell you what,' I said. 'Why don't you discuss this with your hairdresser?'

'Yes but,' she was getting frustrated, 'when I ask for their opinion I never like it. They never give me the opinion I want. I'm paying them a lot of money. I want an opinion I can be happy with.'

And then it occurred to me that there might be more to this. I asked her why she was in such a flap about her hair colour? She had always been quite relaxed about it previously.

She had coped well with her brief orange period two years ago and before that she had a low-key flirtation with red. Why was she so agitated now? Was it – I said – anything to do with the man she had met at Tumble Tots?

She said, maybe. Maybe it was.

Sometimes there is no point in pussy-footing around, so I just said, 'Listen Jen, are you in a flap about the ageing effects of your hair colour because you're dating a much younger man?'

'He's not that much younger,' she said.

So, of course, I had to ask – 'Okay. How much younger?'

She said, 'Just about twenty years.'

'TWENTY YEARS? Twenty years! Twenty years, Jen?'

And she rang off.

I rang her straight back. 'Don't hang up,' I said. 'I'm worried about you. That's a huge age gap.'

She said, 'Plenty of men are with women twenty years younger. Nobody worries about them. People congratulate them.'

I said, 'Yes, but...'

She said, 'Yes but what?'

'It's a bit different, isn't it, the other way around?'

'Is it?' she said. 'Maybe you're jealous.'

'I – what?'

'Look, Sally. Don't worry about me. There's no need, really. I'm fine. I'm in control. So what if he's twenty-two years younger, I— '

'Twenty-*two*? You said twenty.'

'Well,' she said. 'Twenty? Twenty-two? Twenty-five? Who's counting? I'm not going to get hung up about it.'

'So why worry about your hair colour?' I said.

She said she wasn't worried about it anymore, she'd decided to go blonde. Then she said, 'Anyway, enough about me. I hate one-sided conversations. Tell me about you. What are you worrying about?'

But I wasn't in the mood to share my concerns about Laura. Or to carry on the conversation at all, so it was a relief when –

'Hiya!'

Sophie turned up. She was standing in the doorway, looking out towards the road. 'A taxi's just delivered an old lady to the house,' she said. 'Is she yours?'

I told Jen that Sophie and Ella had just arrived and I would have to go, and then I turned my attention to Ella, who was following Sophie into the kitchen. I'd promised to take Ella up to Laura's today, so she could play with little Harry when he was awake. I was hoping we might be able to have a reassuring chat with Laura, although I hadn't yet worked out what form that might take, and it would have to be done carefully. Laura was unsettled by the thought that her grandmother had a more exciting sex life. It was a tricky situation.

Sophie explained she had just popped by to measure the window and door openings in Aspire for nets.

'Nets?' I said. 'Are you setting traps?'

'No,' she said, 'not traps, Mrs Forth. Just net curtains to make it decent.' She borrowed a tape measure and a pen and went off down the side of the house. She left without bringing my tape measure back, but I've no doubt she will return it sometime. She'll probably pop up when I'm on the loo and hand it to me.

I explained to Ella on our way over to Laura's in the car that Laura had been a bit unsettled by Ella's response to her question about sex the other day. Ella needed reminding of the gist of our conversation, so I said it was the one where Ella told Laura about her enthusiastic love life with Grandad.

'Oh yes,' said Ella. 'Those were the days.'

I explained that Laura was just a bit anxious about her own love life at the moment. Her hormones were probably playing up a bit.

'Hormones,' said Ella. 'I remember those.'

I said we should probably soft-pedal any references to the Kama Sutra this time, in case Laura made any unsettling comparisons. Ella agreed, and said it was none of Kama Sutra's business anyway.

We had a lovely afternoon at Laura's. Ella put Harry through his paces, and Harry made all the right responses. I thought she had completely forgotten about our conversation in the car until we were getting ready to come away again.

'Now then,' Ella said to Laura, as I was helping her with her coat. 'Did you take my advice?'

My heart started to sink.

'What advice?' said Laura.

'My recipe for a happy marriage,' she said. 'If you give your husband three or four kisses a day, you won't go far wrong. Mark my words.'

'Kisses?' said Laura.

'Yes,' said Ella. 'Kisses. Like I told you. Three or four a day. That's the secret.'

'Thanks, Grandma,' said Laura. 'That's good to know.'

I congratulated Ella in the car on our way home. 'That was nicely done,' I told her.

'Yes, I thought so,' she said, and then she fell silent, and dozed. A little later she woke up and asked me if we could stop at the Co-op, because she needed some frozen chips.

I was waiting for Ella outside the Co-op when Susan came out with a carton of milk. She saw me, and stopped to talk. 'What do you make of that?' she indicated the newspaper billboard.

Grandma On Murder Charge!

Susan said, 'Not very savvy, was she? Using a knife?'

'How's that?' I said.

She tapped the side of her nose. 'Should have used the rhubarb leaf. Then no-one would have known.'

'Oh yes,' I said. 'Maybe.'

'I looked it up on the internet,' said Susan, 'and it's quite true, what you told me. Anyway,' she said, 'must get on. I'm going out tonight, but I want to make something for Derek's meal before I go. He won't cook anything for himself. Too lazy. If I didn't feed him, he'd starve. He relies on me to keep him alive. Funny that, isn't it?'

***

I thought about Twitter again this morning. I'm strangely attracted to the idea, despite Dan's warning that it's not meant for the likes of mumsy folk like me. But although I'm drawn to it, I'm wondering if the necessity to tweet at regular intervals might turn out to be very demanding?

Would it be like having a voracious parrot in the corner of the room, a parrot hungry for words? An irritable parrot which would bite if it doesn't like the words you feed it? I could be out of my depth on Twitter. There is something dangerously intimidating about the whole idea, I think that's why I like it. I'm attracted to the element of risk. There's no doubt Café Revive with a friend would be safer, but it's flapjack land, and if you're eating a flapjack, you are not living on the edge.

Could I cope with living on the edge? I went to the fridge to rummage around for a chocolate bar to give me courage, and I came across a bag of dried prunes. On the back of the bag it clearly said – 'Why don't you follow us on Twitter!'

I looked again inside the bag, to check that it was full of prunes and not opinions. And then I thought, if a packet of prunes can have a Twitter account, surely I could have a Twitter account? If there are people out there who will follow a bag of prunes on Twitter, maybe the competition for followers is not that strong.

Of course, I don't know anything about this scene at all. It's entirely possible that prunes are more entertaining on Twitter than they are when they float around in a bowl of custard. I had another look in the fridge and discovered that I could, if I wanted, follow a carton of orange juice on Twitter. I looked on the kitchen bench and saw that my tea bags are on Twitter. I hadn't realised there were so many groceries on Twitter. I began to feel I was in with a chance. What can a prune say to a tea bag that would be such a hard act for me to follow?

101

I was looking at a packet of gravy salts to see if they were on Twitter, when Judith rang. She said, 'Look Sally, we haven't spoken since the trifle incident at the dinner party, and I'm ringing to see if we can put that behind us, and carry on being friends.'

I said, 'Of course we can, Judith,' leaving aside the fact that we had never been friends.

She said, 'Looking back Sally, it was a great dinner party, and my dress is none the worse for you throwing trifle at it.'

I said that was good to hear.

And then she said, 'Actually, there is another reason I rang. My youngest, Morwenna – you know, I told you about her – the award winning particle physicist? She's just been promoted on sixty thousand a year? Well, she's home tomorrow for a week between projects. She has no friends here now, and I'm wondering if Dan would take her out, just socially, just so she doesn't have to sit in the house every evening with her dad and me? She gets bored so easily, she's always needed such a lot of stimulating. Dan's a nice enough lad, I wondered whether he could spare her a few hours? They were in the same year at school, weren't they? If he knew she was around he might suggest they meet up?'

'Well, Judith,' I said, pausing for breath as my mind raced ahead to match-make a future where Dan and Morwenna marry and both teach at Cambridge University, she as professor of particle physics and he as professor of the particles left over. 'Yes of course, I'm sure Daniel would be happy to stimulate Morwenna, that is, to take her out and stop her getting bored. Of course, Dan does have a girlfriend, but as you say, if it's just a social occasion, that's a bit different. Sixty thousand a year, did you say? In one so young? Gosh.'

'Yes. She's so successful. I don't know where she gets it from.'

'No,' I agreed. 'Odd, isn't it?'

'Anyway,' she said, 'would you mind speaking to Dan? To see if he would mind taking her out for a drink? Or to the flicks or something? Just for a bit of company her own age. She always liked Dan.'

So that's what I've agreed to do, but now that I've put the phone down I'm not sure Dan will be up for this. I shouldn't really agree to things on his behalf, it always gets me into trouble. I was his social secretary until he was fourteen, and I just can't retire from the role. Probably because it's so manifestly obvious that all single men under the age of twenty-five need a good social secretary. It's difficult to give up on something which makes so much sense.

I gave some thought to how I might approach this idea with him, and decided to present it as a wonderful surprise. It used to work years ago when I told him he had an appointment at the dentist's.

So this evening when Dan came in, and before he had even shut the kitchen door behind him I said, 'Dan! Guess what?'

'You're not on Twitter?'

'No, nothing to do with Twitter.'

'You don't want me to apply for something?'

'No. Dan, do you remember Judith's daughter Morwenna? She was in your year at school.'

'Oh yeah,' he said, with no enthusiasm.

'She's home this week, and I wondered whether you might give her a ring and meet up?'

He looked at me blankly. 'What for?'

'To catch up.'

'With what?'

'Old times.'

'There were no Old Times.'

'Just to be friendly then.'

'I can't ring Morwenna up when I'm going out with Sophie.'

'Morwenna's just a friend. Sophie won't mind you having a friend.'

'You're hoping I'll dump Sophie and start seeing Morwenna. Just because she's a big shot earning lots of money.'

'How do you know that?'

'Facebook.'

'I just thought it might be nice for you two to meet up for a chat.'

'Mum – you have to back off!'

'Hiya!'

'Oh hello, Sophie. Come in and shut the door.'

'Who has to back off?' Sophie said, smiling brightly at me.

'I'll tell you what we were talking about Sophie,' I said. 'I was suggesting to Dan that you and he might like to go out somewhere with an old friend of Dan's who is home this week with nothing much to do. All her friends have left here now.'

'We could do that,' she said, looking at Dan. 'I'll ring her. Just give me her number.'

'Thank you Sophie,' I said. 'I'll get it for you.'

There's a lot to be said for Sophie, really. She's uncomplicated, always cheerful, and her ability to materialise out of thin air is a serious talent.

I gave Sophie Morwenna's number and she asked me, 'What's this girl's name?'

So I told her, and she said, 'Oh yeah. I think I remember her from school. She had plaits and a brace. And she worked really hard. Never mind. I expect she's all right now. I'll give her a ring.'

Simple as that. I felt very pleased with myself. I thought I'd handled that potentially tricky situation well. Sophie was pleased, Judith would be pleased, there's a good chance Morwenna will be pleased, and Dan was not displeased. Very satisfactory. I felt quite the diplomat, quite the expert in man management. Bold enough, even, to text Jen and ask how she was getting on with her much younger boyfriend. That is, if the much younger boyfriend had not already left her high and dry. So at around ten, just before I started thinking about going to bed, I decided to send Jen a text.

Hello, I began, cautiously, How are you? Are things still okay?

Jen replied after ten minutes, Hi! Things are great! Fantasies!! No time for details now but I have to tell you something – a big ball of kapok is a lot of fun when you're with a younger man!! Catch you later!!!

I suddenly felt very tired and started looking for my warm nightie, which I am now wearing, along with a forlorn expression.

***

I was dragging a bag of shopping out of the back foot-well of my car when I heard someone behind me say, 'Sally lass, I haven't seen you for ages. That is you isn't it? I'm just looking at your bum. You could be anybody.'

I emerged from the car with my bag and turned around. Derek was leaning on our partition fence.

'Yes, it's me Derek,' I said. 'Well spotted. How's things?'

'Not so bad,' he said. 'And not so good. I don't like retirement Sally. Don't know what to do with it. Women are better at it.'

'Do you think so?'

'Oh yes, women are good at making work, whether they have a job or not. Susan's always up to something. She's thrown me out of the house today. Says I have to do some gardening.'

I went over to the fence to chat. 'So what has she got you doing?'

'Growing rhubarb, would you believe.'

'Growing rhubarb?' I said, shocked. 'Why?'

'Why? She says she wants some for Christmas, that's why. Funny thing to want at Christmas, but she's a funny woman. Maybe she wants to beat me over the head with it.'

'It's the wrong time of year Derek. Tell Susan it won't grow.'

'Susan is a determined woman. If she wants rhubarb at Christmas, the seasons won't stand in her way. And if it keeps the old bat happy, I'll grow it in the greenhouse. There'll be plenty, if you want some. Anyhow, I'll get on. Don't want her to think I'm slacking.'

I got into the kitchen with the shopping, and considered what had just happened. There are two explanations for the attempt to grow rhubarb out of season next door. Either our conversation about the poisonous property of rhubarb leaves has prompted Susan to murder her husband, or alternatively, she fancies a rhubarb crumble on Christmas Day. It's one or the other.

It's true, Susan was very interested to hear that rhubarb leaves are poisonous, and she was also very irritated with Derek, but even so, her instruction to grow rhubarb does not by itself amount to an intention to commit murder by poisoning.

I decided that for the moment, it's too soon to alert the police. I should just monitor the situation. Nothing can happen in any case until some leaves appear on the rhubarb plants, and I will be able to see them from the bathroom window upstairs with a pair of binoculars. So I will know when I might need to take action of any kind.

I told myself I'd been watching too many crime dramas on TV. Too many re-runs of Midsomer Murders. I'd read too much Agatha Christie. Just because the title sprang so easily to mind – *Deadly Rhubarb* – did not mean this story would ever be written. I told myself to put the kettle on, and chill out.

And surely, I thought, Susan wouldn't make Derek grow the rhubarb she plans to kill him with? She's perverse, but not that perverse. So I had a cup of coffee and tried to relax while I watched Derek potter around in his green house. But to be honest, I felt a bit queasy.

I was in school this afternoon, and they are having another epidemic of humming. We thought we'd seen the last of it, but it's back, in force, worse than before. Whole classes start to hum, in unison, no-one looks as if they're humming and every individual, if challenged, can stop humming and deny humming. But the noise continues. It's impossible to pinpoint who is humming as long as enough of the class joins the hum, and individuals fall silent whenever you approach.

It's clever, you have to admit, and it's effectively infuriating for the class teacher. Of course, it relies on the class working together in unison, but this fact escaped Lee this afternoon. We were studying a Halloween poem about toffee apples, and Lee started to hum loudly all by himself. He kept it up when his teacher approached and so he was easily outed as a solitary hummer. Lee was told off, warned, threatened, warned again, and then just when I thought he would tell the teacher where he could stick his toffee apple, the whole class started to hum. The hum began softly, but rose in volume until the English teacher and I felt as if we were in a room with a swarm of bees.

I hoped the young English teacher wouldn't ricochet around the classroom trying to catch someone out in the act of humming. That would make him much more entertaining than any teacher should ever allow themselves to be in front of a class. I suggested that he just sit tight and appear to be bored while I went to fetch a member of the Senior Management Team. They are, after all, paid more than him to deal with outbreaks of phantom humming. I took Lee with me. He had tired of the class monotone and was singing daa da-da de daa to the 'Superman' theme tune, so was clearly culpable.

By the time I'd tracked down someone from senior management, the lesson had finished, so I went to see the young English teacher during break to have a chat about the incident, and maybe make one or two suggestions. A whole-class detention of some kind might be the answer. Everyone would claim to be innocent of course. They would all insist that they hadn't joined in the hum and were being unjustly punished, but collective responsibility would have to apply, and no exceptions could or should be made. Very sad – even heart-breaking – but unavoidable. Everyone would have to suffer the detention, including Rob, the English teacher, who would have to supervise the class. Rob would have to derive what satisfaction he could from watching the class suffer the loss of their afternoon break, even while he was losing his own. The dynamics of reciprocal punishments in schools is a sometimes difficult to get right. Ideally you want the pupils to suffer more for their misdemeanours than their teachers, but it's a thing easy to misjudge. I was looking forward to talking this over with Rob.

'Hello, Rob,' I said. 'That was a bit of a pain, wasn't it?'

'Bastards!' he said. 'Bastards! How dare they think they can do that to me! Bastards! I hate them!'

'Well,' I attempted a little chuckle to defuse some of the tension in his response, 'we have to remember they're just kids, Rob. I thought we might mull over some ideas about where best to go from here?'

'I'd like to kill some of them. Today, I could have got hold of them and thrown them out the fucking window. Just a shame we were only one floor up. I'd have been really tempted if we were on the top floor, so help me God. Bastards!'

We had a little chat, but I don't think he's in teaching for the long term. It's not a job that suits everybody.

I got home and discovered Sophie fixing net curtains to the window openings in Aspire. She had also hung a little wooden plaque above the door opening which said, 'Home Is Where the Heart Is.' She said it was a surprise for Dan, and asked me whether I thought he would like it. She thought it made the heap look more cosy, more like a little house.

I stood back and cast a critical eye over it, and I thought, this heap of rubbish is going to have to come down. Dan was losing interest in it, and it had served whatever purpose it had ever had. Some of the hay bale cladding had fallen away and the net curtains made it look desperate. The 'Home Is Where the Heart Is' plaque looked heavily ironic. It was looking like a dust bowl homestead from Great Depression. It had to go.

'I've arranged for some furniture to be delivered,' said Sophie. 'So that I can move in next week.'

'What?' Obviously, this was an idea that had to be knocked on the head straight away. 'I'm sorry Sophie,' I said, 'but you can't move in here.'

'Oh no. Why not?'

'Well – it's not habitable. It's just a shell. It's much too cold for the winter. It's out of the question.'

'But I can't afford anything else,' she said. 'I can't stay at home and keep my job because of the shifts. I love my job at the care home, Mrs Forth. I really love it.'

'Sophie, you can't live in this pile of rubbish, it's much too cold.'

'Can I live with you then? In the house?'

I looked at her with what might have been horror, and she said, 'Please, Miss.'

***

Bill was quite relaxed about Sophie moving in. He said it might be easier on the nerves to know she was on the premises, than to have her pop up when we didn't think she was.

But Dan wasn't as happy with the idea. When I told him this morning that I'd agreed to Sophie moving in until she had another more permanent arrangement, he said, 'Oh. We should have talked about this first.'

I was surprised. 'Did you and Sophie not discuss the possibility that she might move in with us?'

'No,' he said, 'never. Actually, I was thinking Sophie and I might not be together much longer.'

'Really?' I said. 'But how will that work? What happens if you split up with Sophie while she's living under our roof?'

'Well,' he said, 'I didn't ask her to move in, Mum. But it should be all right. As long as she has her own room, because I might want to see someone else.'

'Dan,' I said, struggling to get my head around what seemed to be happening, 'we can't stack your girlfriends up in a holding pattern as if they're landing at Heathrow. Your Dad and I – this is our home, not some sort of boarding house for your current and previous girlfriends. This isn't a charitable concern for— '

'Yeah all right,' he said. 'Point taken. But I can't stay with Sophie, just because you've agreed to her living here.'

'She was wanting to move into Aspire. You'll have to take it down, Dan. It's attracting occupants. I want it taken down and cleared away before the winter sets in.'

'Yeah right,' he said. 'Okay. I'll do that as soon as Baz moves out.'

'Baz! Don't tell me we've got Baz in there now?'

'He's not living in there. He's just dossing down in a sleeping bag for a while. He's had a row with his folks. He won't be there long.'

'God sakes, Dan,' I said, 'he won't even have a toilet. How's he going to manage to wash and go to the toilet?'

'Oh that's all right,' Dan said. 'I've told him just to use our loo and shower. He won't mind not having an en suite out there. You don't need to worry about that.'

'I'm not remotely worried about that, Dan,' I said – and I was going to go on to say what I was worried about, when his phone rang.

'Baz!' he said. 'Yeah. Yeah. Yeah, that's right. Yeah. No, she's fine with it. Yeah. Yeah. Yeah, great idea. No, that's okay. See you. See you Baz. See you.' He looked up. 'I told him you're fine with it,' he said.

'I'm not fine with it.'

'Mum,' he said, turning to rummage through a kitchen drawer, 'you can't put Baz out on the streets. Be reasonable.'

Wait a minute – I thought. Hang on. Something isn't right here.

'Reasonable?' I said. 'Did you say be reasonable? I am being reasonable. It's a crazy idea for Baz to move in to that freezing cold heap of junk.'

'Don't stress about it, Mum. It's just a temporary thing. Baz hates being inside anyway. That place is just right for him. He doesn't mind being a bit cold. Baz loves the cold. And he's shit pleased about moving in. Just let him do it, he won't be any trouble. I've told him he can do our garden, and he's a brilliant cook, he'll make himself useful around the place.'

'But, that's worse! It'll look as if we have a household slave banished to a kennel in the garden.'

'It's nothing like that. It's just Baz. I'll chuck him a hot water bottle if you're worried about him being cold. It's not a problem.' He stopped rummaging in the drawer and turned around. 'But what *is* a problem is I've lost my keys.'

When Dan found his keys and went out, I thought, I wish I was still working. Life was easier when I was at work.

I wondered if I could go down to school and ask them to give me my job back. I would tell them they need me. I'd tell them they have too many rookies on the staff, they can't manage without the experienced old hands. I'm expensive, I'll tell them, but I'm good. I'll remind them of how well I silence a class, and how quickly I can make a rubbish cup of instant coffee. I'll prepare a little speech and say,

'Friends and Colleagues, remember my talent for ignoring emails and missing deadlines, my cavalier disregard for performance targets, my knack for falling asleep during CPD evenings? I can still do that. Parents' evenings? I can do Parents' Evenings. I can convince any parent that I know their child when I have absolutely no idea who the kid is. As for New Initiatives, I can throttle those. I can help any New Initiative introduced in September wither on the vine just before Christmas. Christmas? Did I say Christmas? Why wait till Christmas? Let's say by half term. I know how to do this job. I'm a pro. Give me my job back. I didn't mean to take this career break, it was a mistake. Work is so much easier than living with my children.'

I'd say all this and hope they would find me impossible to resist. If I was earning again I could rent a little place for Bill and me on the other side of town. It would be so peaceful, going back to work after working at being unemployed.

I went outside to have a look at Aspire, to determine whether it was likely to collapse on Baz and kill him outright as he lay sleeping. I poked at it here and there, but the basic structure seemed surprisingly robust. It was peaceful standing under the dome, watching the net curtains moving gently in the breeze, and listening to the dry rustle of the hay cladding on the outside. Maybe I could move in myself.

I was imagining my life in a hermitage appendage to the household when Jen rang to update me on the current situation with her youthful beau. I walked back into the kitchen with the phone clamped to my ear while she told me the latest.

'Bit of a shock the other day,' she told me. 'I discovered something when I was talking to Scott – my new friend.'

'Oh yes?' I said. 'What did you discover?'

'I'm older than his mother.'

'Oh bloody hell. That's a tough one.'

'Of course – he doesn't know that.'

'No. How old does he think you are?'

'Late thirties.'

'So, you've given away – at least ten years?'

'Well, I wouldn't have put it like that, exactly,' she said. 'I've just aligned our ages more favourably.'

'It's not quite that simple though, is it?'

'Oh, lighten up Sally,' she said. 'Of course it's that simple. That's the truth. This isn't a serious thing. It's not going to last. I could be dead before he cuts his wisdom teeth. It's just for fun.'

'Okay,' I said. 'Okay. So how are you managing to combine all this with being a grandma?'

'Ways and means. Don't worry about the technicalities. Nobody knows me up here. I can lead a double life.'

Grandma Leads Double Life!

I said, 'Are you sure you know what you're doing?'

'Oh, who cares? I know I'm doing it. I know that much.'

'Right,' I said. 'So are you blonde?'

'Yes,' she said. 'As Marilyn Monroe.'

***

Dan rang me late this afternoon. He doesn't ever ring to chat, so I knew he had something important to tell me. He told me not to make anything for dinner tonight, because Baz was going to cook for us all, to thank me for letting him kip down in Aspire.

I was immediately anxious. I asked Dan what Baz was planning to cook.

'Meat,' he said. 'He's got some meat.'

'What kind of meat?'

'I don't know Mum,' he said. 'Baz just said he'd got hold of some meat. Anyway, he's a good cook. It'll be fine.'

I was still anxious. I'd be happier if Baz had bought the meat, rather than got hold of it.

Baz turned up just after six and knocked politely on the back door. He was carrying two plastic carrier bags, one containing two tins of peas and a bag of frozen chips, and the other a large slab of meat, unwrapped, and dripping blood onto the step. He came inside, and more blood dripped onto the ceramic floor tiles.

'What meat is this, Baz?' I said.

'I think it's venison,' he said.

'You think it's venison? What else might it be?'

'Well, it might be beef, but I don't think so, I think it's venison.'

'Where did it come from?'

'A bloke I know,' he said. 'I've had stuff from him before. It's good. Very fresh. It might need a bit of a rinse under the tap.' He took it out of the bag to show me and I thought I saw something twitch. 'It's venison,' he said. 'I think.' Then he asked me if I had a big frying pan and some red wine.

113

I left him to it. Dan and Sophie came in and I could hear them all busy in the kitchen. Dan asked Baz what the meat was, and I heard Baz say, 'I told your mum it was venison.' There was some stifled laughter. I made a conscious effort not to listen after that. Sophie came into the living room to bring me a glass of wine. She sat down next to me, ready to chat. She smiled at me and made her opening gambit. 'Mrs Forth,' she said, 'have you ever wondered what shape panda bears are under their fur?'

We chatted for a while. The wine helped. Then Bill came home earlier than expected, which was a nice surprise, and soon after that the meal was ready.

So we've eaten it now, whatever it was. We all sat around the table, Bill, Dan, Sophie, Baz and me, tucking in to our badger steaks, celebrating the fact that we are all accommodating and accommodated. We all have shelter, and somewhere to sleep.

***

I saw Susan on the drive this morning, and thought I'd better explain about Baz moving into Aspire temporarily. She might be put out if I don't keep her in the loop.

'Susan,' I said, 'do you remember the young man who was asleep on your lawn with Dan a while back? The one who said you had very comfortable grass, and your lawn has the right contours for his back?'

Her eyes narrowed, 'Oh yes. A bit backward, wasn't he? I wouldn't trust him. Glad he's gone for good. Shifty, I thought he was. Why? What about him?'

'Oh nothing,' I said.

We looked at each other in silence for a few seconds while she registered this, and then she said, 'Right, come round the back, and see what's happened to our lawn.'

I followed her into her back garden. In the middle of her beautiful lawn was a large conical heap of finely sifted earth. 'What do you make of that?' she asked me.

'It's a molehill,' I told her.

'I know it's a molehill,' she said. 'But what I want to know is, how do we kill the moles? Should we use poison, or lethal traps?' She scanned the surface of the grass. 'I'd take a knife to them, but I don't know where they are.'

Derek came out of the house carrying a bunch of what looked like relay batons. He said they were battery operated mole-deflecting sticks which vibrate and make a noise at intervals. Moles hate them, he said. Once he puts the sticks in the lawn, the moles won't be able to leave quick enough.

Susan was unimpressed. 'We don't want to waste time chasing them about with vibrating sticks. No point in playing hide and seek with the bloody things while they ruin our lawn. We need to kill them. I want them dead, Derek,' she said. 'All of them. Dead.' She surveyed the lawn. 'Today.'

Derek dropped the sticks on the grass. 'How am I going to do that, Susan? I can't dig them up and strangle them in front of you with my bare hands.'

'We need traps,' Susan said. 'My father used them years ago. They have a powerful spring inside them. The mole triggers it and – bang!' She clapped her hands together. 'A metal bar comes down and crushes its head.'

Derek winced.

Susan continued. 'Or we could mix rat poison with ground glass and chopped up worms and poke it down into their tunnels.'

'Well,' I said. 'I can see you two have lots to discuss, so I'll let you get on.'

I left them to it. I was rushing off to meet up with Judith this afternoon. She rang me yesterday to suggest it. There was something bothering her, and she obviously wanted to bother me with it. I had been planning to walk as far as the high street, but time was now short, so I set off down the road to the bus stop.

I was there at the rendezvous first, sitting in a coveted M&S booth with two coffees and two flapjacks at the ready. In just a minute or two Judith came bustling up to leave her bags with me before joining the queue for a less calorific snack. I ate my flapjack and was starting on the one I'd bought for her when she arrived with her pot of fruit. She was very agitated, I could tell by the way she started stabbing at her fruit with the little plastic fork.

'What's up Judith?' I said.

She sighed. 'It's Persephone, in America. She's just done something incredibly stupid.'

My ears pricked up. This was exciting news. 'Is this your daughter who lives in a New York penthouse and works for Chase Manhattan Bank for an eye-watering salary?'

'Yes,' she said, stabbing at grapes.

'So, what has she done?'

'She's resigned! Quit her job! She's going to spend a year just following her dream. Can you believe it?' Her alarm was infectious.

'Oh no,' I said. 'A year following her dream? That's awful.'

'I can't believe it,' she said. 'I can't believe she would be that stupid.'

'I don't know what to say, Judith,' I said. 'I'm so sorry.'

'She rang a couple of days ago to tell me what she was going to do. I pleaded with her to reconsider. I told her, this world is so competitive, you can't afford to take your eye off the ball, and you have to keep your nose to the grindstone and your shoulder to the wheel because if you don't, someone will cut you off at the knees. Persephone has her head in the clouds, Sally, but she needs to keep her feet on the ground.'

I tried to follow the argument. 'How tall is she?' I said.

'What's that got to do with anything?' Judith snapped her fork in half somewhere in her pot of fruit.

I gave her my teaspoon.

'I've got nothing against following a dream,' Judith said. 'But it's a question of timing. You have to get the timing right. You don't want to be following dreams when you're young, you should have better things to do. We had better things to do, didn't we, when we were young?'

I thought for a second or two. 'I don't actually recall ever following a dream. Is it too late for me now?'

'No. But wait until your sixties and there's nothing else spoiling.'

'I don't know, Judith. I sort of imagine myself following a dream looking gorgeous in something floaty with my hair blowing in the wind. At this rate I'm going to be hobbling after a dream in an M&S thermal. I think I've missed the boat. How old is Perspex?'

'Persephone for God's sake! It's bad enough her American friends calling her Pussy. She's twenty-six.'

'So she's exactly the right age for following a dream. She'll look great. She could do it on horseback and look fabulous. Honestly, I wouldn't worry about it.'

'Easy for you to say. It would be different if one of yours announced they were going to follow a dream.'

'Actually, I think Dan might be following a dream. Or maybe he's just in a dream. And Laura's always making announcements of one kind or another. None are particularly dream-like. Best not to worry about it, Judith. Drink your coffee and try to relax. We should be thinking about our own dreams.'

We had a bit of desultory conversation after that, but Judith's heart wasn't in it.

Eventually she started gathering her things and said she would have to go. She asked me whether I had remembered to speak to Dan about Morwenna. I said yes, everything was in hand. She said thank god Morwenna was still on the straight and narrow, at least she had the good sense not to have dreams.

I said yes, that was something to be thankful for.

On the way home on the bus, I reflected on our conversation and realised I hadn't asked Judith what Persephone's dream was, and that could have had a bearing on things.

It's Hallowe'en. I was scrubbing some potatoes earlier, prior to putting them in the oven to bake, when I heard footsteps running along the back of the house. I peered through the window behind the sink to see if I could see anything, and then – aahhh! A ghastly face jumped up from below. A ghoulish bride of Frankenstein was inches from the window, her hair matted with blood, her eye hanging forward on her cheek, a knife piercing her neck, a slash to her face exposing the bone. She held up a hand clasping a diseased rat, and said, 'Hiya!' Then she was gone.

Sophie came in through the back door.

'It's just me! Did I give you a fright?' she asked me, her eye bouncing impishly on her cheek.

'Well,' I said, 'I was terrified for a few seconds.'

'Oh good,' she said, 'I hoped it was really scary. We're going to a Hallowe'en party tonight. I've asked the Morwith girl if she'll come, so we're meeting her in the Cat and Fiddle at seven-thirty. There's food, so don't put lots of those spuds in.'

'Right,' I said. 'Where did you get the special effects?'

'Brilliant aren't they? Baz knows someone. He's coming as a dead person. He says he'll be the life and soul of the party! Funny that, isn't it?'

'Yes,' I said, 'dead funny.'

'And Dan's coming as a mad wolf. It's going to be great. Would you like to come?'

'No thank you Sophie.'

'You could come as a crazy housewife.'

'I could stay here as a crazy housewife.'

Then Dan came in with a gorgeous looking girl in a tight black dress and long black polished fingernails.

'Mum – Sophie,' said Dan, 'this is Morwenna. She's changed a bit since she was at school.'

Chapter 6 – November

At six-thirty this morning, someone was urgently tapping on my bedroom door.

'Mrs Forth? Are you awake?'

No use denying it. 'What is it, Sophie?'

'Can you get up? I need some help.'

Bill was taking an early phone call, so I got up without making more enquiries. I put my dressing gown on and went downstairs to the kitchen. Dan and Baz were making some breakfast, and Sophie was sitting at the table with a cup of tea.

'What's the problem?' I said, and Sophie turned around to face me. Her Hallowe'en eye was still stuck to her face and lolling forwards out of its socket. It was very disconcerting. Strikingly authentic.

'I can't get this eye off my face,' said Sophie. 'And now Hallowe'en's finished, it's as if my eye is actually coming out for real. It's not very nice, Mrs Forth.'

I took a closer look. 'Why can't you pull it off?' I said.

'Baz gave me some glue to use yesterday. And it won't wash off.'

'The bloke I got it from said it was good stuff,' said Baz, looking for approval.

'I don't think I can go to work like this,' said Sophie. 'I'll have to ring my boss and explain that it looks as if my eye's falling out. I work with old people and they're usually pretty tough but they expect you to have your eyes properly in your head.'

Sophie made her phone call, and then I tried to cut some of the false eye free with a pair of sharp scissors. But I had to

119

abandon the attempt almost immediately because the scissors were too sharp and pointed, and her real eye was too close underneath the false one, and it didn't feel safe.

After breakfast Sophie had a shower, to see if she could dislodge the thing. Afterwards it was just as stuck, but it looked fresher and perkier, and the bobbing eye had a newly-washed, roguish twinkle, which wasn't helpful. I said I would drive her down to her GP's to see if they had any suggestions.

The surgery was busy when we arrived – there were a lot of cars in the car park. I suggested to Sophie that she held a paper hanky over her eye, in case she alarmed anyone, and we went inside.

The receptionist was on the phone and we waited until she had finished her call. Sophie said she had a bit of a problem around her eye, and we needed some advice.

The receptionist said the doctors were all very busy today, and maybe we could make an appointment and come back? I said we were hoping to see someone today, if that was possible. The receptionist shook her head sadly and said there were no appointments today, but maybe a bit of Golden Eye ointment would help in the meantime?

Then it was my turn to shake my head sadly, 'Unfortunately,' I said, 'Golden Eye ointment isn't going to help.'

The receptionist gave me a weary smile, and asked me if I thought I was some sort of eye specialist.

So I said, 'Show this lady your eye, Sophie.'

Ten seconds later I was sitting in the waiting room with a copy of *House and Garden* and the receptionist was sitting on a low stool with her head between her legs. Sophie was being attended to in a treatment room. Very satisfactory all round.

It took about half an hour. Sophie's face was a bit blotchy afterwards, and she has lost a segment of eyebrow, but she was free of the rollicking eye. We went back home, and I made her an early lunch before she went to work for the afternoon.

Sophie was pleased to have just two eyes now, both in the right place, but she was not happy with the way the Hallowe'en party had gone last night. In particular, she was not happy with Morwenna.

She said that she herself had worn a proper Hallowe'en costume, with her eye hanging out and her cheek wound sticker and the dead rat over her shoulder and her hair all back -combed with red paint. But Morwenna had only worn pale foundation and purple eye shadow, and she was wearing a really nice dress instead of a regulation shroud. So Morwenna had looked gorgeous, but Sophie looked as if she had been attacked by a wolf and died three weeks ago. 'It's not fair,' Sophie said, and she sounded as if she might get a bit tearful. Poor thing.

So I set to and gave her a little pep talk about life not always being fair and the important thing being to pick yourself up and learn from the experience so that you're better prepared next time, and it was upsetting but she would get over it. I had a little personal anecdote which I thought might be helpful, so I said, 'You know, Sophie, all this reminds me of the time when I—'

But she cut me short. 'Actually Mrs Forth,' she said, 'I've got to go now or I'll miss my bus.'

After she had gone and I had finished my lunch, I felt like talking to a proper grown-up. Someone who would think twice before supergluing an extra eye to their head. I thought I would give Jen a ring, even though her hold on adult status was precarious at the moment. I thought I might suggest I go up to see her. It's a long way north but I could go on the train. I rarely get to go up north and I thought it would be a bit of an adventure.

'Jen!' I said, when she answered. 'How about this for a plan? How about if I come up to you and spend a few days?'

'Oh,' she said with no enthusiasm at all, 'that would be wonderful. But – there might be a problem. If Scott sees me with you, he might realise I'm a bit older than thirty-nine. You might give me away. Unless...'

'Unless what?'

'Unless you pretend to be my mother. That might work. In fact, that might be a good idea. Do you still have that tweedy skirt and grey angora cardigan?'

'Pretend to be your mother? Would you like to re-think that?'

There was a slight pause, during which I assumed she was coming to her senses.

'Sally,' she said. 'Can I speak frankly? It's not a good time for you to come up. My flat is full of kapok and testosterone. My days are very complicated. I have rigidly timetabled slots, sometimes I'm a jolly grandma, and at other times I'm Maggie May. They're very different roles. There's not a lot of overlap. I'm very busy. It's difficult to keep track. When I go out I don't know if I should be buying Play-Doh or sexy knickers. Can we postpone your visit until everything has gone tits up and I need a shoulder to cry on?'

'Okay,' I said. 'That's fine. Just keep me posted. And don't ever suggest I could pose as your mother again, or you won't be crying on my shoulder.'

'Sorry, it was a crazy suggestion. Do you forgive me?'

'I'm thinking about it.' I put the phone down and stared into space.

What exactly am I for these days, I thought? What is the purpose of my life? When I was teaching English, the purpose of my life was to de-mystify the apostrophe. But now? What is my life's purpose at the moment? Jen doesn't need me, I'd embarrass her. Dan doesn't need me. Laura doesn't need me – she is probably even now agreeing with her therapist that I'm the reason she's nuts. Sophie doesn't need me, apart from very occasionally to help her remove the extra organs she glues to her head. My husband needs me, of course, but he doesn't need to be with me much, it seems. What exactly is the purpose of my life?

And so, sitting there among the remains of my lunch, I had an existential crisis.

***

I've heard of existential crises of course. But I never imagined I would be clever enough to have one of my own. I'd always thought they were for poets and intellectuals. I'd have been quite chuffed with myself, if I'd been in the mood.

At first I thought it might just wear off, like a headache. Last night I thought an episode of *Holby City* might cure it, and maybe an episode of *Only Connect* would jolt me out of it. But it was there again this morning. Existential angst. After breakfast, I mooched around the house, looking for one of my leather gloves which has been missing for weeks, and also for some meaning to my life. I found the glove.

Maybe, I thought, very tentatively, I should embark on a programme of Good Works, to see if I could do something worthwhile with my increased leisure time. I thought about it until my body gave a little involuntary shudder, which I took to be a sign that this might not be the right path.

I don't think this is an uncommon problem among people who have recently left work for whatever reason, this search for a meaningful existence. I think Derek next door is suffering from it. His wife Susan is dealing with her existential angst by plotting to kill things. It's counterintuitive, but it's working for her, she seems energised by it, but it's not working for Derek, not least because he may be one of the things she is plotting to kill.

Jen is dealing with her angst by looking for love on a ball of kapok. She may be misguided, and she may be heading for heartache, but I've never lived on my own with a ball of kapok so I have no right to judge.

Judith is looking for confirmation of her life's meaning through her children's lives, but this only works when your children know and care about what your life's meaning is. If they go off-piste, and start living their own lives without any reference to yours, it can be very difficult, and make for some pretty heavy discussions in Marks and Spencer's café requiring a booth and strong coffee.

Bill hasn't retired yet, and is well protected from existential angst by his job. But it's lying in wait.

Last year at this time I was much too busy to have an existential crisis, it would have seemed like a massively frivolous over indulgence. Leisure was what I craved a year ago, time to think and relax and look about me and take stock. Well, I've done that now. I've looked about me and taken stock, and there's not much in the cupboard. Last year I rebelled against the school timetable which dictated every minute of my working day and well beyond, but this year, without that timetable, my days are unfocused and lack purpose.

Personally, I think it takes extraordinary courage and strength of will to be idle, and have no particular purpose in life. Very few people can handle it. It's a skilled job and it takes nerves of steel. And if you do succeed in being idle and staying sane, don't expect anyone to give you credit for it. Don't expect anyone to say, 'Well, she's done absolutely fuck-all since she stopped work, and you've got to admire her for that!' No. Your achievement will go unrecognised.

I only just held myself together this morning because I had to go into school after lunch to help Lee in an art lesson, so I could persuade myself that I was going to do something useful.

But I'm not of course. I'm not really doing much for Lee. He regards me as an amusing eccentricity of the School. I pop up every now and again and concern myself with his education, which confirms for him that I am not right in the head. He humours me if he feels like it. Lee won't be troubled by existential angst, because his raison d'etre is to hate school and he does that very well. However, this takes up a lot of his mental strength, so he doesn't have energy left over for learning.

Art is one of Lee's favourite lessons. It has a lot going for it as far as Lee is concerned. He can move around the class room. He can be very creative with scissors. He can spill things by accident, and cover things in paint, and at the end of the lesson he can soak his work in water and reduce it to a brown pulp. I've been in lots of art lessons with Lee, and I can't remember many where he didn't have a pile of brown pulp to show for his efforts at the end of the hour's work.

Maybe today would be different.

'Lee,' I said to him at the beginning of the lesson this afternoon, 'just for a change, why don't you make something we can pin up on the wall today, instead of a pile of brown mush?'

He didn't reply, but I thought I might have planted the germ of an idea. Maybe this notion of leaving a legacy after an art lesson will appeal to him. It may have novelty value. Lee can surprise sometimes. There was that time about six months ago when he said he liked my new hairstyle.

In our lesson today, Lee set about his brief and painted a picture of an autumnal tree. It was a good picture, I thought it was one of Lee's best efforts, and I commented on it to give him appropriate encouragement. 'This tree's really very good, Lee,' I said. 'I particularly like the shape. It's a very good shape for a tree. Well done.'

He immediately added an appendage to the tree which altered the shape entirely and made it lop-sided.

'Well, maybe I should have waited till you'd finished. Still, it's an interesting shape. Oh!' I said. 'It's a flowering tree. I see you're covering it with red flowers.'

He continued working. Concentrating on the tree.

'Right,' I said, keeping up an interested commentary. 'The tree is completely covered in red blooms now. So many flowers you can hardly see the leaves. It's looking quite dramatic.'

Lee paused his efforts with the red paint, and contemplated his tree. 'It's blood,' he said. 'The tree's covered in blood.'

'Oh God,' I said. 'Why? I thought it was blossom.'

'It ain't no blossom,' he said. 'It's blood.'

'Oh no. What's caused that?'

'There's something dead in there.'

I recoiled slightly from the tree. 'Something dead?'

'Yeah. Something died in the tree. And that's its blood.'

'Oh my god, Lee. This was a nice tree and now it's soaked in blood. It's starting to scare me.'

'Yeah,' he agreed. 'It's not a good tree.' And I sensed that the tree was beginning to unsettle even its creator.

'I thought there might be birds nesting in it earlier,' I said. 'But now I'm hoping they're not. '

'Ain't no birds in that tree,' said Lee, very solemn, shaking his head. 'Won't last long in there.'

We both looked in dismay at the blood-drenched tree. 'What are you going to do with it now?' I asked him, because I wanted no responsibility for the massacre among its branches.

'We could put it up on the wall,' said Lee. 'Like you said.' He picked it up, and a surfeit of blood ran from the foliage down the page and dripped onto the table.

I hesitated. 'We could. We could put it up on the wall with the others.' I glanced around the room at the innocent trees painted by the others in the group, which were now being pinned onto the display board. Some had birds perching on their branches, some were framed by rainbows, one had a perky little squirrel peeping out of a hole in the trunk. Lee carried his tree across the room to the board, trailing blood on the floor. I followed him with some drawing pins.

'It'll have to go near the front,' he told me. 'Or the blood will drip over the other trees and most probably kill them.' He glanced at little Nutkin peeking from the branches of a tree nearby. 'It'd definitely kill that sodding squirrel.'

So we put it near the front. Carnage in a Walt Disney landscape. The bell went soon after, and we were both relieved to leave the scene.

When I got home, there was a full scale row going on next door. I heard raised voices before I opened my car door to get out. Susan shouting at Derek.

'You idiot! I told you this would happen! You and your vibrating stick!'

I opened the car door quietly and tried to slither into the house unseen.

'Sally! Over here!'

So I went over to the fence. I could see what looked like a ring of four or five molehills encircling one of Derek's mole deflecting sticks.

'They love the bloody things!' said Susan. 'Come round, have a proper look.'

So once again, I stood at the back of their house and surveyed their lawn, and it did look as if the sticks had attracted more moles.

'Look at that!' said Susan. 'They're dancing around the bloody things like a maypole. I told him – we need to kill them! We need to nip their heads off in traps! But he wouldn't listen.' She stamped her foot in frustration.

'Where is Derek?' I said. I looked around, and thought – poor Derek, has she nipped his head off? In a trap?

But he came out of the house carrying something.

'What the hell is that?' said Susan.

Derek was grim faced. 'It's a radio. They don't like noise. I'm going to put it down one of the holes. That'll fettle them.'

'What!' She looked at me incredulous. 'He's going to serenade them now! Music while you work. They'll be doing square dances under the turf. They might like music, Derek. Have you thought about that?'

'It's Radio One Susan,' he said. 'Give me some credit. They'll clear off in a few hours.'

I left them violently disagreeing about moles and their taste in music. I had nothing to contribute, and I needed a cup of tea after the gruesome tree earlier, so I made my excuses.

I heard Baz arrive around six-thirty, and decided to ask him in for a chat about whether or not he was working towards healing the rift with his parents, with a view to moving back home. Having him living in Aspire is a concern I could do without. It isn't habitable, and while he's in there I feel responsible for him.

He sat opposite me with tea and biscuits, and emptied the sugar bowl into his mug.

'Well Baz,' I said. 'How are things with your parents now? Have you managed to patch things up?'

'Yeah,' he said. 'We get on much better, now that I've left home.'

'Left home?'

'Yeah. We were always arguing before.'

'What about? If you don't mind me asking?'

'The usual stuff. They said I drank too much, and smoked too much, and did too much other stuff.'

'And do you?'

'I did, yeah. But since I left I'm not drinking as much, and I don't like to smoke next door. I'm much healthier now I've got my own place. And happier. And my folks are really pleased. It's great.'

I nodded. Not trusting myself to speak in case I gave way to despair.

'And,' he said, 'when I get hold of some more meat, I can cook us all dinner. So it's win-win!'

***

Sophie curled up on the sofa with me this evening. We chatted while watching television. Sophie's doing long day shifts this week, so she came in, had a quick bite to eat and a bath, and came down in her jimjams and dressing gown. She slumped next to me on the sofa. Bill was having an increasingly rare evening at home, and was in the armchair by the stove. We made a very cosy tableau.

Sophie chatted to Bill. 'Mr Forth,' she said, looking over at him, 'you know you're on the telly sometimes?'

'Mmm?' he said.

'Do you think you'd ever do Strictly?'

'I don't know, Sophie. I've never been asked.'

'You should,' said Sophie. 'It would make you more famous.'

Dan, meanwhile, has gone out. Not for him the comfy fireside evening with mum, dad and girlfriend. He's gone out to the local Amateur Dramatics Society to talk to them about the staging of their next play, which is set on a space ship. It's quite a thriving group apparently, with lots of young people, which is unusual for an Am Dram Society. I've known a few groups that had to cast around for someone under seventy to play Peter Pan.

'Sophie,' I said. 'Did you not fancy going with Dan down to the Am Dram meeting this evening? There's lots of young people there apparently. It's a lively group.'

'No,' she said. 'I was too tired. And it's nice and cosy here with you and Mr Forth.' She repositioned herself on the sofa, and I thought for one awful moment she was going to put her head in my lap. 'I trust Dan, you know,' she said after a pause. 'I know he wouldn't get too friendly with any of the other girls down there.'

Oh dear, I thought. This girl knows nothing. She is a complete innocent, and she's on my sofa in her pyjamas telling me she trusts my son, who has just told me he doesn't see a long term future for their relationship. Could this be any more awkward?

'Mrs Forth?' she said. 'Would you mind if sometimes I called you Mum? "Mrs Forth" seems a bit teacher-y.'

My heart, which was already somewhere near my hips, sank further to my knees. Bill tried to come to the rescue by suggesting a cup of tea and creating a general disturbance with enquiries about types of tea and sizes of cup, and biscuits or no biscuits. I thought we had headed the whole thing off at the pass, but shortly after Bill went into the kitchen to put the kettle on, it came back.

'So, shall I call you Mum then, Mrs Forth?' said Sophie.

I could have said, 'Actually Sophie, I'd rather you didn't, if you don't mind.' I could have said that, but it would have felt like kicking a baby guinea pig across the room. Alternatively, I could have said, 'That would be lovely Sophie, yes, call me Mum whenever you like.' But, sadly, that would have felt like shit.

So instead I said, 'Actually Sophie, I really like the way you still call me Mrs Forth, like you did when you were at school. It means a lot to me, because it reminds me of all the good times we had when you were doing GCSE English.'

Sophie sat up straighter and looked faintly puzzled. 'Did we have any good times when I was doing GCSE English, Mrs Forth?'

Bill arrived with the tea, and I busied myself with that to indicate that this discussion was over. Sophie got the message, and drank her tea, and reverted to her usual line of discourse.

'It'll be Christmas soon,' she said. 'Mrs Forth, have you ever wondered whether a robin looks like a kiwi fruit under its feathers?'

My phone rang and, as I was juggling a cup of tea and a plate of biscuits, Sophie said, 'I'll get it for you!' and she answered it. 'Hiya! Mrs Forth's phone! Sophie is taking her calls.' The caller said something and Sophie replied, 'I live here now! Yeah. Don't know how permanent. I'm supposed to be looking for somewhere else. Yeah, I'll put her on. Who's calling please?' She handed me the phone, and said, 'It's someone called Laura.'

I stood up and went into the kitchen to take the call.

'Mum,' said Laura, 'what's going on? Who was that Sophie person?'

'Sophie is Dan's girlfriend. She's spending some time here until she can find somewhere more permanent.'

'Whose idea was that?'

'I don't know how it happened, to be honest, Laura.'

'What happens if she and Dan split up?'

'Well, she has her own room. Dan seems to think it could still work.'

'What room is she in?'

'Your room.'

'My old bedroom?'

'Yes.'

'But I don't know her.'

'I don't think she's in there all that much, actually, Laura.'

'Still. It feels like an invasion of my space. You should have asked me first. Have you still got that heap of junk stuck to the side of the house?'

'Yes, it's still there. For the moment.'

'Isn't it time you got rid of it?'

'It is yes. But there's someone spending a few nights in it just now.'

'What! Who?'

'Baz.'

'Baz? Oh God. You haven't eaten any of his meat, have you? Put Dan on. I need to talk to him.'

But of course I couldn't put Dan on, because he was the only one of us not at home.

Minutes after Laura's call when I was back on the sofa in possession of my tea and biscuits, and just a little shaken, Dan came home. We heard the kitchen door open, and the sound of two people making an entrance.

'It's Dan!' said Sophie, sitting up straight and looking expectantly towards the door, ready to greet him.

And in he came, with Morwenna. 'Hiya!' said Sophie, and then, 'Oh.'

Once again, Sophie was at a disadvantage alongside Morwenna. This time she didn't look like an autopsy, but she looked like a close relative of Christopher Robin with the sex appeal of a piglet. Morwenna looked like a proper grown-up woman with more sex appeal than Christopher Robin could possibly hope to handle.

'Hi!' said Morwenna, smiling radiantly at us all. 'Sorry to disturb your evening. I just wanted to thank Sophie for inviting me to the Halloween party. I don't think I thanked her properly the other night, and I'm going to be away until Christmas. I saw

Dan when I was out, so I thought I'd just drop by.' She looked around. 'But maybe she isn't here?'

Sophie said, 'Hi Morwenna.'

'Oh you're there!' Morwenna looked more carefully at the advertisement for hot water bottles and flannelette sheets perched on our sofa. 'You're a master of disguise Sophie! Last time I saw you, you looked as if you'd had some botched plastic surgery. Of course – you had an excuse – it was Halloween. Anyway, thanks so much for inviting me along, it was a great party. And I hope I'll see you all when I'm back at Christmas. It's been so good to catch up with everyone, and to meet Sophie of course.'

Both Dan and Bill were smiling foolishly and seemed lost for words. Sophie was trying to rearrange her terry towelling dressing gown to look more alluring, so I said, 'It's been good to see you too Morwenna, maybe there'll be another fancy dress party to go to at Christmas? That would be fun.'

'That would be great fun,' said Morwenna. 'You'd be up for that, wouldn't you Sophie? You might get a chance to wear that eye again. Ghost of Christmas Past or something. It certainly put my purple eye shadow to shame. I was seriously outclassed. What happened to it? The eye? Have you still got it?'

'It's been incinerated,' said Sophie.

'Oh, right! Well, never mind. Anyway – must go – it's getting late. Early start in the morning. Bye all, oh – and keep up the good work Mr Forth.'

We smiled and waved. Then Dan saw Morwenna out, and Bill sat down. Sophie pulled her dressing gown around her with impressive dignity and announced that she was going to bed.

***

Thankfully, there is a distraction this morning from the search for meaning in my life, in the form of an email. The email is from Sandra Perkins. The last time I saw Sandra Perkins was over thirty years ago, on my last day as a pupil at school. When I think of her, I see in my mind's eye a fresh faced girl of eighteen in a school regulation white blouse and tie, and a bottle-green, tight but approved-length school skirt.

Well I never. Sandra Perkins. Well, well, well. Good Lord. How amazing to hear from her after all these years. Difficult to say for sure, of course, looking back after this much time, but I'm pretty certain we couldn't stand each other.

What could she possibly be emailing me about? I read on, and discovered that Sandra is organising a reunion of our school year group. I hadn't heard that Sandra had done particularly well since leaving school, but obviously she has. We've never had a reunion, and Sandra thinks this has been very remiss of us, and *it's past time we put that right!*

Very remiss? Well, I'm not sure about that, Sandra. I'm not sure whether we should mess with the arrangement we have had up to now. It seems to have worked pretty well all these years, this previous plan of ours just to ignore each other. Why spoil a good thing?

I read on. What seems to be bothering Sandra is that if we don't get a move on and organise a reunion *while we are all 'relatively' young and fit and active, we'll risk leaving it until it's too late!!! Because*, she hates to remind us, *We're not getting any younger!!! And time flies! Let's not wait until our numbers start to dwindle!!*

Marvellous. Fantastic. Thank you Sandra, you've made my day. No – really – you certainly know how to cheer a girl up. I suppose you weren't to know I was having an existential crisis, but still. Have you included a thoughtful link to a funeral planning service somewhere in this email, Sandra? Let's make sure we are all adequately prepared because you never know the day or the hour. Oh – there doesn't seem to be a link to Cremations R Us. An oversight, surely.

I was about to press 'delete' when my phone rang. It was Judith, in a state of high excitement. 'Sally? Have you seen

Sandra's email? Isn't that a great idea? I think it's good of her to go to all this trouble to get us together, don't you?'

'Oh. Is it?'

'Of course it is! It's a great idea! I'm glad she's making the effort.'

Okay, I thought. Perhaps I've been a bit hasty in judging Sandra's email. If Judith-the-Annihilator-of-Young-Dreams is grateful for her efforts, that suggests I'm being a bit harsh.

Judith burbled on. She had read the whole email, and she told me that when we arrive at the venue for the reunion we will be given a name badge with our first name and maiden name on it, so that we will know each other easily, without trying to remember names after all this time.

I wondered whether this might in fact be a bad idea. It might lead to us circulating around, reading name badges, searching faces, and trying to dig out of wrinkles and layers of foundation the bonny-cheeked girls we used to know. I thought it would be better to go incognito, and only own up to who we are, or rather were, if we felt like it.

Judith said I was being a miserable sod, and I needn't think I was getting out of it, because we were both going to the reunion. She said I had nothing to worry about because it wasn't until December. This will give us plenty of time to lose some weight and do something with our hair, and maybe even do a bit of running so that we can tell everyone we're doing a bit of running. 'But we needn't keep that up,' she said, 'obviously.'

Sophie came back from work just after two this afternoon. She had been doing an early shift, so was finished for the day. She was planning to have a bowl of soup, and then catch up on some sleep. I told her while she was eating her soup that I was going to a reunion of the girls I was at school with, and I was wondering what to wear.

'A reunion?' said Sophie. 'That's nice.'

I said it was a long time since we had all been at school together. I wasn't sure whether it would be nice, but I supposed it would be interesting.

Sophie said, 'Were you a suffragette when you were younger, Mrs Forth?'

'No Sophie I wasn't. I was a David Bowie fan.'

'Were you?' she said, intrigued. 'Well, anyway. I bet you had much more fun before the internet was invented and people just had biros.' Then she filled a hot water bottle, and took it upstairs, and I was left wondering whether Ofsted was doing its job properly.

Baz was the next one back, knocking on the door at about six-thirty. I hoped he wasn't carrying a bag with some very fresh meat thrashing around in it.

'Should have told you last night, Mrs Forth,' he said. 'Next door have left a radio out somewhere in their garden. I've heard it playing. I went round there this morning to tell them about it. She's a funny woman, isn't she, next door? Sort of menacing but in a flowery apron.'

I asked him in, and he carried on talking while he took his boots off. I was glad there were no bags of meat bobbing about at his feet. 'I spoke to Mrs Next Door,' he said, 'and she asked me if I was the character who had slept on her lawn, so I said yes, and she told me to clear off, so I didn't get a chance to mention the radio.'

I gave Baz a cup of tea and a sugar bowl, and explained that the radio was playing to the moles in Susan's back garden, in the hope that it would encourage them to pack up and move away.

Baz said they used traps at work for moles, not radios. He said he didn't know anyone who used radios for moles.

We might have continued to discuss traps versus radios, but it was very difficult to ignore the smell of Baz's feet, now that he had removed his boots. He mentioned it first. 'God – my feet stink!' he said. 'I think I'd better go.'

I asked him how he was managing to do his washing, and he said he would be taking it down to the laundrette at the weekend. He said until then he was just airing his clothes overnight, to freshen them up, because he thought that worked quite well. Particularly when there's a bit of a breeze. But he said, to be honest, the socks he was wearing now could do with more than a good airing.

I suggested that he put some washing in our machine this evening, because I thought it might be unwise to let his things go unwashed any longer. I said there was already some potent biology at work in his socks, and I was worried about them evolving and becoming conscious.

He said thanks, it would be great if he could put his washing in our machine, and he would come round with it later on. I said no problem, and now that his socks knew their way into our kitchen he could probably just send them round on their own.

Baz laughed, and said that was quite funny. He poured the sugar bowl into his tea, drank up and left, saying he would see me later. I sprayed some disinfectant on the kitchen floor and gave it a wipe after he'd gone. Those socks couldn't possibly make contact with any surface without leaving something behind, and I didn't want to be in the same room with whatever that was.

Bill is going to be away for a few days, so there was just Dan, Sophie and me at home this evening, with Baz popping in and out with his washing, and making us all cups of coffee and tea.

At around ten o'clock, Sophie said, 'Let's watch the news. We might see Mr Forth.'

Dan left the room. He doesn't like to watch the news.

Sophie and I watched, and after a while she said, 'Mrs Forth, does it make you angry when people say bad things about Mr Forth?'

I told her we should switch channels and watch the wildlife programme on the other side. Sophie got up and went into the hall to give Dan a shout: 'We've turned over Dan! We're watching elephants now!'

She came and sat down on the sofa, and we started to watch. The elephants made more comfortable viewing, and Sophie settled in to the programme.

'Mrs Forth,' she said, 'have you ever wondered whether people would still like elephants if they were covered in spikes?'

I quite like having Sophie around.

***

I had a tricky conversation with Susan from next door today. I noticed as I was leaving the house just after lunch that she was kneeling on her lawn, and stabbing it repeatedly with a long-bladed knife. She didn't see me, and I was going to walk by, but I hesitated because I thought she might have gone mad, and there might be some sort of civic duty for me to intervene.

'Susan!' I called over to her. 'Are you okay?'

She jumped up and hid the knife behind her back. 'I've got a bone to pick with you, Sally. Come round, we need to talk about it.'

But I didn't fancy going round. Not after witnessing her frenzied attack on the lawn. I felt safer with the fence between us. 'Actually Susan, I'm in the middle of something at the moment,' I said. 'Can you just tell me over the fence?'

She came up to the fence, still with the knife behind her back. 'You've got someone living in there, haven't you?' She indicated Aspire. 'I know you have.'

'It's just Baz, Susan. Dan's friend. He's camping in there for a few nights, it's not a permanent arrangement.'

'I don't like it Sally. It's not right. Having people sleeping rough on my doorstep. I'm surprised at you, to be honest, allowing it. Does Bill know about this?'

'I think I might have mentioned it,' I said. But actually, I'm not sure I did.

'Well, I don't think Dan's friend should be in there. He smokes, you know. I've seen him out in the garden. Suppose that thing burned down when he was in it? That would be a bit awkward, wouldn't it? For you and Bill? And from my point of view, I don't know him from Adam. He's wandering around at night.' She forgot about hiding the knife, and brought it around in front of her and held it upright like a light sabre. 'He might not be safe. How do I know what he's capable of?'

'He's fine, Susan, honestly,' I said. 'He's perfectly safe. But leave it with me. I'll sort something out.'

'I'm thinking of you and Bill as well as myself, Sally. That's no place for anyone to live in. It's a pile of rubbish, basically, isn't it? I don't know what the Press would make of it.'

'Yes. Yes, I see what you mean. Leave it with me.'

'Good.'

We both turned our attention to the knife, which was now resting along the top of the fence. 'I suppose you're wondering what I'm doing with this?' she said.

'Were you trying to stab moles?'

'I was, yes. I thought I might get a few if I stabbed into their tunnels. But I don't know if I'm hitting any. I thought I might be able to hear something if I got one.'

'Like a squeak or a cry?'

'Something like that, I suppose.'

I looked across at Susan's lawn and pictured her kneeling there, stabbing wildly into the ground, listening to squeaky cries of 'Ow!' 'Ow!' 'Oo that hurt!' coming from under the turf.

'Did the radio not work then?' I asked her.

'No it didn't. Derek wants to try it again with Radio Four instead of music. He thinks voices might put them off more than music.'

I risked a little joke. 'They might like The Archers.'

'What do you mean?'

No. Too risky.

'Anyway, Susan, must be off. And I've got the message about Baz.'

'Good. I've got nothing against that lad. Apart from the fact that I don't like him at all. But he can't be living in there.'

'No, you're right,' I said. 'I'll deal with it.' And I set off.

'Sally!' she called after me.

I turned around.

'What are you got up like that for?'

I looked down at myself. 'I'm going running, Susan. This is my running gear.'

'Oh is it?' she said. 'Well, if you say so.'

I waved, and set off up the hill along the quieter end of our road. I thought I'd jog slowly to get warmed up. It's years since I've run anywhere, but I assumed I would still be able to do it, even if it was just for thirty seconds at a time. My plan was to run for as long as I could, then walk, then run again, by turns until I got back home or dropped dead.

But when I started jogging I became very aware of my internal organs. After just a few yards they were bobbing around inside me like giant corks in a washing machine. They are not anchored down as firmly as I remember. They seem to have come loose in my forties. I had to stop when my ovaries slung themselves over my stomach and wanted to stay there like a cat on a warm car bonnet.

I stood still for a minute, while my insides slid over and around each other and repositioned themselves anatomically. It was a relief to find that I hadn't done any permanent damage after jogging twenty yards. Obviously, I should learn to pace myself, to avoid my small intestines lassoing my heart to my liver.

So I abandoned running in favour of brisk walking, which had to be very brisk to justify the purple knee-length leggings and skimpy top I had persuaded myself it was appropriate to wear. I marched along, legs scissoring up the pavement, arms like pistons, and my face as red and as shiny as the setting sun. I decided I would turn around before I reached the chip shop on the corner at the top of the road. I was grunting a bit with the effort, and my hairband was slipping forward on my head and was very nearly a blindfold. So I didn't see who was shouting, 'Miss! Oi Miss! Fancy a bag of chips, Miss? Might make you go a bit faster!' But there was no mistaking the voice.

Lee. It was Lee. I considered my options. I could turn around and scarper, pretending I hadn't recognised him, or I could stop and chat, talking to him easily and nonchalantly as if I wasn't looking and behaving like a plonker. I decided to stand my ground, and tried to muster up some older-person cool.

'Hi Lee,' I said, casually jogging on the spot as if I didn't want to lose precious momentum. 'How are you? Those chips look nice.'

He held out the bag and I took one. 'What the fuck are you doing, Miss?' he said, looking at me with slight concern as if I was a malfunctioning wind-up toy.

'I'm running Lee. To get fit.'

'Running! That's not running,' he said. 'You didn't think you were running, did you?'

'I have been running,' I said, 'but just then I was power-walking.'

'Power-walking?' he said. 'What's power-walking?'

'That's what I was doing Lee. It's called power-walking.'

He considered this. 'Your knees look fucked.'

An older friend of Lee's came over to investigate the phenomenon bobbing around on the pavement in front of his pal.

'What's this?' he said to Lee.

'It's my special needs teacher,' said Lee.

He looked from me to Lee and back, and said, 'Who's got the special needs?'

'I'm off now guys,' I said, jogging around in a circle so I was pointing down the hill. 'I'm timing myself so I can't hang around. See you later, Lee!'

When I got home I stood in the drive for five minutes, hanging onto the fence while my heart-beat returned to normal and my face stopped throbbing with pulses of radiant heat and light. When I could stand upright unaided again, I thought I should have a quick look inside Aspire, to see how Baz was living in there. Susan was right, he shouldn't be living rough on our doorstep in the middle of winter. I stepped inside, and looked around.

I was stunned. Aspire lived up to its name. It looked like a double page spread in *House and Garden* with the strap line, 'Shed Chic'. There were rows of herbs hanging from the roof, there was a little kitchen corner with a camping stove and two shiny copper-bottomed pans, a comfy bed arranged over hay bales and covered with a crimson wool blanket, a pine cupboard with a china bowl on top, full of big fir cones. Baz had a bookshelf, a clothes rail artistically fashioned from a section of wrought iron garden trellis, and even a Persian rug on the floor, for God's sake. There were bunches of lavender hanging from the walls. It was immaculate, tidy, colourful, aromatic and stylish, and it put my own insipid living room to shame.

How could I evict Baz, when his was the only living space on site with any panache? I should move in here myself and employ him to redecorate my entire house.

Baz came around, latish-on this evening, with another load of washing and a fiver which he insisted on giving me for the use of the washing machine and tumble drier. He wanted to talk about Christmas trees.

He leant against the kitchen bench with his arms folded and asked me whether we usually had a real tree, or an artificial one.

I said we usually had one of each.

'Right,' he said. 'I'm asking 'cos I'm planning to get a nice little tree in a pot and a holly bough for my place, and I wondered if you wanted anything?'

'Well, that's very kind of you Baz,' I said, thinking, 'my place'? This sounds like him digging in.

'I could pick you out a nice tree and a holly bough from work, and bring it back the week before Christmas.'

'Yes please, that would be lovely.'

'And what about a bird?' he said. 'I can get you a really good bird for Christmas dinner. Turkey, goose, duck – whatever you like. You name it, and I'll get you a really nice one.'

I remembered Laura's warning about not eating Baz's meat. 'Oh, well, Baz, I usually just get a turkey from Marks and Spencer. We aren't very adventurous really, when it comes to Christmas dinner.'

'How about I get you something different to try? You name the bird, and I'll put my order in,' he said. 'Or should I just bring something as a surprise? I'll cook it, if you're not sure how to tackle it.'

A bird that needs tackling? I wasn't sure. 'That's very generous of you Baz, but—'

'Spot on,' he said. 'Don't worry about a thing. I'll pop in tomorrow for my washing.'

I read recently that some people don't have a 'mind's eye'. They can't visualise things, they can't conjure up pictures in their head. But I have a particularly good mind's eye. I have no difficulty conjuring pictures in my head. I conjured a picture of Baz turning up on Christmas Eve with two plastic bags dripping blood, one containing an owl, and the other a brace of budgies. I saw Baz with his sleeves rolled up, stuffing the owl with the budgies, and telling me not to worry about a thing.

I could do with talking to Bill about Baz, but obviously, that's not an option at the moment. Politics is never a happy place, but it seems to be particularly vicious just now, and Bill is fighting on all fronts, his own side as well as the opposition. I wonder why he bothers. There must be far easier ways to make a living that don't involve being tied to a rack, or hauled over the coals, or pilloried in the Press, or any other kind of punishment bad enough to justify a medieval metaphor. I did once suggest to Bill that he give up politics and train as a science teacher. He said, 'God Sally, after everything you've told me about teaching? No thanks, I wouldn't survive my first week.'

***

Fortunately, Jen provided me with some light relief this morning when I needed something to lift my spirits. She rang to tell me that her daughter Emily had arrived at her place without warning last evening, to borrow her pressure cooker. Emily has a key to Jen's flat, so she knocked on the door and then let herself in.

Jen said she was not quite fully dressed, and worse, neither was Scott, her new, much younger boyfriend. Jen's daughter Emily is the same age as Scott, and they haven't met each other yet, but Jen didn't feel last night would be a good time for introductions. She said if she ever introduces Emily to Scott she will wait until Scott is wearing clothes. I agreed, and said that introducing Emily to all of Scott, all at once, was not a good idea. And then I asked how this particular scene had played out.

'Well,' said Jen, 'that ball of kapok saved the day. I put the sofa throw around me, and Scott lay low behind the kapok. I said I was just going for a shower. Emily didn't suspect a thing.'

'You got away with it then? And did you laugh about it afterwards?'

'We did, yes, but...' There was a reflective pause on the line. 'You know, Sally, this isn't how I imagined my life would turn out. I thought I'd be in the Rotary Club, or maybe on the committee of the Inner Wheel or the Spinning Jenny, organising fund-raising coffee mornings and ceilidhs to raise money for good causes. I didn't think I'd be hiding a lover less than half my age behind a ball of kapok when my daughter called round unexpectedly to borrow a pressure cooker. When all this started I thought it was fun, but sometimes I wonder whether actually I'm quite a sad case and I just think I'm having fun. Which is it, do you think? Do you think I've got life sussed, or do you think I'm a fool? I can't work it out. I'm either a success or an idiot. Which is it? What do you think Sally? Help me out here. Oh, hang on. There's a call from Scott waiting. Speak later. Bye.'

I contemplated our phone call while I was making a shepherd's pie. It's sometimes surprisingly difficult to know if you are being an idiot or if you are living life to the full. You'd think it would be easy to establish, but it's not. Consider the plan to sell your house and take to the open road in a motor home. Would you be an idiot or would you be living life to the full? I suppose if you got as far as Folkestone and the back axle of your motor home packed up and you caught a cold and lost your bank card, you might then think you'd been a fool and should have stayed at home. But if you got down to the south of France and the sun was shining and the wine was flowing, you'd think you were living life to the full. There's an important point here somewhere, but I lost sight of it between chopping the onions and making the gravy.

I'm in bed now and almost ready to go to sleep. But before I do, I will record in my diary that I met Chrissy today for the first time, because I think we may be going to see more of her. I was in the garden scraping potato peelings off my chopping board onto the compost heap in the dark earlier this evening, when someone came up the drive and said, '*Arise fair sun, and kill the envious moon!*'

'Don't come any closer!' I said. 'I've got a knife.'

'Sorry!' said the voice. 'So sorry! Hello! Mrs Forth, isn't it? I'm Chrissy. Dan's friend from amateur dramatics. Sorry about that, I'm just brushing up on my R&J. I have to learn it for a performance in February and I'm living and breathing it at the moment. It's a method acting thing. Just ignore me if I sound a bit strange. Can I leave this for Dan? He's expecting it.'

'Oh, right,' I said. 'Well – that did sound a bit odd. Listen, Chrissy, do you want to step inside for a minute, I can't see a thing out here.'

'Absolutely,' she said. '*So please you, step aside.*'

'Right,' I said. 'This way.'

We stood in the kitchen, and she showed me the book she wanted me to give Dan. I explained that he wasn't home yet, but I'd pass it on.

She said great, fantastic, then she said she was looking forward to seeing him next Friday. I asked if there was a rehearsal on Friday, but she said no, they were going to see Romeo and Juliet streamed from the Globe, and showing in the cinema in town.

I said, 'That sounds nice. Is Sophie going?'

And she said, 'Who's Sophie?'

'Well,' I said. 'Sophie is Dan's girlfriend.'

'Oh really? Is she? Dan hasn't mentioned her. I wonder why? Do you think they're still together?'

I hesitated, 'I have to say, that was my understanding. Although, I might not be bang up to date. I suppose there might have been some recent developments, I'm not always in the loop.'

'I see.' Then she sighed and said, '*Is your man secret? Did you ne'er hear say, two can keep counsel putting one away.*'

I was completely stumped for any sort of intelligent reply. I'm not often completely stumped, but on this occasion I was. Thank God for Sophie, who made one of her visionary appearances.

'Hiya!'

'Oh hello Sophie, this is a friend of Dan's from amateur dramatics. Chrissy. She just popped in to lend Dan a book. Chrissy, this is Sophie.'

Sophie said 'Hiya!' to Chrissy, and asked her if she would like a cup of tea.

But Chrissy looked at her watch and said she would have to be going, it was getting late. Then she said on her way out, '*It is so very late that we may call it early by and by.*'

'What did she say?' said Sophie, after Chrissy had gone.

I told Sophie I wasn't sure what she'd said, but I thought it was a line from a play she had to learn.

'She needs to be careful, doing that,' said Sophie. 'People might think she's a nutcase.'

***

I have decided to speak to Dan about Sophie. He's spending three evenings a week with the Highfield Players, and Sophie and I are watching a lot of television. I'm more than happy to watch television with Sophie, but I'm wondering where we are all going with this routine. Is this arrangement to become a way of life, or are we in some sort of transition period? Or what?

Sophie and I watched TV together again last night. At the same time I sorted through some Christmas cards unused from previous years, to see how many more I might need to buy this year. Sophie helped. She looked at cards depicting robins and reindeer and pheasants and penguins, and I felt sure these scenes would precipitate one of her searching wildlife enquiries.

Eventually Sophie asked me whether I thought a penguin egg would taste the same as an ordinary egg. I said yes it would, it would taste exactly the same. I said it with confidence as if I regularly had one of each at breakfast and challenged myself blindfold to detect a difference. Sophie was impressed, and said I knew lots of really interesting stuff.

No – I don't mind at all having Sophie around, I'm just wondering why she is around me more than she is around Dan. She must wonder the same, but so far she hasn't said anything.

I spoke to Dan this lunchtime, and asked him how things were going with Sophie. He said things were going fine, Sophie seemed to like staying in with me in the evenings when she wasn't working, so he thought she was happy living with us.

'No Dan,' I said. 'I mean how are things going between you and Sophie, not between me and Sophie.'

'Oh right,' he said. 'Between me and Sophie? Yeah. We get on fine. Great. Well, okay. Okay-ish. Most of the time. Well – some of the time. Actually though, we might have a few compatibility issues.'

I asked him what sort of compatibility issues.

'Oh. Nothing much,' he said. 'Nothing too serious. We laugh at different things. We don't like watching the same telly. We don't like doing the same things. We're not really interested in the same stuff. We don't talk much. That kind of thing.'

'That sounds like more than just a few compatibility issues, Dan,' I said.

'Yeah, well, it's not all bad. We both like liquorice allsorts.'

I sat down at the table opposite him to talk. 'Dan,' I said, 'a mutual love of liquorice allsorts, while very important in any relationship, is not really enough to compensate for being completely incompatible.'

'Yeah, I know that Mum,' he said. 'Leave it with me. It's just a bit difficult, Sophie living in with us. Now that I've met Chrissy.' And then he started to fidget and look around the kitchen for an escape hatch, so I knew this conversation wasn't going to last much longer.

I would have asked him about Chrissy, but I sensed my time was up and I was right. He said he had to go, as he and Baz were constructing an ornamental lily pond this afternoon. He had designed it and, once they had finished work on it, Baz was going to source the fish.

I made a rapid mental readjustment from love triangles to lily ponds, and said that sounded like a really interesting job, and I asked him to take a photo on his phone to show me.

After he left I decided I had to be more proactive in managing the lives of the three young people living under, or almost under, my roof. I don't like the role of bystander. I prefer to take action. I don't like to wait and see.

So, I'm going to indulge in a bit of innocent matchmaking. I'll wait until I know Dan will be out, and then I'll invite Baz to share a meal with Sophie and me. I'll make my signature dish, fish pie, and make a bit of an occasion of it. I'll tell Baz and Sophie it's a formal dinner, and they have to dress up. There will be candles, wine, soft lighting and love potions primed and ready. I've never attempted matchmaking before, and now that I've had this idea I'm keen to give it a go.

Because it's the ideal solution. Baz has no girlfriend and Sophie may soon have no boyfriend. They just need a little encouragement to fall in love with each other, and why shouldn't they? They have interests in common. They both share an interest in the natural world. Baz has an interest in eating animals, and Sophie is fascinated by how animals might look if their outer layers were missing or radically altered. It's a starting point.

The situation called for a shopping list. I got started on the back of an envelope and was writing 'candles, wine, fish, cheese, penguin eggs' when there was a banging on the front door. Not a knocking, a banging. Who the hell is this, I thought, and went to open up.

I opened the door just as Susan was going to give it another thump, so she stumbled forwards a bit into the hallway, and then straightened up.

'Susan!' I said. 'What the hell?'

'Sally – I'm upset. You promised me that lad would be gone from the heap of junk, and the whole thing would be coming down. But I saw him having a smoke in the garden again last night, and when I looked inside the pile just now I see he's got it all done up like a tart's boudoir. He's not going anywhere, is he? You're not playing straight with me, Sally, I'm going to have to make a complaint to the council. I'm just giving you fair warning.'

'All right, Susan,' I said. 'But before you go, tell me, have you got rid of those moles yet?'

'No. We haven't. And that's another thing. The bastard things are all over the lawn and the flower borders. I hate them Sally, I hate the sodding things. They are ruining my garden. I could spit.'

'Have I told you that Baz is an expert at trapping moles? He's caught hundreds of them. He's got certificates to prove it.'

Susan looked at me steadily. 'You don't say? Ha! I know what you're doing here. I'm not so easily fooled. You're hoping that if you tell me that lad can catch moles, I'll let him stay so that he can set traps in our garden.'

'It's up to you.'

'Certificates, did you say?'

'He has the equivalent of an A-level in Mole Management and Eradication.'

'I don't believe you.'

'Suit yourself.'

'All right.' She thought about it, weighing up her dislike of the moles against her dislike of Baz being in Aspire. 'All right then – if he can catch the moles, he can stay. For the moment.'

'He'll catch the moles Susan, don't worry about that.'

'He'd better. He's got a week. He needs to show me a mole within the week.'

'Okay Susan, it's a deal.'

'I don't know why I listen to you.' She stomped off down the path and I shut the door.

I had a dizzying feeling of triumph. Power is so intoxicating. I had a plan to save Dan, Chrissy, Sophie and Baz's love-lives with one boldly orchestrated move, and I had got the better of Susan. I was pleased with my magnificence and I wanted more. But there was no more, so I went back to the kitchen table to continue writing my shopping list. I massaged my temples before I added anything, and confirmed that my existential crisis was feeling much better today. I seemed to be throwing it off.

School rang me early this evening. They were ringing to let me know that Lee had been given a one day suspension from school, and he won't be in school tomorrow. I asked what he'd done to warrant the suspension.

Apparently, a newly qualified young drama teacher had thought it would be a good idea for Lee to join the cast of the Christmas Show as a pirate. She thought he would like dressing up with a sword and an eye patch and a parrot on his shoulder.

He has a natural swagger which made her think he would make a good swashbuckling pirate, and she knew it would be good for him to succeed at something. So she had tried to persuade him to take part.

But she had reckoned without Lee's dignity, which would not be safe in fancy dress with a parrot on his shoulder. Lee had declined her kind offer, but when she persisted in pushing her agenda there had been a full and frank exchange of views on the subject, which ended with Lee telling the drama teacher she could fuck off if she thought he was going to ponce around the stage with a twat of a parrot.

Telling a member of staff to fuck off in this much style has consequences – schools find this difficult to overlook – so Lee has been suspended. But, on the plus side, he has seen off the threat of humiliation and he will be able to hold his head up outside the chip shop. So my guess is that Lee will cope well with his day's holiday.

School doesn't need me tomorrow, thanks to Lee being on gardening leave, so I will be able to concentrate on my plan to encourage Sophie and Baz to fall in love with each other. Basically, I would be using the same methods employed by romantic novelists down the centuries to facilitate a relationship. I have read enough Jane Austen to know how these things are done. I will put Sophie and Baz in the same room together and initiate some conversation. Then I will withdraw, ostensibly to attend to an urgent household task such as disciplining the parlour maids, or quelling a brouhaha in the servants' hall. By the time I return Sophie and Baz will be gazing into each other's eyes and exchanging tokens of affection.

Or maybe despite the candles and the wine and the dressing up and the effort I put in, they just won't fancy each other. It will all come down to chemistry in the end, as indeed most things do.

So I told them separately that I would be cooking dinner for them this Friday, and to make it more fun I thought we should dress up for the occasion. Sophie wanted to know what we were dressing up as, and wondered whether her shroud might be due a second airing. Baz was a little anxious at first because he got the idea that it was just going to be him and me. Maybe he wondered whether I was planning to jump him over the fruit crumble.

However, all misunderstandings are now sorted out, and the stage is set.

***

I chose this Friday evening for the matchmaking dinner because I knew Dan would be out seeing Romeo and Juliet with Chrissy. Dan had asked Sophie if she would go with them to see the film, but she had said no. Sophie told me that she hadn't liked Shakespeare when she was at school, and she didn't think he would have got any better in the few years since she left. So she wasn't interested.

I told Sophie and Baz seven-thirty for eight, and we would start with drinks in the lounge.

Baz arrived first. He had dressed up – he wore tight jeans and a clean white T-shirt. He looked very nice. A bit like the physicist Brian Cox after 700 hours in the gym and a bang on the head. I thought Sophie would be very taken with him, she had probably never seen Baz look this smart. While we were waiting for her to come downstairs I decided I would ask him about his experience of catching moles. 'Baz,' I said, 'how many moles have you caught since working for the landscape gardening firm?'

'Moles?' he said. 'I can't catch moles. I've never even seen one. I'm pretty sure I've never eaten one. Unless they put them in burgers.'

'Right,' I said. 'Do you think it's a skill you can learn? Catching moles?'

'Oh yes, there'll be some skill to it. And I suppose if you caught one you'd be able to see how much meat there was on it.'

'Hiya!'

Sophie was wearing a very fetching black dress, it was fitted and strappy, but the overall effect was tempered by the four large rollers she had in her hair. There were two on top of her head and one above each ear. 'I heard you talking about moles,' she said, 'they shed their skins don't they, like snakes? My mum had a moleskin jacket once.'

'Actually,' I said, 'I don't think they do shed their skin. Not voluntarily, anyway. They need some encouragement. But moving on from moles, we'll be ready to eat in about ten minutes. Do you want to take your rollers out Sophie? Before we have our meal?'

'Oh,' she said. 'I thought you said we were dressing up. But yeah, I'll take them out now.' She went back upstairs, and Baz and I looked at each other.

'She's a bit of a fruit cake, isn't she?' he said. But there was warmth in his voice.

We sat down to our meal shortly after Sophie came back down. We had a pleasant chat over our first course. It wasn't entirely animal focused, because the conversation moved on from wild life to eccentric family members. Sophie said her grandmother tells fortunes. Baz's grandmother can cure hiccups. My grandmother could stand on her head well into her seventies. We all come from good stock.

I made a tactical withdrawal after the apple crumble, and left them to talk and finish their wine. I heard them murmuring away companionably to each other while I loaded the dishwasher. So far, so good.

But not for long. I put the kettle on for tea, and heard raised voices. What on earth? They were practically nuzzling each other when I left to put the dishwasher on. I went back into the dining room.

Sophie was very close to tears and Baz was trying to put his arm around her shoulders, although she was shrugging him off.

'What's up?' I said. 'Something wrong?'

'Baz thinks Dan's going to dump me,' said Sophie. 'That's not true, is it Mrs Forth?'

'I – actually, Sophie – I just came in to see if either of you wanted tea or coffee?'

Baz said he wouldn't have anything, thanks. He was obviously distressed to see Sophie so upset, and was trying to put things right. 'Cheer up Soph,' he said. 'It wouldn't be the end of the world.'

'It would,' she said, crying now. 'It would be the end of the world. Don't say that, Baz.'

Poor Baz stood up and said he would have to go. He thanked me for the meal on his way out, and said he wouldn't have said anything to Sophie if he'd known how upset she'd be. He thought she was going off Dan, he said. He'd obviously got that wrong.

It was a cold night, so I asked him if he would like to stay in our spare bedroom tonight. He said no, he'd be just fine in his own place. I wanted to give him a cuddle, but daren't risk it in case he thought again that I was just after his body, so instead I gave him a comradely pat on the back and asked him if he would like a hot water bottle. Baz said no thanks, he was too warm, and he went outside, a disappointed man.

I went back to Sophie, who was now wiping her nose on a napkin and dabbing her eyes in turn. I asked her if some tea might help, and suggested she went into the lounge and made herself comfortable while I made us both a cup.

She was still sobbing when I brought the tea in. 'Dan would have said something if he was going to dump me. He's never said anything. I don't think he will dump me. I don't want him to dump me, Mrs Forth.'

I tried to console her. 'You poor thing,' I said. 'I hate to see you this upset. To be honest Sophie, I didn't realise you were so fond of Dan. You seem to be quite happy for him to go out without you. I thought you were drifting apart. I hadn't realised you were so much in love with him.'

'Oh no!' she said, tears now streaming down her face. 'I feel terrible, Mrs Forth. If Dan dumps me, I'll have to leave here and go back home. My cousin Julie is in my bedroom now and if I move back home I'll have to share with her and she sings all the time and she really gets on my nerves. She's doing her A-levels and I just know she's going to pass them all. I don't like her. I want to stay here. I've got my own room here and it's got its own little washbasin in the corner and everything.'

'Oh,' I said. 'I thought you were upset because you were in love with Dan?'

'No,' she gave a dismissive wave of her hand, and then she thought about it. 'I mean, I like Dan. Dan's all right. He's really nice. I don't *not* like him or anything. We get along okay.' She blew her nose. 'We don't hate each other or anything. But – I don't know. Does that sound like being in love?'

'No. That sounds like being in the same house.'

She turned towards me and I sensed she was going to ask me one of her earnest questions. 'What's it like being in love, Mrs Forth? Is it like how you feel when you see a really cute little puppy?'

'Actually no, no I wouldn't say it was like that. No.'

'So, what's it like?'

'Well, it's a bit like having a happy, excited feeling like butterflies in your stomach, and sometimes feeling a little bit sick, and light headed, and off your food.'

'I had a tooth out once and it felt like that.'

So I suggested to Sophie that she drank her tea first and then went to bed with a hot water bottle. Dan wasn't back yet and there was no point in her waiting up for him. While she was filling her bottle, I asked her if she had enjoyed her evening with Baz. She said yes, she had, and then she asked me whether I thought Baz was good looking. I said I thought he was very handsome and sexy. Sophie grew thoughtful, and patted her hot water bottle dry on the kitchen towel and reminded me that I'm married to Mr Forth.

Bill rang me later, when I was in bed. He was obviously calling from an office somewhere, still busy at this time of night: there were voices in the background. No point in asking him how things were going, he wouldn't be able to tell me and they're always in crisis anyway. I had finished off the red wine and was feeling quite mellow and drowsy, so instead I asked him, 'How does it feel to be in love with me, Bill?'

He said, 'Thanks Shelley, just put the file on the desk with the others and I'll check it over with Steve.'

***

I'm having a break from thinking about other people's relationships. They can sort themselves out, I have other things to do. I have a reunion to think about, and Christmas to prepare for, and a relationship with my own husband to breathe life into when I next see him.

There are only two misunderstandings I must consider clearing up before I leave people to get on with how they feel about each other without my interference. I must think about letting Dan know that actually Sophie is more attached to the washbasin in her room than she is to him. Although I am not sure how I would do that without having some negative impact on his chutzpah. And I must tell Baz that despite how things appeared at dinner the other night, Sophie seems not to be in love with Dan or with any other human being, but he might have a chance with her if he can emphasise anything he has in common with a bathroom sink.

I must also tell Baz that he is now responsible for catching the moles in Susan's garden, and if he doesn't do this, I will have to pull his house down. Unfortunately, given Susan's temperament, that is how it is.

Judith wants me to help her choose a dress for the reunion. I tried to get out of it by protesting that I don't have much dress sense and I couldn't be sure I would be giving her the right advice. She said that's okay, because she knows if I'm really keen on something she might have to think twice about it, and that would be very helpful.

So I met her this afternoon and we started in House of Fraser and moved on to John Lewis. For two whole hours nothing was right with any garment I held up for Judith's consideration. Not the colour, the style, the length, the fit, the sleeves, the lack of sleeves, the price, or the washing instructions. Every garment she looked at was blighted by something. I'd have bought ten dresses in the time it took Judith to reject a hundred. She's almost fifty, but I'm amazed she isn't still going around in the vestiges of her school uniform for lack of anything she considers more suitable to wear.

As the afternoon wore on Judith became more and more frustrated. She held dresses up for me and asked me, 'What fool put that bow on the front of this bodice?' 'What idiot thinks yellow looks good with maroon?' 'Who in their right mind designs sleeves like this?' No matter how often I told her that I did not know which idiots in the fashion industry were making these mad decisions, she continued to interrogate me. She was desperate for answers. She wanted the perpetrators' names, so she could hunt them down and garotte them with a length of lace.

Judith selected two dresses in almost four hours that she was prepared to try on, although without much hope of success. I went into the changing rooms with her, to try some things on myself, and we were in adjacent cubicles. After about a minute of sounds corresponding with undressing and dressing, Judith thumped on our partition wall.

'Sally,' she said. 'It's no good, they're using distorting mirrors in here. I don't recognise myself in this mirror. What's yours like?'

I looked at my reflection. 'Not good,' I said. 'There's something wrong with the way I look in here. I can't quite put my finger on it. I can see my reflection, but it's altered. I'm looking at my less fortunate identical twin.'

'You're right,' said Judith. 'That's exactly right. A less fortunate identical twin. That's what I'm looking at. And I can see myself from behind. My back view. So peculiar. I don't recognise myself from behind. My legs are too short. Shorter than they are from the front.'

I studied my own back view. 'It is strange,' I said, 'to see yourself from behind. It's giving me an out-of-body experience. This is the first time I've really looked at the back of my own head. I can imagine it now, in a basket at the foot of a guillotine.'

'The lighting's very harsh,' said Judith. 'I don't need to see myself this clearly. It's unnecessary. I know what I look like, I just need the gist. What's your lighting like?'

'Savage,' I said. 'Brutal. There's nowhere to hide in here.'

'Something's very wrong, Sally. The lighting's all wrong. And when I'm not looking at the back of myself, there's an old woman pulling faces at me in the mirror. I'm getting out.'

'Things aren't great in here either,' I said. 'Let's go.'

We were too badly shaken to buy anything, or to continue looking for anything when we came out of the changing rooms, so we went for coffee to steady our nerves.

We found a table and sat down, and after a few sips of coffee we started to feel more like ourselves, and less like the strangely altered doppelgangers we had left behind in the changing rooms.

'You might have noticed,' said Judith after ten minutes or so, 'that I'm a bit out of sorts today.'

I hadn't actually. It would be very difficult to notice when Judith is out of sorts. Her sorts are unpredictable and not easy to diagnose. I couldn't say for sure what she's like when she's in sorts.

'What's up?' I said. 'You're not still thinking about the weird changing room woman with the short legs claiming to be you, are you?'

'No. It's not that. It's Morwenna. She's ditched Hugh.'

This was a sudden change of topic. I tried to catch up. 'Morwenna?' I said. 'She's ditched who?'

157

'Hugh.'

'Me?'

'Not you. Hugh.'

'You?'

'Oh for god's sake Sally. Not me. Not you. Her boyfriend, Hugh.'

'Well,' I said, irritated myself. 'She mustn't like him. If she ditched him.'

Judith pointed her spoon at me and said, 'Listen to this, and explain to me why she doesn't like him. He's good-looking, he's doing well at PWC, his parents are wealthy, they have a place in Geneva, he likes to cook, he's athletic. What do these girls want? What do they want Sally? What? When they seem to have everything, what the hell is it that they haven't got? Why don't they want what they've got? When they've got what everyone else wants?'

I searched for answers and said, 'I don't know.'

'When she told me she'd broken up with him, I said, Morwenna, what went wrong? Hugh is such a lovely man. And she said – and I can hardly believe it – she said he was *a bit controlling*. I said to her, I said – Look Morwenna, *I'm* a bit controlling. I am! I freely admit, I'm a bit controlling. That's the truth! And I told her – if I hadn't exercised some control of her father over the years, God only knows what he might have been doing now. I dread to think. He'd have bought that sailing dingy, and we'd be living on the Isle of Skye. He needed controlling and I controlled him, and thank God I had the presence of mind to do it. He could have been running around out of control for years. He's much better when he's under control. Don't knock a bit of control, Morwenna, I said. Marriage can't be a free-for-all.'

So then, after a trying afternoon, I decided to exercise some control myself, despite my determination this morning not to interfere in other people's relationships.

'You know what I think?' I began

'What?' said Judith. 'What do you think?'

'I think you should stop thinking about those girls of yours, and start living your own life.'

'Oh do you?'

'I do, yes. And changing the subject slightly,' I said, 'maybe we have something to learn from Jen Spencer, because since she moved away she has been very much in control of her own life.'

'Oh has she?' said Judith. 'What's she doing now? She moved north didn't she, to be closer to her daughter Emily. She was going to help look after grandchildren. Doesn't sound as if she's in control of much.'

'You couldn't be more wrong there, Judith,' I said. I wasn't planning to say much more, but then I thought – Jen has moved away now, and she and Judith don't know each other well, I could risk spilling some sensational beans here. So I carried on. 'Jen is having to juggle looking after her grandchildren with having a secret relationship with a man half her age. How's that for control? She's having a great time.'

Judith's eyes grew wider and rounder, and for a few seconds she was lost for words. I felt the warm glow which comes with imparting scandalous news.

'God Almighty!' she said. 'That's amazing! Half her age? In his twenties? And Emily doesn't even know? I must tell Morwenna. She and Emily are such good friends.'

Chapter 7 – December

Obviously, I extracted a promise from Judith that she would not say anything to anyone about Jen's relationship with the firm-buttocked Scott, especially to her daughter Morwenna. I bought Judith an extra cup of coffee from the café to delay her departure. Then I sat opposite her and pointed out at length how unfair it would be to drop Jen in it with her daughter Emily by letting anything slip. As indeed I had just done.

It was not lost on me that if Judith tells her daughter Morwenna, and Morwenna tells Jen's daughter Emily, and Jen identifies me as the source of the leak, then Jen will never confide in me again. And that would be terrible, because Jen is the only one of my friends doing anything interesting at the moment, and her confidences are the only ones worth having.

Judith has promised not to say anything to Morwenna, but my mind is not at rest. Being in possession of sensational news which you have to keep to yourself is not something everyone can handle. As things have turned out, it's not something I can handle.

What an idiot. Why didn't I keep my mouth shut? I just couldn't resist the temptation to have someone boggle at my news. And now I'm hostage to Judith's mood swings, which is like being a butterfly held between the finger and thumb of a toddler, and as precarious as fortune gets.

Possibly as a consequence of this preoccupation, I wasn't as diplomatic as I could have been later in the day, when I outlined to Baz the agreement I had made with Susan next door about his living arrangements, which now depend on his ability to catch the moles ravaging her lawn.

I went around to see him this evening, to put him in the picture. He was just about to go up the road to get fish and chips. 'Baz,' I said, 'I don't know whether I've mentioned that Susan next door wants me to evict you so that I can pull this place down. But I've persuaded her to agree to you living here for longer, if you can trap the moles in her back garden. So—'

'What?' said Baz, looking down at his Persian carpet on the floor, and up at the bunches of lavender hanging from his walls, and across at the pine cones in the china bowl on his chest of drawers. *'What?'*

'Yes, I'm sorry Baz. But that's about the size of it, I'm afraid. Susan's never liked this construction, and I've always told her it was just a temporary thing. It has a stay of execution while you can be useful to her in the garden, starting with the moles. I told her you would be able to catch them. Can you do it? Sorry – I realise I'm springing this on you.'

Baz put his hand out to steady himself on his art nouveau wrought iron trellis clothes hanger. 'Shit,' he said. 'I've never caught a mole in my life. Are they the ones with the front paddles?'

'It can't be that difficult to catch them, surely?' I said. 'They can't see.'

Baz pulled off his beanie hat and ran his fingers through his hair. 'How many moles has she got?'

'I don't know Baz, they're under the ground. Difficult to judge.'

'Shit,' he said again. 'They're underground. I can't even shoot them.'

'Can you get some advice from work?' I suggested. 'Someone will advise you on how to set traps, surely? Obviously, you won't want to catch them all at once, you might want to spin it out a bit so you can stay in here longer.'

'Right,' he said. 'Yeah, right. I'll speak to someone.'

He looked very despondent, so I tried to cheer him up. 'You never know Baz, you might be able to charm Susan into letting you stay here. Especially if you offer her some help in her garden. She's very proud of her garden, that's why she hates the moles so much. If she starts to like you, and you make yourself useful, she might not mind you being in here for longer.'

'Should I go round now and ask if she wants some fish and chips?'

But I said I didn't think that was the way forward. I suggested that he discovered as much as he could about how to catch moles, and then arranged to call on Susan for a consultation before he set the traps. I said I'd already told her he was an expert mole catcher, and the more clued up he could sound when he was talking to Susan, the better. So for example, I said, it would be good not to ask Susan if moles are the ones with the front paddles.

'Right,' said Baz. 'But last time I saw her she told me to clear off. She doesn't like me.'

'You could change that, Baz. She's a woman, she'll be susceptible to charm. If you play this right, she could be putty in your hands.'

Baz frowned. Perhaps he wasn't sure about the analogy. 'I don't know, Mrs Forth. I'll try, but...'

'Listen,' I said. 'You find out about the moles, and then before you go over there to discuss what you plan to do, I'll tell you what you need to know about charming women of a certain age.' I had a fleeting image of Baz sitting astride Susan with a mole between his teeth, but I dismissed it instantly.

I watched him pull on his hat again, and I felt some sympathy for him. He had thought all he had to do this evening was to buy fish and chips, but now he knows he has to get the fish and chips, catch an animal he's never even seen and seduce a woman who hates him before he can be secure in the pile of very stylish rubbish he calls home.

I told him to bring his fish and chips back to our kitchen, and I'd make him a cup of tea to have with them.

Life is very tough now for young people. It was easier for my generation. Look at how lucky we've been. We had more jobs, more affordable housing and Lovejoy on the telly. We started out with Yogi Bear and we've ended up with the internet.

After Baz had left for his fish and chips, I sat down to watch an episode of Yogi Bear on You Tube just to perk myself up, and convince myself that I'm smarter than the average woman. But as everybody knows, one You Tube clip can so easily lead to another, and I was watching something else when Sophie came in from work.

'What are you watching, Mrs Forth?' said Sophie, looking over my shoulder.

'It's the Woodentops,' I said. 'They're a family of little wooden puppets. They look like old fashioned clothes pegs, and they've got little painted faces. They just hang off their strings and potter about with their hands out in front of them, doing ordinary things and being nice to each other. It was one of the first children's programmes on television and it's lovely, Sophie. Very soothing to watch if you're feeling a bit stressed.'

Sophie watched for a few seconds as the little wooden puppets slowly articulated their way around their garden, their little round feet hovering just above the ground. 'Do they have magic powers?' she asked me.

'No,' I said, 'they don't. Not unless you count their ability to walk about without actually touching the ground. They've got a great sense of humour though. They're always having a good old chuckle about something. Particularly Daddy Woodentop. He's a real character,' I said, gazing at the screen.

Sophie watched the fuzzy grey and white images with me a little longer, trying to see what I was seeing. She started to lose interest once it was obvious that these puppets were not going to spin around 360 degrees, thrust a little wooden fist into the air, and fly off to fight extra-terrestrial invaders.

'Do these Wood Tops have weapons, or vaporisers to fight with?' she asked me.

'They don't fight Sophie. They're Woodentops. They just bumble around their garden chuckling and looking for things they might have lost.'

She drifted away. But I stayed and watched until Daddy Woodentop found Baby Woodentop's blanket under the tree.

Half an hour later, there were four of us sitting around the table having dinner. Dan and Baz were eating fish and chips, Sophie and I were eating what Baz refers to as women's food, by which he means quiche and salad. Baz was fretting about his interview with Susan next door. His brief was to ooze charm while offering his services as a neighbourhood mole catcher. He said he'd never had to charm anyone before in his life, and he didn't know how to do it. 'What do you have to do to charm someone?' he asked me. 'Do you need to play an instrument? 'Cos if you do I'm fucked.'

'In the olden days,' said Sophie, 'in the time of Pride and Prejudice, the men used to kiss the ladies' hands. It's a shame they don't still do that. If someone kissed my hand I'd think – crap, I must be really special.'

'Is charm even a real thing?' said Dan. 'Or is it something people only think exists.'

'Oh yes,' I said. 'It's definitely a real thing.'

'So what is it?' said Dan. 'How do you do it?' He was sensing it could be useful in certain circumstances.

'When you charm someone,' I said, 'you make them feel as if you like them, and they're important to you, and what they say is interesting, and you enjoy being with them. And if you can do all that with a smile, they will like you in return, and be more likely to be well disposed towards you.'

'That's very cynical. That's just fooling people so they'll do what you want,' said Dan.

There was a knock on the door, and when I went to open it Chrissy stood on the step. 'Hello all!' she said cheerfully. 'I just thought I'd call by. Great to see you again, Mrs Forth. I enjoyed our chat a few days ago, but 'Parting is such sweet sorrow' and all that. Good to see you again.'

Dan stood up. 'Chrissy!' he said. 'Hi! Come and tell us what you've been doing today. I bet it's really interesting.'

***

Disturbing news. Jen told me on the phone about nine-ish this evening that she had left her grandchildren with Scott while she nipped out to the shops for a bottle of wine and some vitamin E tablets.

I said, 'Ah – so Emily knows about Scott now?'

'God no,' said Jen. 'I haven't introduced them. Thing is, Sally, if I introduce Scott to my daughter, he might fancy her more than he fancies me, and then it'll be coo-coo-ca-choo Mrs Robinson all over again. Why take the risk?'

'Won't the kids tell Emily about Scott?'

'No, I've got them with me overnight. They're asleep in the spare room. They won't see Scott, but he's there in case of emergencies while I've nipped out.'

'Jennifer,' I said, because this was serious, 'I think Emily should know about Scott, if you're leaving her kids with him.'

'But they're asleep.'

'Even if they're asleep.'

There was a puzzled silence on the line, during which I decided that I would have to tell Jen I had been indiscreet about her much younger lover.

'And also… ' I said.

'What?'

'And also, I accidentally told Morwenna's mother, Judith, about you and Scott. And I mentioned he was practically an infant.'

'You didn't! Oh god, Sally! Emily and Morwenna are close friends!'

'I know that,' I said. 'I wasn't thinking. Sorry. Judith has promised not to say anything.'

'Will she keep her promise?'

'Maybe for a bit. But she'll blab eventually. You need to get in first.'

'Oh god. What am I going to say to her? – Emily, meet my lover Scott, he'd like to play with the Lego when your kids have finished with it.'

'You'll think of something,' I said.

And she will. But after she rang, Bill came home, and I put the Emily-Judith-Jen dynamic to the back of my mind. Bill says he's suffering from meeting fatigue. Apparently, he's been in a series of meetings and none have gone well. Everyone hated everyone else, no-one trusted anybody, and even at his diplomatic best he couldn't get the main players to see eye to eye. All they've agreed on is that they will have another meeting. He said he'll convene the next meeting beside a river and take a ducking stool and see if he can get some agreement by the end of the day.

Then he said, 'But never mind about all that, what's been happening here? I see we still have Esperanto clinging to the side of the house. I thought that was going?'

'Aspire. It was going, yes,' I said, 'but Dan's friend Baz has taken an interest in it.' I stopped short of saying he was living there.

Bill frowned, 'Baz? Which one is Baz? Is Baz the one who was expelled from school for trying to sell cannabis to one of the school governors?'

'No that was Chaz.'

'Oh yes. Chaz. So Baz must be the one who peed in the maths teacher's brief case?'

But that was Traz. Dan has such a colourful friendship group, and they've all had lively and fascinating school careers. It's easy to get them mixed up. I reminded Bill that Baz was the one who planted seeds in the big flower border at the front of the school which grew up and spelled the word 'Bollocks'.

'Oh yes,' said Bill. 'Nice lad.'

The phone started ringing. Bill spent the next half an hour pacing up and down with the phone to his ear starting sentences with, 'There is another way of looking at this ....' and, 'We still get most of what we want ...'

After the calls, Bill had a small glass of red wine, and told me that it was eleven thirty pm and he was going to make a perfectly reasonable suggestion about how we should spend what remained of the day, and he'd be grateful if I would just agree with him.

So I did.

***

I thought I'd pop over and see Laura this afternoon. We've spoken on the phone a few times this week, and she sounds fine, but I'd like to see the whites of her eyes. Laura and Ben have had some problems with equal and opposite amounts of enthusiasm for their sex life. Laura told me some weeks ago that Ben was enthusiastically chasing her around the house at bedtime, and she was just as enthusiastically running away from him. Sounds like fun to me, but who am I to say? There was talk of her seeing a counsellor a while back, and I don't know whether she has actually gone ahead with that plan.

When I arrived at Laura's she was putting her Christmas tree up. We spent a companionable half hour or so placing the baubles on it while I worked up the courage to ask her anything more searching than 'Where shall I put this big red one?'

Eventually I took a deep breath and said, 'So, Laura, how are you and Ben now? Have you got everything sorted out? In the bedroom department? You certainly seem a lot happier.'

'Yes, I think we are a lot happier.'

'That's good,' I said, and I really didn't want any more detail. So I don't know why I asked, 'Are you and Ben understanding each other better now?'

Laura sat back on her heels and gave me an appraising look. 'Well,' she said. 'Promise you won't be shocked?'

Promise you won't be shocked? What kind of question is that to ask your mother? Promise you won't be shocked? I was already shocked. I was shocked before I knew why I should be shocked. I was shocked to know I might be shocked.

'Shocked?' I said. 'What about? How shocked? Shocked about what? What do you mean, shocked?'

Laura paused. 'I'm not going to tell you if you're going to get all uptight, Mum. I have to know you can take this in your stride. Otherwise, it would be better for you not to know.'

'Not to know what? Tell me. Quick.'

'Well,' she watched me closely before saying, 'Ben and I are thinking about having an open marriage.'

'An open marriage?' I said. 'What's that? Is it like an Open Day? Will people come in and have a look at your marriage? Will you show people round? Will there be flip charts and wall displays? How will this work?'

'You know perfectly well what an open marriage is, Mum. But we're just thinking about it. We haven't made any decisions yet. Actually, Ben's not keen on the idea at all.'

'Neither am I,' I said. 'I'm not keen on it. I don't know how on earth it could possibly work. How open would it be? Would it be wide open or just ajar? Would it be open all week or just at weekends? Would it open late on Thursdays? Or shut on Sundays? Would it be open at both ends? I think this idea is unworkable, Laura.'

'God! I shouldn't have said anything,' she said, picking up a blue bauble and hastily giving it to the tree. 'Don't worry. I'm probably just thinking these things because I feel a bit trapped. I don't think I'd be feeling so trapped if I had a job. But you'd have to look after Harry full time for me to do that.'

Harry put his fist in his mouth, and started to squirm about and cry, and I wanted to put my fist in my mouth and squirm about and cry, too. But Harry was doing a really good job on his own and I felt he was speaking for both of us, so I let him run with it. He wanted feeding, and I wanted an anaesthetic, so it was almost an hour and a half before I felt able to return to this open marriage notion. I wanted to nip it in the bud. If that isn't too painful a simile in the circumstances.

'Laura, I must say, I really don't think this open marriage idea is a good one. Honestly, I think it would end in tears.'

'Yes, you're probably right,' she said. 'Actually, I'm not sure if I really mean it. Did I tell you I've been seeing Gene, the counsellor?'

'No you didn't tell me that. Is she any good? Does she blame me for everything?'

'He. Gene's a he. It's short for Eugene. He doesn't blame you for anything, and yes, he's great. Really good. We agreed that I might just be a bit bored. He's lovely, Mum, you'd like him. He's not a bit like Ben.'

'But I like Ben. Ben's lovely. I don't think I would like someone who isn't a bit like Ben.'

'Yes, and I like Ben of course. And he is lovely, yes. But this man is, well, he's not like Ben at all. And I really like him. Funny that, isn't it? Does that sound normal to you?'

'Laura,' I said, 'I'm going to give you some very good advice, and I want you to follow it. I want you to stop going to counselling and join a choir.'

'Mum,' she said, 'that's really weird. Why would I do that?'

'Because,' I said earnestly, 'I have a very strong feeling that it's in your best interests.'

Laura looked at me for a few seconds and then she laughed. 'That's crazy, Mum. But if it makes you happy, I'll think about it.'

Driving home, I had the distinct feeling that Laura was not going to be taking my advice. And I thought – while grinding my gears and my teeth – how frustrating that is. Here I am, I've been knocking about for a while now, I've learned a thing or two, I've acquired a gut instinct for how the wind is blowing, but I cannot pass on what I have learned for the benefit of my children. I am – if not a fountain of wisdom – a small sprinkle of wisdom, but nobody wants to drink or become even slightly damp, to benefit from what I know.

Of course, I'm a realist. I don't expect my children to sit at my feet and say, 'I thirst for your guidance Oh Wise One. Show me the way.' But it would save us all a lot of hassle if they did.

***

Dan asked me this morning whether I would be in tonight. He said he thought he might have to speak to Sophie, and it would be good if I was on hand.

'On hand for what?' I asked him. I don't usually have to be on hand when people speak to each other.

He said, 'Mum, I think I'm going to have to break things off with Sophie, because I'm getting on really well with er... '

'Chrissy,' I said.

'Chrissy. But I'm worried Sophie will throw some sort of wobbler when I tell her it's over. I don't know how she'll take it to be honest. She can be a bit – what's the word? Not crazy. I don't mean crazy. Nuts. She can be a bit nuts. It might be useful if you were around. She might need a shoulder to cry on.'

'She might need your shoulder to cry on, Dan, not mine.'

'No,' he said, anxious to explain, 'yours would be best because mine won't be here.'

'Where will yours be?'

'Out. I have to go out at seven-thirty. I might only have a couple of hours to hang around after I've told her, and then it would be really good if you could sort of take over from me. I don't think she'll want me around for long anyway, after – you know. It'll be too painful for her.'

I realised then that I had forgotten to tell Dan that Sophie is actually more attached to her little washbasin than she is to him. It seemed a bit awkward now to mention it, so I just said, 'Dan, I don't think you need worry too much about Sophie, I think she'll be fine – once she gets over the initial shock.'

Dan shook his head. 'Believe me Mum, she's going to be devastated. Poor girl, I feel terrible. But I have to say something soon. I'm getting really friendly with Chrissy, and I have to end it with Sophie now. If you could be around to help tonight that would be great. Maybe you could go up to her room after I've gone out, in case she's really upset and she can't manage the stairs?'

'Can't manage the stairs? Are we expecting her to lose the use of her legs?'

'Yeah, well. Not permanently. But if you could go up, just in case. Thanks. I should be home about five-thirty tonight, but I won't need a meal because I'll be going out for a curry later. I'll probably just have a sandwich or something before – before the thing with Sophie.'

He picked up his house keys and his packed lunch, and before he left he said, 'Chrissy will probably want to spend the occasional night with me here. But I think that will work okay, even if Sophie doesn't want to move out. I mean, obviously, I'd wait a while before I ask Chrissy back here, to give Sophie a chance to start getting over me. I don't want them fighting over me or anything.' A thought occurred to him. 'Am I sounding a bit conceited?'

'Maybe just a little,' I said, sounding a bit sarcastic.

'So is it okay if I borrow your car?' he said, and that was that settled.

After he'd gone, dragging his enormous ego with him, I thought about this new turn of events. I wasn't surprised by them, obviously. I was expecting Dan and Sophie's relationship to end, but I wasn't expecting to be recruited to help. But maybe this is how things are now, when more than one generation of adults live together in the same house.

I went out to do some Christmas shopping this afternoon. I bought something for Sophie and Baz. For Sophie, a DVD of Jurassic Park and an illustrated book on dinosaurs. For Baz I bought a red and gold duvet cover.

Just as I was sitting down for a cup of tea in John Lewis I heard a text bounce into my phone. It was from Jen and it said, Am in terrible trouble. Ring.

I rang. And the trouble was that Jen's daughter Emily had been shocked and horrified to discover that her mother was having a fulfilling and lustily invigorating relationship with a man half her age. Kids, eh? They've got no idea at all.

'You'd think she'd be happy for me,' said Jen. 'Wouldn't you think that? But she's not. She refuses to meet Scott, and she says she doesn't want me to have him in the house at the same time as her children. I asked if that meant I couldn't invite Scott to hers for Christmas dinner, and she rang off. She hung up on me.'

'She's upset about the age gap,' I said. 'Scott must be about her age.'

'Well yes, of course,' said Jen. 'That's what she's upset about, it's the age gap. Actually, I think Scott might be a year or two younger than Emily. If Scott was my age she'd be happy for me. I hope. But she says it's creepy, the age difference. That's the word she used, Sally – creepy. How does that make me feel? I'm hurt. Why can't I just enjoy this thing while it lasts? What's the big problem, exactly? I'm an adult, and Scott's an adult. No-one's getting hurt, why does it have to be creepy? It's not going to last long, is it? Me and Scott? Once his mother finds out he'll probably be grounded. The thing is Sally, Emily liked me better when I was knitting vegetables. Now that I'm having sex with a man half my age on a ball of kapok she's gone off me. But I can't just sit around and knit vegetables to keep her happy, can I?'

'Of course not,' I said. 'Of course you can't.'

I thought about it while I was finishing my tea. 'Creepy' does seem harsh. Judgemental. But Emily is probably just trying to come to terms with the fact that her mother has a sex life, and doesn't get her kicks exclusively from knitting carrots. I suppose the problem from Emily's perspective is that having sex on a ball of kapok with a much younger lover is just not a very mumsy thing to do.

When I got home around six thirtyish, Dan was in the kitchen making two cups of tea. 'I'm taking these upstairs for Sophie and me,' he said.

'How is Sophie?'

'Well,' Dan lowered his voice and spoke confidentially. 'I've told her. I've done the hard bit, and I've tried to let her down gently. But I think there might be some sort of delayed reaction. Delayed shock or something. She's being very strong, but I think it's going to hit her any time now.'

Dan went back up with the cups of tea, and I hid my Christmas presents in the cupboard under the stairs. I listened. All was quiet upstairs. No anguished wails, no beating of breasts, no audible rending of garments. I crept back into the kitchen.

When Dan came down about half an hour later, he was puzzled. 'She's being weirdly quiet and self-contained,' he said. 'It's not good, she needs to let it all out and then she'll feel better. It's almost as if she didn't care about us splitting up,' he smiled ruefully at the absurdity of such a notion. 'She might get a bit hysterical after I've gone, then she might go quiet again, but she'll bounce back in a week or so. Maybe. Anyway Mum, chances are she'll open up to you more. And I've got to shoot off now, so I'll see you later.'

I went upstairs and knocked on Sophie's door. 'Come in!' she said.

I opened the door and she was sitting on the edge of her bed filing her nails.

'Are you all right Sophie?'

'Well, I'm a bit upset, but Dan says you're fine with me staying here like before, so that's helping me to be brave.'

'Would you like to come down for another cup of tea?'

'Oh yes please,' she said. 'And we can have some of my biscuits. I didn't like to have one with Dan, in case he thought I wasn't upset enough about us breaking up.'

At this rate, I predicted Sophie would bounce back before I made the tea. Hysteria did not seem to be on the cards.

Baz knocked on the door as we were finishing our tea and Sophie let him in.

'Hi Baz,' she said. 'You were right. Dan's just chucked me. I'm staying here though.'

'Oh,' said Baz. 'Are you okay then, Soph?'

'Yes, I'm all right. I have to be strong for Mrs Forth. What have you got there, Baz?'

Baz had come into the kitchen with a tangle of metal contraptions which he put down on the kitchen floor. 'They're mole traps from work. I'm just trying to see how to use them. I thought there'd be more light in here, so I can have a good look.'

He and Sophie knelt down to inspect them, and were soon absorbed in the mechanics of the traps. I left them companionably discussing levers, springs and triggers, and went to watch television. I thought, this is just the kind of thing to take Sophie's mind off her recent emotional mini-trauma. A bit of mole execution paraphernalia is just what she needs. She'll soon forget she's supposed to have a broken heart once she gets a good look at the jaws on those traps.

After Baz left, Sophie came in for a chat before she went upstairs to bed.

'I had a really good idea Mrs Forth, to help Baz with catching the moles in next door's garden.'

'Oh yes?'

'I said he should bring a dead mole back from work, and put it in the trap so it looks as if he's caught one.'

I nodded thoughtfully. That might actually be a very good idea.

'And then if it works,' she said, 'he could do it again, until it looks as if he's caught them all.' She handed me a cup of tea and a biscuit.

'You might be on to something there Sophie,' I said, and I hoped she had washed her hands since the trap inspection.

She chewed her biscuit thoughtfully, 'I'm glad I can stay here Mrs Forth, even though Dan's chucked me. I don't think I could leave now that Mr Forth is having such a bad time. He needs our support.'

'That's very thoughtful of you Sophie, thank you.'

'And it's getting really exciting here now, with the moles.'

'It is,' I said. 'Very exciting.'

***

I'm not entirely sure whether it's a good idea to have a reunion of a group of people who haven't seen each other for about thirty years. It is an event designed to bring your own mortality home to you, and to demonstrate beyond dispute how much we need the cosmetics industry.

An 'old girls' reunion' was exactly the right description for the group gathered in the foyer of the hotel. We 'old girls' spent the first half hour before lunch drifting among each other, trying to match the image of the girls we once knew with the women in the room. Faces were just about recognised, but names eluded us, and not many of the old girls were wearing name badges. Most of us must have thought we would be instantly recognisable and just as unforgettable. Mistakes were made, and Judith was first to put her foot in it. She marched up to Veronica Taylor and said 'Mandy Thompson! You haven't changed a bit!' Veronica was offended, but Mandy was okay with it because she's been dead five years.

Judith herself was offended a little later when a thin woman neither of us recognised told her that she hadn't really changed in all these years. Judith started to preen and say –surely, she must look just a little older than she did at eighteen? The thin lady said, 'Well not that much Judith. That's one of the advantages of looking middle-aged when you're young. You age well.'

Soon after, a confused looking woman collared me and asked me who I used to be. I said I was Sally Bailey, now Forth. She said she couldn't remember a Sally Bailey the Fourth, the Sally Bailey she remembered was definitely a one-off and she owed her three pounds fifty.

I should have handed over three pounds fifty and stayed with this confused woman, because the next woman I bumped into knew exactly who I was, and drew a small crowd while she reminisced about every stupid thing I had ever said or done in the whole of my school career. God – did that woman have a good memory.

As I edged around the room, more than one former classmate put a sympathetic hand on my arm and said how dreadful it must be to be married to Bill at the moment. Which was kind.

An hour or so into the event a woman who looked as if she might have eaten a younger version of herself announced that there was a buffet in the adjoining room, and invited us to take a glass of wine and help ourselves to the delicious food.

While we were eating and drinking, photographs were projected onto a screen in a continuous loop showing group pictures of us from age eleven up to sixteen. Now this was an inspired idea. I could recommend it for any school reunion. We all, every one of us, laughed at ourselves and each other, and particularly at our girlhood hair styles. It was a tremendous bonding thing, and we started to feel like friends again.

Either it was exceptionally blowy in the 1980s, or we had no idea what to do with our hair. It grew out of our heads into fantastical shapes. We all looked like Marie Antoinette in a wind tunnel. We must have been hypnotised out of our wits by fashion, or maybe we couldn't resist sticking our fingers in electric sockets, but something wasn't right. We couldn't stand very close to each other because everyone's hair stood out six inches from their head in all directions. Our faces looked as if they had been snared by tumbleweed. Makes you wonder whether what we are doing with our hair now will look just as funny in twenty years. The passage of time seems to make all hair styles a joke.

The photos and the food and particularly the wine improved the atmosphere dramatically. While I was chatting to someone else, I heard Judith behind me telling a small group that her daughter Persephone had taken the bold step of giving up her well paid job to follow her dream, and she, Judith, was so proud of her. 'That's interesting,' said one of the women Judith was talking to, 'what dream does Persephone have?' Judith said she didn't know all the details, but it was something very exciting.

'Judith doesn't change much, does she?' I said companionably to the woman I had been chatting to.

'Oh,' she said. 'I'm afraid I don't know Judith.'

'You must know Judith,' I said. 'The whole school knew Judith!'

'Well actually,' she said, 'I didn't go to your school. I went to school in Chipping Norton. I was just walking through the hotel lobby and I saw there was wine and thought you looked like a nice crowd.'

When I got back, Bill was home, trying to remember how the coffee machine worked. I took over from him before he blew the thing up, and he told me he had been talking to Baz. He said he hadn't realised Baz was living in the rubbish heap. He said he'd seen inside it, and it looked very nice, but Baz couldn't live there, it was too cold, and basically, the whole idea was ridiculous.

'Oh,' I said. 'Poor Baz. He's a bit stuck for accommodation. He fell out with his parents, and the only way they can get on together is if he never sees them. They're best of friends if they aren't living under the same roof.'

Bill shrugged. 'He can't live out there, Sally. It's crazy. He'll freeze to death. What made you agree to it? You didn't suggest it, did you? Tell me it wasn't your idea?'

'No, it wasn't my idea,' I said, and then right on cue Baz himself knocked on the back door.

He came in and stepped onto the door mat, and began to take his boots off. 'I've been thinking, Mr Forth,' he said, straightening up. 'Would it make any difference if I paid rent? I could manage fifty pounds a week, possibly more.'

'I don't want any rent, Baz,' said Bill. 'It's just, that place you're in isn't habitable.'

Baz, usually so upbeat, looked defeated for the second time in a week. He stood on the door mat, his arms limp by his sides, deflated and defeated. I couldn't stand it, so I made a suggestion.

'Look. How about this? Maybe this would work. Why don't you spend as much of your evenings as you want in Aspire, but sleep overnight in our spare room here on the top floor? That could work, couldn't it?'

Baz nodded, hopeful, and we both looked at Bill, who was now well and truly on the spot. I should have discussed this idea with him first, but I didn't.

Bill thought about it, and while he was thinking Baz took off his beanie hat and used it to wipe his brow as he waited for the verdict. Bill said, 'You'll need a back door key. Stay here for now, Baz, until you get yourself sorted out. I know we've got a housing crisis but I don't really want to solve it single handed.'

'Thanks Mr Forth,' said Baz. 'Thanks a lot. I really appreciate it. That's a fact. And I've got that bird, Mrs Forth, for Christmas dinner. It's a beauty.' He put his hat back on. 'Right! Stuff to do! I'm going over to see Mrs Clenched Fists next door about the moles. Don't worry though – I'm going to be so charming she'll start to think she likes me. And I'll convince her I can just whistle moles up right out of their holes. I might actually catch one and not need to bring a dead one back from work.' He rubbed his hands together with relish. 'Yup,' he said, 'I've been practising on Sophie. Putty in my hands eh, Mrs Forth? Like you said.' Baz tied his boot laces and was ready to go. 'See you later folks!' He swept his thick black hair to the side. 'I'm armed with charm,' he smiled, and did something with his eyebrows, and left.

Bill looked at me. 'Have I missed something?' he said.

We were watching television later, Bill and I. David Attenborough on primates. Bill finds it very relaxing and entertaining. He says there are so many ways humans behave just like animals, and of course he notices it particularly when he watches chimps, especially when they start whooping and yelping and running around in circles. We were both together on the sofa. It was lovely to share an evening, just the two of us, and we were lost in the undergrowth of an African jungle when –

'Hiya you two!' Sophie was home from working her late shift. 'Guess what!' she said.

'What?'

'Baz is moving in!'

'We knew that, Sophie,' I said.

'Oh yeah,' she said. 'I bet it was your idea.'

'It was, yes.'

'It's going to be great, isn't it? Us being all together in the same house? At Christmas? We just need a little baby Jesus now, don't we?'

***

I was taking some sausage rolls out of the oven, when I heard what might have been carol singers at the front door. I rushed through the hall, anticipating a treat.

Two young men in hoodies stood on our garden path. One larger than the other. They stopped singing as soon as I opened

179

the door. The smaller one held out his hand, and mumbled, 'Merry Christmas.'

'Merry Christmas to you too,' I said. 'Are you going to sing me a carol?'

'Just done one,' said the smaller chorister. 'Just now.'

'Lee?' I said. 'Is that you?'

He looked up, and I saw him under the hood. 'We're just doing a bit of carol singing,' he explained.

'That's good,' I said. 'Are you doing this for charity?'

'Who?'

'Are you raising money for charity?'

'No,' said Lee. 'We're just raising a bit of cash.'

'For presents,' said the taller one.

'Yeah,' said Lee. 'For presents.'

'Okay then,' I said, 'what are you going to sing?'

'We just sang something, just before.'

'I didn't hear it when I was in the house. Sing something else.'

'We only know the one about the lass.'

'That'll do. I like that one.'

Lee sighed, and he and his companion shuffled about on the path, there was some clearing of throats, and then they began:

'Good King Wensus' lass looked out,
On the feet of Stephen,
Snow lay on the roundabout,
It was friggin freezin.'

They stopped. 'We don't know the next verse,' said Lee. 'That's all we learned.'

'Lovely,' I said. 'Well done. Look, I haven't got any money on me, but would you like to come in and have a sausage roll? I've got some just out of the oven.'

The members of the alternative angel choir looked at each other, nonplussed. Things were not going to plan.

Lee tried again. 'We're collecting money though.'

'But we'll have a sausage roll,' said Lee's companion.

'Come on then.' I stepped aside, and we all walked through the hall into the kitchen. Sophie was in the kitchen, leaning against the bench top, absorbed in her phone. When the choir came in she looked up, and was alarmed half way through giving her usual greeting.

'Hiyaaaap! Who's this?'

'Sophie, this is Lee, and his friend...? I'm sorry, I don't know your friend's name, Lee.'

'Spew,' said Lee. 'He's called Spew.'

'This is Lee and Spew, Sophie. They're carol singing, but it's a bit cold outside so I've asked them in.'

Sophie looked stricken. She turned aside and muttered at me behind her hand, 'Oh no. You're not going to let them live here, are you?'

'No,' I said. 'I'm going to give them a sausage roll.'

'Oh thank God,' she said. 'Give them one each to go.'

'Are we getting a sausage roll then?' said Lee.

'Of course,' I said. 'Would you like to sit down, guys, and have a glass of Coke with your sausage rolls?'

Sophie gave a squeak of alarm and left the kitchen.

The boys sat down, all wooden and shifty, ready to bolt. I gave them a glass of Coke and two sausage rolls each.

Spew looked around and said, 'I bet this house is worth a packet.'

I agreed. 'A small fortune, I should think.'

'How much do you reckon it's worth?'

'Oh, probably somewhere between a million and a million and a half. Maybe more.'

'Pounds?'

'Yes.'

Both boys shook their heads in wonder at the crazy housing market.

'What's that weird thing round the side?' said Lee.

'It's an impromptu annexe.'

Spew frowned and nodded, as if he was very familiar with the concept of the impromptu annexe. 'It's a bit shit though,' he said. 'It needs to come down. Whatever you call it.'

'You're right Spew,' I said. 'But it's not a permanent arrangement.'

'We could take it down for you if you like. We could do that after we finished carol singing.'

'Ain't we already finished?' said Lee.

'Might be,' said Spew.

'The annexe has to stay up for a bit longer,' I said. 'We don't want it to come down yet.'

'You'd need to get a skip, but we could take it down. Just have to lean on it.'

'Thanks Spew. But I want it to stay up for the moment.'

Spew shrugged. 'Up to you,' he said. Which it was.

'How are the sausage rolls?' I asked them. 'Are they good?'

'They'd be better with some red sauce,' said Lee, looking slightly embarrassed at his own audacity. 'Just saying.'

Spew finished his Coke. 'We better be going,' he said, pushing his plate away.

'Well, thanks for the advice guys. And good luck with the rest of your carol singing.'

'Oh, I think we've finished now,' said Lee.

'Yeah. We done enough now,' said Spew. 'We don't know that many carols.'

'Happy Christmas then, both of you!' I said, once we had negotiated the hall, and they were back outside.

'Yeah, all right,' they said, and gave me a wave, and headed back up the road.

I went along to the kitchen and was clearing away plates and glasses when Sophie put her head around the door, 'Have they gone?' she said.

'Yes, they've gone.'

'Mrs Forth, you shouldn't invite people in like that. What if they had a gun?' She bustled around the kitchen getting ready to go to work and fretting about carol singers packing heat. After she'd gone, I sat down and ate the rest of the sausage rolls.

**

Derek from next door called late this afternoon, with a Christmas card and a bunch of rhubarb. He said he'd picked me the first of the crop and he was going to pick some for himself and Susan in a day or two.

I asked him in and we sat and had a cup of tea and a mince pie. He was in reflective mood. 'Beats me, Sally,' he said, shaking his head. 'The longer I live, the less I understand. That young chap came round with the traps, for the moles. Baz. The young chap you've got living out there, among the rubbish. And it was the oddest thing, but he took a real shine to Susan. Would you credit it? A real shine. And she got all kittenish with him after a bit. I couldn't believe my eyes. I haven't seen her like that for years.'

'Well,' I said. 'Baz can be very charming.'

'I'll say. They were really hitting it off, both of them. And that's not easy. Well, you know Susan, of course. Turns out they both hate moles, so they have something in common.'

I offered him another mince pie. 'Thank you for this lovely rhubarb Derek. You do know that you can't eat the leaves, don't you?'

'Yes of course. Everybody knows that Sally. Did you think I was going to slip one into Susan's chopped cabbage?'

He laughed, and I joined in, and we both had a good old chuckle over it. And then I said, 'All the same Derek, take the leaves off yours and bury them in the compost heap before you take the stems into the house.'

He looked at me strangely, as if I had spoken suddenly in Greek.

'Just in case Susan mistakes it for cabbage,' I said. 'The leaves look very similar.'

183

'Oh right! I thought you meant she was planning to poison me!'

And we laughed again.

Dan and Baz brought my Christmas tree back with them this evening. It's huge. It would look more at home in a railway station. They brought it in through the front door, stump first, and it simultaneously swept clean every surface in its path, leaving behind it an aroma of pine-fresh cleansing products. They grappled with it manfully in the hall – 'Bastard thing's stuck, Baz' – 'Lift the fucker up, Dan' – until they managed to stand it upright. It's now in a pot the size of a beer barrel, and it's lashed to the banisters half way up its length. It has baubles on it up to head height, and I have managed to lasso it with a string of lights from the landing. Its topmost branches are whisking clean the corners of the hall ceiling that have never seen a duster.

Sophie came back from work and was amazed. She said it looked like a Christmas tree off the films. She said it made her feel like singing 'O Come All Me Faithful.'

So! Here we all are, almost ready for Christmas. I gave myself a glass of wine to celebrate the tree, and made some shortcrust pastry for more mince pies. Towards the end of the rather generous glass of Gewurztraminer, I was putting mince pies in the oven, and humming 'Good King Wensus' Lass'.

And then my phone rang.

'He-llo!' I said, trailing clouds of Christmas cheer. 'And a Happy Christmas to one and all!'

'Fuck that for a lark,' said Jen. 'You got me into this mess, now I need a favour.'

'Jen? What's the matter?' I said, as Santa farted, and Rudolph's hooves made a hole in the roof.

'You said I should tell Emily about Scott, and now I've done that and she's not speaking to me. So I'm upset, and Scott's taken himself off in a little teenage huff. All in all, there's a significant lack of Christmas cheer up here, Sally. Not a bauble in sight. I was going to decorate the kapok but now I haven't the heart for it. Anyway. Here's the thing. How about I come to you for Christmas? You've got loads of room, just tuck me away somewhere in one of your attic rooms and give me a bottle of sherry. Send one of the kids up with my dinner on a tray and I'll pull a cracker with myself. Don't expect presents. It's not very nice up here Sally. Nobody loves me. I want to come home. For Christmas. Tomorrow.'

***

Jen arrived with a small bag and a large suitcase this morning, and looked up at the tree in the hall, 'Jeez, Sally. How much Christmas do you need?'

'Lovely, isn't it?' I said.

'Bloody marvellous. Where shall I put my bags?'

I told Jen I've put her in the room next to Sophie. It's not as big as Sophie's room, but I daren't part Sophie from her little washbasin.

Jen and I had a backbone-stiffening cup of strong coffee after she had settled her stuff into her room. We talked about where she was with Scott and Emily at the moment, and which party felt the most hostility towards her. We looked for positives, and agreed that any one of a number of things may happen to improve her life. Scott could leave, and Emily may forgive and forget. Or Scott could stay and Emily may have a change of heart. Or the world could be overrun by enormous man-eating Christmas robins and give us all something else to focus on. Things could be worse, and they may soon be better. It's just a case of finding the right perspective

And fortunately, we have some distraction, because we're all going out tonight. All of us, apart from Bill. We're going to see the Highfield Players production of their latest play, 'The Warning', written by one of the cast. The set, of course, is designed and built by Dan.

I have learned to have confidence in Dan's ability to construct things. He constructed Aspire, and she still stands. He gave her a cupola, and the cupola still dominates the structure as plump and firm and well-anchored as the matronly breast it resembles. He has designed and constructed a lily pond, and the lily pond now gives life to fish and frogs and lilies. Baz says it is universally admired, and no-one need know about the tiny puncture in the lining which will drain the contents, but very, very slowly.

So I wasn't worried when Dan came home this afternoon and started turning the place upside down looking for a large, stout safety pin, of the kind you see in gentlemen's kilts. He said he knew we had one somewhere. I found other safety pins, but they were all dismissed as being sorry excuses for a safety pin. He had his heart set on finding the big one, which he said was a much safer pin than all the rest.

I said – ever the joker – 'I hope you're not holding the set together with a safety pin, Dan!' But worryingly, he left without denying it.

Chrissy came for a meal with us before the performance. After Dan and Sophie's break-up, she and Sophie have circled around each other cautiously. Chrissy thinks Sophie is nice enough, but a bit simple, not worth taking too seriously. Sophie thinks Chrissy is dangerously psychotic and in need of urgent medical help.

Chrissy arrived at about quarter to six. She swept open the kitchen door and said 'Greetings! One and all!'

Jen was standing next to the door slicing tomatoes to arrange on top of a pizza, 'Well yes, why not?' she said, looking around for support.

'Don't mind me,' Chrissy said to Jen. 'This lot here know what to expect. I'm trying to get my head around Romeo and Juliet and time is running out. So, greetings, greetings, greetings?' She frowned and placed her finger to her forehead. 'Greetings? Come on Chrissy, you can do this,' she urged herself on. 'Ah yes! *Patience perforce with wilful choler meeting makes my flesh tremble in their different greeting.* Phew! I thought I wasn't going to manage it that time.'

Jen looked on in admiration. 'Good for you,' she said, politely.

Sophie glanced at me and shook her head.

During the meal, pizza and salad, we tried to establish from Chrissy what the play this evening was about. She wouldn't give much away. We knew there was a spaceship so we guessed there might be aliens, but we didn't learn much else.

Sophie couldn't believe there wasn't a seasonal theme to a play this close to Christmas, and neither could I. I asked the questions Sophie was desperate to ask, to save her any embarrassment. 'Are these Christmas aliens, Chrissy? Does one of them turn into Santa Claus? Are there any elves? Does someone start singing 'White Christmas'? Is the space ship really a Santa's sledge? What's the link with Christmas?'

Chrissy gave me a sympathetic look, 'Sorry Mrs Forth. No link with Christmas I'm afraid. But there's a link with the universe if that's any good. And human nature. Because,' she smiled at us all around the table and held up her forefinger to call us to attention, '*There are more things in Heaven and Earth Horatio than are dreamt of in your philosophy.* Oh, hang on,' she frowned. 'Wrong play.' And soon after that she and Dan set off, because they had to be there at least an hour before curtain up.

After the meal we ran around the house getting ready to go. Sophie filled the dishwasher; she said wouldn't need a shower because she was just going to use her little washbasin. Everyone else had showers, and I messaged Laura to see if she was going to make it. She sent me a reply to say she was having a session and would be there if things didn't overrun by much. Fortunately, I didn't have time to think about this for long. We were on the road by 6.30 and in our seats by 7.15. Sophie was passing sweets along the row a minute later.

The curtains opened at 7.30, and dominating stage left was a spaceship, in every way out of this world. It was magnificently silvered, lights flashed on and off inside it, it was sleek and futuristic, it was authentically dented here and there to suggest brushes with meteorites and sundry planetary bodies. It emitted a low hum mixed with fretful static, as if it had landed on stage as a result of an embarrassing mix-up and would be gone as soon as it had wiped the egg off its face. Bravo Dan! I burst into spontaneous applause.

The play was good, in the way that plays written by amateur playwrights are good, which is to say, not very good. The players were a little eclipsed by the spaceship, it was almost the main character, particularly when from time to time bits of it started to warble and vibrate in some sort of internal monologue. Chrissy did well. She made an especially convincing alien, having as she did a head start in that direction. There were jokes which the audience were kind enough to find funny, and which Sophie in particular thought were stonkingly humorous. By the interval we had all been entertained, and unusually for an amateur production, we thought we could probably stand another hour.

I glanced through the programme in the interval while the others were getting drinks, and saw in the blurb about the play that the cast were grateful to Dan Forth for his 'fantastically creative efforts with the ship, especially the wow (!!) event at the end of the last act!! It'll be all right on the night, Dan!!'

Ah. The 'wow' event at the end of the last act can mean only one thing: the space ship is going to take off at the end. A nagging anxiety began gathering strength in my head and loins, and it had to do with the search for the safety pin a few hours earlier which I now wished that we had found.

The second half of the play was in fact a little better than the first. There were more jokes and one of them was actually funny, which was a lovely surprise, and produced its own round of applause from a grateful audience. As the action drew to a close, it was obvious that the ship was in fact, going to take off. It was throbbing and pulsating as if it had an astronomical headache, and the cast were having to raise their voices to compete with it. I looked for wires or pulleys, and noticed that what was once an aerial waving about above the space ship was now being pulled taut in preparation for a hoist.

The final few speeches were delivered on stage. Then Chrissy stepped into her craft and I realised she was going up with the ship and there's a safety pin in this mix somewhere which is not fit for purpose.

Chrissy waved to the Earthlings, the Earthlings waved back. Chrissy waved again, and blew us all a kiss. The audience waved back. We were all waving – alien, Earthlings, audience –but no-one was going anywhere. The aerial was now taut and taking the strain. Jen leant towards me and said, 'Don't look.'

Slowly, the space ship was winched by some unseen mechanism into the air. Chrissy was ecstatic, messianic, blowing kisses across the audience as if ascending into heaven. The ship rose six feet, and then stopped. Chrissy glanced down and then up, but seemed generally unfazed by the fact that her space ship was of the variety which took off and then changed its mind. The cast took their bows, Chrissy continued to embrace the audience from on high, the audience applauded, and then there was a sudden jolt and the ship dropped about a foot.

Fortunately, the curtains were then whisked shut. There were signs of commotion behind the curtain, but no cries for help or requests for a doctor in the house, so the audience considered itself off the leash and stood up, and made ready to go.

We walked over to the adjoining bar while we waited for Dan and Chrissy to emerge from theatre land, and Jen got talking to a pleasant looking man who turned out to be Chrissy's father. They were getting on well so I drifted away and left them to it. I switched my phone back on and there was a message from Bill which I had to read twice.

> Shit's going to hit the fan here in a day or two.
> We'll need to talk.

And Laura hadn't turned up.

***

Christmas Eve. Jen had much to report after the evening at the play. Chrissy's father, Sam, was a lovely man. Friendly, interesting, divorced, bitch of a former wife, not too fascinated by himself. All good, especially the latter. He and Chrissy were on their own over Christmas. They don't have a Christmas tree up, their place doesn't look very festive, so Jen has invited them both over here on the day after Boxing Day for drinks and mince pies, and to admire our tree. And – let's be perfectly frank – because she's hoping to get off with Sam before she has to go back to kapok villa, and Scott the Incredibly Young.

***

Christmas Day, and it started off pretty much as always. There was the usual chaotic mix of fizz, wrapping paper, too many vegetables and the debate over whether the turkey was cooked. Baz thought it was, Ella didn't think so, Bill said it might be, Dan said after a couple of glasses you wouldn't notice anyway, Jen said don't mummify it for God's sake, and Sophie said if you eat uncooked turkey you could have diarrhoea for six months.

Yes, it was the usual mix, until about three in the afternoon.

Laura, Ben, Little Harry and Gene joined us then. I was expecting them, of course, although Gene was a surprise. Laura swept in with her menfolk in tow, 'Hi everyone! Lovely to see you all! Merry Christmas! This is Gene – he's my therapist!'

There was a bit of a hubbub. Everyone hugged and was hugged. Dan and Ben slapped each other on the back and Dan asked him, 'What's with the therapist?' Ben said, 'Search me.'

Ella grasped the nettle. 'Therapist?' she said. 'What do you need a therapist for? What kind of therapist?'

'I was feeling quite low grandma,' said Laura to Ella and everyone else, 'so I went to see Gene here, and now I feel great, and Ben and I are so much happier that we're thinking of taking him into our marriage, and giving him a second home, with us.'

The hubbub died down, Bill froze in the act of filling some glasses with champagne, and Sophie said quietly, 'They must have got him from a refuge.'

'Don't look so shocked everyone,' said Laura. 'Think of it as a different sort of marriage arrangement, a more generous marriage if you like, but still a marriage. A better marriage, overall, just different.'

'Different all right,' said Ella. 'Taking him into your marriage? Who's put this ridiculous notion into your head?' She turned to Gene, 'Must be you,' she said.

'Grandma!' said Laura. 'It's not a ridiculous notion! It's a new, inventive, creative interpretation of post-marital bonding. It frees some couples from stultifying pair bonds, it's liberating and enriching. It's to be celebrated, that's why I've brought Gene along today. I want you to welcome him, everyone, because this is important to me. And Ben.'

Ben said, 'Actually, I— '

'So what we thought was,' continued Laura, 'this would be a good chance, while we're all here, just to tell you about it, and answer any questions you might have. I want us to be totally up front and honest, so no-one will be confused or feel as if we're doing weird things behind your backs. I want everyone to be happy about this.'

We all fell unhappily silent. Sophie, who was wearing Rudolf antlers and holding a plate of mince pies said, 'It's just, this isn't very Christmassy. You haven't even had a mince pie yet. And there's crackers.'

'Crackers?' said Ella. 'I'll say.'

Laura looked at Sophie and appeared to notice her for the first time. 'I'm sorry,' she said, 'but who are you?'

'This is Sophie, Laura,' I said. 'Remember? You've spoken on the phone?'

'Oh yes, of course, sorry. Hello Sophie, you're Dan's girlfriend.'

'Well, not now,' said Sophie. 'We've had an unconscious coupling.'

Ella sat down and said, 'Why don't we just watch the tail end of the Queen?'

'You mean a conscious uncoupling,' said Laura.

'Oh okay,' said Sophie agreeably. 'Can't be much difference.'

Bill handed glasses of champagne around and Laura took a bite of mince pie and said, 'So I expect you'll be moving out of my room now Sophie, if you and Dan have split up?'

'No,' said Sophie. 'I'm staying. And Baz is too.'

'Really?'

'Yes, because,' Sophie looked around for inspiration, 'because this house is an open house, like your marriage. Only we don't have a therapist.'

'Cheers!' said Bill. 'Let's drink to that.'

The afternoon drinks and nibbles family gathering continued more agreeably for a while after that. People were standing around drinking and nibbling, although there was of course, still an elephant in the room. I tried to ignore this elephant and pretend it wasn't there, because that is what you are supposed to do with elephants when they come into your room. Especially at Christmas, when elephants are so prevalent in people's rooms. There will barely be a room in the land today without an elephant lumbering around in the corner somewhere, and most households will just carry on as if it isn't there.

However, it is a fact that after a glass or two or three of fizzy wine, you develop a heightened sensitivity to the presence of elephants. You find yourself thinking, 'What the hell is that? What is that large, grey, flappy-eared thing with a trunk on its head in the corner of the room there?' You peer over the top of your glass and then – 'Holy shit! It's an elephant! Clearly visible now. What the hell is this all about? Someone needs to explain to me – what does this elephant mean?'

So, benefiting from my fizz-fuelled 20/20 elephant-spotting glasses, I crossed the room and engaged Gene in some festive conversation.

'Gene! Hi! Hi Gene! Hygiene? Gene. Hi! Now then, Gene. What I need to know from you,' I wagged a tipsy finger approximately in his direction, 'what I need to know from you, is, what the hell are you playing at. Hmm?'

'I'm sorry?' Gene inclined his head slightly in my direction, as if he must have misheard me.

'I said. What I said was,' I lowered my voice, because although there was music and lots of people talking in the room, I didn't want to risk being overheard. 'What's going on Gene? I'm old enough not to be born yesterday. So, something's up. Obviously. And I want to know what it is. Because I don't like it. One bit.'

Gene looked very concerned. 'Are you worried about my relationship with Laura and Ben?'

'I am! That's it! That's exactly what I'm worried about. Personally, if you want my opinion, what you should do, and I'm going to be very frank here Frank, is piss off and leave them alone. I'm sorry to be this blunt Prank, but you asked my opinion, and there it is.'

Laura appeared at my elbow. 'Mum?' she said. 'Are you okay?'

'Ah! Laura—' And then suddenly, thanks to our bottles of Tesco's *Chateau de Voyez le Blindingly Obvious*, I had an insight which I felt I had to share. 'Laura, I think this man is married, and his wife is even now wondering where the hell he is.'

'Mum,' said Laura, exasperated, 'you're just not getting this! Of course he's married! I know he's married, his wife is a good friend. She couldn't come with Gene today because she has to help her sister. We don't have secrets from each other, and I don't want us to have any secrets from you. We – how can I explain this?' She looked to Gene for help.

Gene spoke to me irritatingly slowly and clearly, almost as if I was an out-of-touch middle-aged woman who had drunk too much fizz, 'We are pushing at the boundaries of marriage, Mrs Forth, not to destroy – definitely not – but to expand its horizons and make it less confining. Why would love leave a relationship if it isn't trapped there? We think of it as strengthening a relationship by being more generous with our love.'

Gene was standing very close, making it difficult for me to focus on his face. I tried, but his eyes began to move towards each other until he had one whacking great eye in the middle of his forehead, and his nose divided in two and moved apart, and then he had two noses, one on each cheek.

I thought, I'm not standing here wasting good drinking time talking to this man who can't even organise his own face. What's needed here, I decided, is a withering and scathing, yet intelligent put-down, a body blow which will stop this bollocks in its tracks once and for all.

'This sounds to me,' I said with heavy significance, 'this sounds to me, like a stupid thinking thought. And you, Gene, are a talking plonker.' And then, dazzled by my own wit, I turned to go.

I seemed to be heading towards the kitchen, which was a surprise because that wasn't where I was going, but I maintained course to appear purposeful and focused. The alternative would have been to mill around in circles and look dazed, and I didn't want to be doing that so soon after delivering my *coup de grâce* above.

Laura caught up with me in the kitchen. 'I can't believe you just said that, Mum. How could you be so rude to my guest?'

'He's leading you down the garden path without a paddle, Laura. You need to wake up and smell the roses. I'm warning you, scales need to fall from your thighs before it's too late.'

'You're drunk.'

'I beg your pardon, I am not drunk!' But unfortunately I was so annoyed I threw half a glass of fizz down the front of my dress, which is something that sober people don't do.

'You're drunk, Mum, and I'm going home.'

'All right then,' I said. 'Go home if you want to. Go.'

She snatched Harry's bottle off the kitchen bench and went back into the living room.

I looked around the kitchen at the hastily cleared remains of our lunch. Goodwill to All Men. And I had just told my daughter to go home.

***

The day after Boxing Day, and Jen was anticipating the visit this evening from Sam and his daughter Chrissy. Jen is looking for a new romance. She says the kapok-fuelled relationship with Scott was never a meeting of minds. It was a lively, springy relationship, but she suspects it has now run its course. Finding romance in your late forties is a wonderful thing, similar to finding treasure at the back of your fridge. So Jen was excited but very apprehensive before Sam and Chrissy's visit this evening. She said she had felt a connection, an attraction, when she had been talking to Sam after the play, and she thought he felt it too. She said it was as if they both knew they should have met each other years ago.

I thought this was a lot to read into a twenty minute conversation snatched in the aftermath of an indifferent play about aliens, but Jen disagreed. She said it only takes that long to know if you are on someone's wavelength. She said she knew twenty minutes after meeting her husband that they weren't on the same wavelength, and after that they had spent the whole of their married life trying to tune into each other and wondering what weird frequency made the other one vibrate. But this could be different.

To be honest though, I was more interested in the events of two evenings ago than in middle-aged love at first sight. I wanted to discuss my falling out with Laura. I couldn't believe that I had sent my daughter out of the house on Christmas Day. It was distressing and I needed to talk about it, to try and make it seem less so.

So Jen and I helped ourselves to another warm mince pie to further extend our leisurely mid-afternoon cup of coffee, and to get to grips again with the upsetting events of the day before yesterday. We applied generous amounts of double cream, which felt like balm to the soul. Jen agreed after a mouthful of pie, that it was unfortunate it happened to be Christmas Day when I had cast Laura out. It had a regrettable Dickensian ring to it. What made it especially poignant, she said, was the fact that little Harry had to go too. Bad enough to send your daughter out into the night on Christmas Day, but to cast out a daughter and her tiny child was particularly bad form for the time of year.

I thanked Jen for her valuable insights and said now I felt like Mrs Herod weaned on bile.

'The trouble is,' said Jen, 'you're not used to falling out with Laura. So it really upsets you when you do, and you end up getting your timing wrong and telling the girl to piss off on Christmas Day. Emily and I fall out all the time. Always have. We're used to falling out, we know the routine, we understand the rules. We'd have known we were about to fall out over this whole open marriage thing, so we'd have planned when we were going to do it. We would pencil it in for the day before New Year's Eve, when there's nothing else happening. But you and Laura just went for it on Christmas Day, like a couple of amateurs.'

So I asked Jen, since she was the expert, what I should do now to patch things up.

She took another mince pie. 'Well, if you're in the right and she's in the wrong, you have to say you're sorry you weren't able to sort things out more amicably, but now that you've both had a chance to think things over you should meet up and have a much calmer chat about it.'

'And if she's in the right and I'm in the wrong?'

'If she's in the right and you're in the wrong, you say you're sorry you weren't able to sort things out more amicably, but now that you've both had a chance to think things over you should meet up and have a much calmer chat about it.'

While I was considering this advice, Susan from next door tapped on the window. She was carrying a cardboard box. I went to the door and asked her in.

'Susan,' I said, 'come and have a cup of coffee with Jen and me. There's mince pies and cream. You remember Jenny from further down the road, don't you? She's staying with us over Christmas. Oh, Susan,' I said eyeing the cardboard box, 'have you brought us a present? How lovely! How kind of you!'

'It's not a present,' said Susan. 'It's a dead mole.'

'Oh right. Definitely not a present then.'

'No,' she said. 'It's a dead mole and I want you to take a look at it.' She lifted the lid of the box and showed it to both of us. 'What do you make of that?'

'Well,' said Jen, 'it looks as if it's seen better days.'

'Exactly,' said Susan. 'That's what I thought.'

There was a mole in the corner of the box which looked as if it might have been embalmed along with Tutankhamun, to give him something to be annoyed about in the after-life.

'Your lad Baz reckons he caught this on Christmas Eve,' said Susan. 'But this mole's been dead a lot longer than that. Look at it. It must have been dead for months. Maybe even a year or more.'

All three of us studied the mole, and I remembered Sophie's plan for Baz to impress Susan by putting dead moles in her mole traps.

'This could have been a very old mole when the trap got it, Susan,' I said. 'I don't suppose they age particularly well.'

'You're kidding,' said Jen. 'It's practically a fossil.'

Susan tilted the box and the mole slid easily along the base and struck the far side like a piece of dry wood.

'It might have been very sick before it died,' I said.

'Very sick?' said Jen. 'Worse than that. If it died two days ago it was very dead before it died.'

'Well, anyway,' I said. 'Enough of this morbid conversation. Put the box away Susan and come and sit down and have a coffee and a chat. Actually, the coffee's cold. Have a glass of sherry.'

Mild intoxication agrees with Susan: I have known her laugh after a glass of wine. It can be unnerving if you're not prepared for it. She stayed for an hour and her mood improved with every sip she took. She should be prescribed sherry medicinally. Before she left for home, she actually told a joke about a giraffe in a shower cubicle. At least, I assume it was a joke. Why else would a giraffe be in a shower cubicle?

I hoped that the sherry would make her forget about the desiccated mole. But no, she remembered it and took it away with her, so that particular chicken will probably now come back to roost. When she sobers up she will remember that she has a grievance and will suspect us of pulling a fast one. I must tell Baz if he is going to use this tactic, to bring back fresher specimens to put in the traps.

After Susan had gone a little unsteadily back home, Jen spent almost an hour preparing herself for Chrissy and her father's visit this evening. She was nervous, and she was making me nervous. I thought the evening would go better for her if she was more relaxed, and didn't have such high expectations of this new friendship. I told Jen to take it easy, and take it slowly, and warned her not to sound too intense or she might frighten Sam off. But she was fraught and irritable. She said she heard what I was saying, but could I please just leave her alone to fiddle with her false eye lashes? I offered to help but she said she could manage and I would just poke her in the eye.

At seven-thirty Jen came downstairs looking great, with eyelashes as long as a giraffe's in a shower cubicle. While she was upstairs she had obviously decided that the way to Sam's heart was through his daughter, so she had something prepared when Sam and Chrissy arrived minutes later.

'Ah, Chrissy!' said Jen, when Chrissy and her dad came inside and were taking their coats off in the hall, 'Good to see you again, Chrissy, *I pray you, know me when we meet again, I wish you well.*'

'Sorry?' said Chrissy, looking at Jen and seeming confused. 'What did you say?'

'I said,' Jen continued bravely, '*I pray you, know me when we meet again, I wish you well.*'

'Oh,' said Chrissy, shrugging a little. 'Right. Yeah.'

'See?' said Sophie quietly to me. 'She doesn't like it when people do it to her.'

But after this shaky start, the evening went surprisingly well. Jen, Sam and I talked about amateur dramatics and evening classes and dating websites. Jen asked Sam if he had tried dating websites, and then he asked her if she had. Jen said she had asked first, and Sam said so she had, and they both thought this hilarious. Jen was fluttering her eyelashes without a care for their moorings.

I left them to it and went to talk to Sophie and Baz about the status of the moles they were inserting into Susan's traps. Sophie agreed with me that the mole Baz put in the trap was not fooling anybody, she said it looked like a slipper that had been under the bed since you were ten.

I heard my phone ringing in the kitchen, and went to answer it. It was Ben, asking to speak to Laura. 'She isn't here Ben,' I said. 'Did you think she was with me?'

'Yes,' he said. 'She left here at lunchtime, and she said she was coming to you.'

So naturally, I rang Bill. I never ring him at work. Never. I would hesitate to ring him if the house was burning down. But this was a serious emergency, so I rang.

'Bill,' I said, 'Laura's gone missing.'

'From where? For how long?'

'Ben rang to say she left home at lunchtime today, and said she was coming here. But she hasn't been here. Ben's worried, and I'm worried. Harry's with Ben's mother. Where on earth can she be?'

'Have Laura and Ben had any sort of row?'

'I didn't ask.'

Has Ben been in touch with Laura's friend, Maz?'

'I don't know.'

'Did Laura pack a bag before she left?'

'I didn't ask.'

'Does Ben think Gene has got anything to do with this?'

'I don't know.'

Bill hesitated and said, 'This whole thing seems a little under-researched.'

'Well it's just happened,' I said. 'Ben's just rung.'

'Okay,' said Bill. 'Here's what I think you should do. Get in touch with Maz, and see if she knows anything. Speak to Ben, and see if they had an upset which might have made her flounce off. Ask him if he's spoken to Gene since Laura left at lunchtime, to find out if he's seen her. Try not to panic, Laura can be a drama queen sometimes but she's not daft. And she won't leave Harry for long. Ring me in an hour if I'm not home by then and let me know what you've found out.'

So Dan rang Maz, who hadn't seen Laura. I rang Ben who said there had been some tensions between him and Laura, but no row this morning. He said he was on his way to see Gene. He said normally they would be evenly matched, but he had the advantage of being bloody furious, and he had a baseball bat in the car with him.

Jen put the kettle on and Baz made some large turkey sandwiches. Chrissy said there would be something from R&J that would sum this whole thing up if she could just bring it to mind. Sophie said her grandmother was clairvoyant and could probably help, so she would give her a ring. 'I lost my phone once,' she said, 'and my gran told me where it was.'

'Really?' said Chrissy, deliberating but not dismissing. 'Well, I suppose *there are more things in heaven and earth* and all that. Where did your grandma say it was, your phone?'

'She said it would be in the house somewhere,' said Sophie. 'And when I looked, there it was, in the house just like she said. I'll go and phone her now.'

I rang Bill back in half an hour. 'It's nearly nine o'clock Bill,' I said, 'and we're not much further forward. Maz hasn't seen or heard from Laura, and Ben is on his way to give Gene a thrashing. He said things have been strained between him and Laura but no row today.'

'Did Ben say specifically he was going to give Gene a thrashing?'

'Not in as many words. He said he had a baseball bat in the car.'

'I don't like the sound of that, Sally.'

'No,' I said. 'Get back here, Bill.'

Everyone was standing around in the kitchen, which had become the operations and command centre. Everyone except Sophie, who had gone upstairs to ring the Oracle in the person of her grandma. I wanted to send them all out to look for Laura, but we didn't know where to look. We'd had all drunk too much to drive, and were reduced to searching unsuccessfully by phone. None of us knew what to do next.

We needed to elect a strong leader to take control and make some sensible, clear headed decisions. There was good manpower here standing around doing nothing because they had drunk a few glasses of fizzy wine. The situation called for someone on site with a lifetime's experience in people management to grasp the reins.

'Right everyone,' I said. 'Listen up. We have two problems here. We don't know where Laura is, and Ben is on his way to see Gene, and that might come to blows.'

'Ben and Gene?' said Dan. 'What kind of fight would that be? They'd probably throw cushions at each other.'

'No,' I said. 'When I spoke to Ben he said he was furious. I think he intends to do Gene some damage.'

Dan shook his head. 'I don't see it myself. They'd push each other over then sit and talk about it for half an hour.'

'Ben has a baseball bat with him.'

'There might be some action then,' said Baz, hopefully.

'We don't want that,' I said. 'We don't want Ben in a police cell when Laura turns up. So, Dan and Baz – ring Ben and find out where he is and what he's doing, and then if necessary get a taxi over there and make sure he doesn't get into any trouble.'

'Now?' said Dan, looking at his unfinished turkey sandwich.

'Now. Right now.'

Sophie came downstairs, excited, and with news to share. 'She's surrounded by water. My gran says. I've just been speaking to her.'

'Your gran is surrounded by water?' said Sam.

'No,' said Sophie. 'Gran says Laura is surrounded by water.'

'Is she having a bath?' said Chrissy. 'Did Ben look in the bathroom?'

'I didn't ask if she might be in the bath. I'll ring Gran again.' Sophie ran back upstairs.

Jen was handing around cups of coffee. She handed me a cup and said, 'Is there any truth in the myth that coffee counteracts alcohol?'

'No,' I said. 'None. We could really do with a driver. Does anyone think they might be sober enough?'

No-one did. 'I haven't had that much,' said Chrissy. 'I'm definitely not drunk.'

'But you don't drive,' said Sam.

'Oh yeah,' said Chrissy.

'How about if we ask Susan from next door if she could be a driver?' said Jen.

'Might be worth a try,' I said. 'Could you go next door Jen, and suss Susan out? If she's sober and willing, bring her round and she could drive Dan and Baz to find Ben before he commits an offence.'

Sophie reappeared. 'Laura's not in the bath! There's more water than that.'

'Sophie,' I said, 'I'm very grateful to your gran, but honestly I'm not sure this is helping.'

'But – she was right about my phone!' Sophie said urgently. 'She was right about that, Mrs Forth. You have to admit.'

'Yes, that's true,' I said. But really I wished Sophie would shut up.

Dan and Baz were making progress. They managed to contact Ben on his mobile, and had established where he was.

He was trying to gain entry to Gene's house but Gene wouldn't open the front door and was threatening to call the police. Ben said he was going to try around the back. I didn't recognise the address but Sam knew where it was and said it would take less than fifteen minutes to get there from here.

Jen came back from next door accompanied by Susan, who came into the kitchen and looked around and said, 'What now? Jen here says you need someone to drive a car because you're all too drunk.'

'Susan,' I said, 'you owe me a favour. Can you drive Sam and the boys here to an urgent appointment? Are you ready now? Have you got your keys? I'll explain when you get back.'

'What favour?' she said. 'I don't even know where I'm going.'

'Sam will tell you where to go. Won't you, Sam?'

'Who's Sam?' said Susan, 'I don't know any Sam.'

Sophie suddenly had an idea. 'How far away is the seaside?'

'I'm not going to the seaside!' said Susan. 'You can forget that for a game of soldiers.'

'For Christ's sake Susan,' I said. 'We need your help – will you drive the car?'

'All right all right,' she said. 'But I want a full explanation when I get back.'

They faffed around in the kitchen doorway letting in blasts of freezing cold air and putting on shoes and coats. Baz said, 'We need to take some sort of weapon, in case we have to defend ourselves.' Dan said, 'It's Ben and Gene, a roll of newspaper would be overkill.' Baz said, 'But Ben has a baseball bat,' and Dan said, 'Yes, but he's on our side.' Susan said she didn't like the sound of any of this. Sam promised he would look after her, and she said that was all very well but she didn't even know who he was.

And then they were gone, and there was just Jen and Sophie and me left in the kitchen. There was a brief lull while our heartbeats slowed a little, then five minutes later Bill arrived. It was well after nine, and still no sign of Laura. No-one had seen her, or heard from her since lunchtime. She'd vanished. I could see Bill was worried, and that made me more worried than before he came home. We sat down and tried to think of friends of Laura's we might be able to call, friends she might have spoken to if she was upset.

Sophie explained to Bill, who was looking dazed, that her grandma had made a contribution to our search for answers. 'Mr Forth,' she said, 'my grandma's clairvoyant and she says Laura's surrounded by water. I told Mrs Forth, but she's not taking any notice.'

I cursed myself for falling out with Laura on Christmas Day. This was starting to feel like my fault, and it was just a matter of time before everyone would be contemplating this bleak fact. I should have been more understanding, more sympathetic. Why, why, why hadn't I just talked to her calmly instead of –

The phone rang. I snatched it up.

'Mum? I've just got home and I can't find Ben and Harry. I'm starting to get a bit concerned.'

'Laura? Laura!' I looked up at Bill, 'It's Laura. Thank God.' And then, overwhelmed with relief and ecstatic that she was home and safe and well, I said, 'Where the hell have you been Laura? Why in God's name didn't you say where you were going? What were you thinking of, being so stupid not to ring? We've been out of our minds with worry! Why didn't you ring when it was getting so late? Ben thought you were coming here. He rang and asked if he could speak to you, but of course you weren't here! We've been frantic here, Laura. Absolutely frantic. I rang your dad and told him to come home. I never do that but I was mad with worry. I still feel really anxious. You've put ten years on my life.'

Bill put his hand out to request the phone. I gave it to him. 'Hi Laura,' he said. 'How're you doing?'

Chapter 8 – January

A pparently Laura had needed some time to herself, so she had gone to the sales, and then she'd gone swimming. She met a friend she hadn't seen for ages and they had gone for a drink. She hadn't said she would definitely be coming here, she only said she might call in, and she had told Ben that she would be a while. She felt a lot better for her day out until she went home to an empty house, and rang me.

Susan isn't happy either. She holds me responsible for a speeding offence she was given on the night of the mercy dash to Gene's house, and wants me to reimburse her if she has to pay a fine. She was speeding because she panicked when the police turned up at Gene's just as she was pulling away.

Apparently, she was spotted by the police car which was on its way to Gene's place in response to his call for help. Susan saw blue lights heading down the road towards her just after she had dropped Dan, Baz and Sam off outside Gene's. She was perfectly innocent, but felt guilty, so she turned tail and took off at speed for home. She was intercepted doing 38 mph in a 30 mph zone, charged with speeding, and then crawled home at 20 mph, cursing me.

Dan said when he and the others got out of Susan's car there was no sign of Ben at the front of Gene's house, so they went around the back and found him lying on the ground talking to Gene through the cat flap. The conversation was animated but not overtly aggressive, so Dan and Sam sat on the patio furniture to monitor the situation. Baz meanwhile, rearranged the Christmas lights on an acer tree in Gene's garden, to achieve a more pleasing artistic effect.

When the police arrived after booking Susan, Gene's wife Wendy was passing cups of tea out through the cat flap to the al fresco gathering on the patio, so it was apparent that this was not a life-threatening situation.

Gene then opened the back door to explain to the two policemen why he had rung them for help. He said Ben had turned up at his house offering to give him some marriage guidance with a baseball bat. Gene said he was trained in conflict resolution and he knew the baseball bat would not be a useful negotiating tool, but Ben had insisted that it would. Ben said his wife Laura had gone missing and he held Gene responsible, and one of the policeman got the idea that Gene might be holding Laura hostage. They were initiating a search of his house when I rang Dan, to say that Laura was at home, safe and well.

Both Gene and Ben were a little shaken afterwards. When he had calmed down Ben said he hadn't thought himself capable of taking up a baseball bat in anger, and Gene said he'd never imagined that couples counselling would be a dangerous career choice.

I'll have to go and see Laura later this week, to see how this whole thing is shaking down.

***

Jen's extended Christmas visit has come to an end and she has gone home, but she and Sam are going to keep in touch. Jen went home resolving to end her relationship with Scott the Younger than Her, and she had a little speech prepared which was designed to let him down gently. But she hasn't made the speech because Scott has not shown up to listen to it. Jen thinks she won't ever see him again because it must have occurred to him that a man with his skills on a ball of kapok could play the field.

Jen has tired of the kapok, and wants rid of it. She has found a good home for it and is delighted because she didn't want to drag it with her any further into the New Year. After making extensive enquiries she discovered that a local charity are happy to come and collect it and take it away. They have a use for quantities of kapok which they were reluctant to share with Jen over the phone, other than to say they were making modesty pads for people with exotic requirements, which they said was sensitive but useful work, as anyone who has used a modesty pad for something exotic could confirm.

So, it has been a less than tranquil start to the New Year, and of course, things are not likely to improve. The political landscape is in upheaval. I'm not writing about it in any detail here because it is so well documented elsewhere, but as everyone knows there is a leadership challenge and Bill is among the challengers. He expects it to be a bumpy ride. He will announce this week that he is running, so I have had a word with Dan, Baz and Sophie. I told them that there may be reporters outside the house at some stage, and asked them to be polite and cheerful always, but please, please, not to make a comment on anything they may be asked. I told them they should say, 'Hello,' or 'Good morning,' or 'Lovely day,' or 'Awful day,' but absolutely nothing else.

Dan and Baz seem to have got the idea, but Sophie is beside herself with excitement and doesn't see this as a situation requiring caution or restraint. She sees this as a 'Strictly' situation without the dancing, and is desperate for Bill to win. We are both very touched by Sophie's loyalty and enthusiasm. Bill said to me in bed last night that he hoped he deserved it.

***

As a welcome distraction to recent events, I was in school today to help settle Lee down. He goes a bit feral after a school holiday of more than a few days. There is a wonderful new initiative being launched this term to tackle low-grade disruption in lessons. Children who demonstrate sustained concentration during lessons can now gain points, and after a certain number of points they will be awarded a certificate. If they gain three certificates in a term they will win a gold medal, and a letter will be sent home to parents to let them know that their child is an Olympic athlete in terms of their powers of concentration.

It was my job to impress Lee with this scheme at the very beginning of term, before all the usual negative influences take hold of him. I spent ten minutes with him during registration this morning, before lessons began.

'There's something different about school this term Lee,' I began.

'Not another bollocks behaviour initiative,' he said.

'No, it's different this time. This time you can win a gold medal.'

'For what?'

'For concentrating in lessons.'

'Gold?'

'Yes, gold. Like in the Olympics.'

'Real gold?'

'No, not real gold.'

'So not gold.'

'Not real gold, no. But it looks just like gold.'

'Well it sounds just like shit.'

'Come on Lee. You could win one of these medals. It's a competition. You just need to concentrate more in lessons, and you'll gain some points. When you get enough points you get a certificate, and when you get three certificates – you win a medal. And then school sends a letter home to tell your parents.'

'What happens when you win three medals?'

'I don't know, Lee, maybe you inherit the Earth. I'll find out.'

So at lunchtime I asked Amy Sanders, deputy head in charge of bollocks behaviour initiatives, what happens if someone gets three gold medals in a term. I said Lee wanted to know. She said it was academic as far as Lee was concerned. I said yes, but,

I'd like to be able to tell him if he asks again. 'Oh, I don't know Sally,' said Amy. 'Maybe three gold medals equals an Oscar, and three Oscars equals a Coronation. Tell him what you like, just get him to shut up in my geography lesson.'

This afternoon Lee had a French lesson. This was a good opportunity to practice his powers of concentration. Lee has to concentrate very hard to convince himself that France exists. Today's lesson was called *'Allez au Supermarché!'* about a visit to a French supermarket. Lee's concentration deserted him in the *Fruits et Légumes* aisle when he realised that all French vegetables were called something different from ours. He couldn't believe it at first, and thought I was joking. We didn't get very far around those supermarket aisles after that, but at least by the end of the lesson the full implications of speaking a language other than English were beginning to dawn on Lee, and he had a lot of sympathy for the French, having such a poncey name for potatoes.

When I got home, Sophie was standing in the kitchen wearing her coat. 'Have you had a good day, Mrs Forth?' she said. She was smiling broadly.

'Yes, thank you Sophie, I've had a very good day. How's your day been?'

'Very good. Really good. I've got a surprise for you.'

'Oh have you?'

'Yes, and it's brilliant.'

'Is it? Oh,' I started to feel anxious. 'Actually Sophie, I'm not too keen on surprises.'

'You'll like this one.'

'Will I? I'm not sure.'

'You will. You'll love this one.'

I looked around. 'Where is it? You haven't bought a dog, have you Sophie? Because I'm allergic to dogs.'

'A dog? No! It's nothing like a dog!'

'So what is it then? Tell me quick.'

'All right then,' she said. 'Guess what?'

'What?'

'Ta-da!' She flung open her coat to reveal her T-shirt. Written across the front was *Mr Forth First!*

I was speechless, but despite that I said, 'Where did you get that?'

'I got it made, today after work. Brilliant, isn't it?'

'I – . God – '

'It's brilliant, because it says Mr Forth, like fourth, and then underneath it says, first! Like coming first. Like we want him to win. It's brilliant! I'm getting some more made.'

'Oh – what? More?' I couldn't take my eyes off the slogan stamped across Sophie's chest. 'Not too many, I hope, Sophie,' I said faintly. 'They must be expensive.'

'Just fifty.'

'FIFTY?'

'Yes, fifty to start with. We should all wear them. You too, Mrs Forth. You can have yours free, but everyone else will have to pay five pounds. Apart from Mr Forth, of course. I've got a brilliant one for him, it says Mr Forth First on the front like the others, but his has got a thumbs-up sign on the back! Fantastic! He'll love it!'

***

Things have been a bit tense around here today. Bill is a little anxious. He tells me that our living arrangements are deemed to be eccentric by those who know about these things. They are 'problematic', the problem being that we have young people living with us who are not related to us in any way, and who are not lodgers paying rent. Apparently, this could be awkward. There have been rumours, and rumours of rumours, nothing definite, but enough to cause unease in some quarters. Anything eccentric on the home front could be seen as suspect.

I said to Bill, it's not our living arrangements that are eccentric, it's the cost of rents and the price of houses. Bill said

– yes, that's true – but back at base, or HQ, or the Mother Ship or whatever the campaign command and control centre is calling itself, they just want to be prepared. So, they want to know who's living here, and what their living arrangements are, and whether or not they are sexually active.

I said, 'Is that anyone else's business?'

'Well of course it isn't,' he said. 'But since when did that matter? Please don't get all fired up with righteous indignation now, Sally. Obviously, they have to ask these questions, let's not be naïve. Look – don't worry about it. They probably just want to be sure we're not running a bawdy house.'

'A bawdy house? Isn't that a Tudor brothel?'

'Anyway, I've told them that Baz and Sophie are living with us. But I didn't mention Chrissy. She's not living with us, is she?'

'She stays the occasional night. With Dan.'

'Rarely?'

'Perhaps more than rarely.'

'Right,' said Bill. 'So, remind me, why is Sophie living with us?'

'She's living with us because it's very expensive and time-consuming to get to and from her shifts at work if she lives at home with her parents, and she can't afford alternative accommodation closer to her job. She moved in when she and Dan were an item, and now that they're not she wants to stay because she is very attached to her room here, particularly its little washbasin.'

'And Baz?'

'He fell out with his parents and can only get on with them now if he's not living with them. He can't afford alternative accommodation because he's saving up for a Vespa scooter upon which to build his business empire. He moved into the mound of rubbish when I wasn't looking, transformed it into a bijou residence, and then I didn't have the heart to pull it down around him. As long as he catches moles for Susan next door, he can have the use of it in the evening. But we've suggested he sleeps in the house overnight, because as Susan pointed out, if he freezes to death out there it won't look good.'

'And Chrissy?'

'She just has the hots for Dan.'

'How long do you see these circumstances continuing? Are we going to be living with them all when they're middle aged and we're having our hips replaced?'

'You tell me, I suppose,' I said. 'How long before they can afford to set up on their own somewhere? There could be some advantages to them being here for the long haul. Baz would do the garden for us, when we have dodgy hips. Sophie's a trained carer, so we're quids in there. We're quite well set up, really. Dan might be able to do something with the loft space for him and Chrissy or whoever he's with at the time.'

'Seriously though, how much of a commitment are we making to house these kids? What's our longer term plan?'

So I told Bill my longer term plan for Baz and Sophie was for them to fall in love and very soon afterwards buy a winning lottery ticket and move out and set up home together. My long term plan for Dan was that he should morph into someone who has a bank account with some actual money in it.

And we left it at that.

Money isn't everything – that's what they say, isn't it? But what concerns me more and more is that maybe they're wrong.

***

I was in the Co-op this morning buying biscuits to take up to Laura's with me this afternoon, and I noticed the billboard on the pavement outside. It said, **Insurers Will Pay Says Triumphant Flood Gran**. At last, some good news. I know of this particular gran, because a few weeks ago I saw an earlier billboard which said, **Distraught Flood Gran Loses Everything**. This must be the same **Flood Gran**, surely, transformed from a **Distraught Flood Gran** into a **Triumphant Flood Gran**. Wonderful.

Of course, if they had wanted to tempt me to buy a paper, the billboard should have said, **Flood Gran Drama Latest!** Then I'd have thought – oh no! What's happened to the **Flood Gran** now? Has she suffered a house fire? I would have rushed to buy a paper, anticipating the following day's billboards, **Former Flood Gran Now Fire Gran 'Critical'**.

But as things stood, the **Flood Gran**'s story was known to me without buying a paper. I lingered inside the shop though, to look at her photo on the front page of the newspaper. She looked younger than me. She's achieved **Flood Gran** status in her late thirties. I lost all sympathy for her. A **Flood Gran** should have white hair, rimless glasses and webbed feet, she shouldn't look like a chuffed-to-bits Fiona Bruce.

I was a little apprehensive on the way up to Laura's. The last time I saw her was when I banished her from the house on Christmas Day, and the last time I spoke to her was when I told her over the phone that I couldn't believe she'd been so stupid. Things were bound to be a bit tricky at first.

I decided to tackle things head-on when I arrived, rather than pussy-footing around awkwardly, so I came out with it straightaway while she was making the tea. 'Look Laura, I'm sorry we fell out on Christmas Day, and I'm sorry I was a bit annoyed with you on the phone, but I was so worried about you, and it made me angry. Try these biscuits they're very nice.'

Laura took the biscuits. 'Thanks. The whole thing was Ben's fault really, for over-reacting. But I don't need you to worry about me, Mum. Especially if it's going to make you angry.'

'The truth is Laura, I thought Gene might have seriously unsettled you. I never thought Gene was a good idea.'

'I know that. It's a shame because he's a really nice man, but obviously there's been a cooling off between us. Since the baseball bat.'

'That's probably just as well,' I said. 'So do you feel any more settled?'

'Settled? Not particularly, no,' she said. 'That's just it. I don't feel settled. I feel as if there is something missing in my life.'

'You mean, like fulfilment? Are you looking for meaning and a sense of purpose?'

'No,' she handed me a mug of tea. 'Like parties. I'm looking for excitement and a sense of freedom.'

'I think that might just be a reaction to having a baby. It takes a little while to come to terms with the fact that you don't get parties and a sense of freedom when you have a baby.'

'I feel a bit trapped. Did you feel trapped when you had me?'

I thought back. The answer was yes, I did. 'No, not really. I felt committed, not trapped.'

'Interesting,' said Laura. 'So when would you say you got your old life back? After having me? How long did it take?'

'My old life?' I said, stalling for time.

'Yes, you know, how long was it before you started to feel like you did before I was born? Free and properly independent?'

'Free?' I said. 'Independent? Oh, difficult to say really.'

'Just a rough estimate.'

'Gosh. It's all a long time ago now, isn't it? But when you started school, I was definitely a lot freer. I was able to nip along to Jen's and we'd have a quick bite to eat together and then rush along to the shops before it was time to pick you up. That was fun. Then Dan was born and it all started again of course. But once he was at playschool I was free as a bird for two and a half hours, three mornings a week.'

'Oh,' said Laura. 'That's not what I meant. What I meant was, when did you actually start to feel independent and free again, like you did before? When did you get that feeling back? That feeling that you were your own person again?'

I reached for another biscuit. 'Well,' I said. 'I think the truth is that post-natal freedom is different from pre-natal freedom. Pre-natal freedom is something we don't even realise we have, until we experience post-natal freedom. Post-natal freedom isn't something we can take for granted, like pre-natal freedom.

Post-natal freedom is a different sort of freedom, a more confined sort of freedom.'

'A confined sort of freedom? What does that mean? I'm confused. Confined freedom sounds like trapped to me. Maybe I'm suffering from post-natal bewilderment.'

'You are Laura,' I seized on this. 'You're definitely suffering from post-natal bewilderment. It can last for a while. I still get bouts of it.' I'm having one now, I thought.

Laura continued, 'And it doesn't help that Ben's driving me mad.'

'Is he?' Oh fuck.

'He comes home, and he complains about his work. And I think – but you've actually been out of the house, talking to people and moving around freely! You haven't changed a nappy all day and, *and* – you can go to the loo whenever you want to! What have you got to complain about?'

I looked at her pained expression, a duplicate of the expression worn by her sisters down the ages, and I tried to formulate a satisfying reply.

'Have another biscuit,' I said.

She took one. 'But it's good, isn't it, that we can have these discussions, don't you think? You and I? I always feel so much better once I get things off my chest talking to you. I can just dump the whole lot on you, the despair, the loneliness, the boredom, the anger, the frustration, the feeling of slowly going mad, and then I feel a whole lot better. I don't know how you feel?'

'Great,' I said. 'Tip top.'

'I wouldn't like to unburden myself to you, and think you were going to end up feeling terrible. Actually, I do feel a bit better, now that I've told you I can't stand my life.'

'Oh good. Is that good?'

'Well I feel better now anyway.' She poured us both another cup of tea. 'So, I was thinking, would you be able to make me some curtains for the kitchen if I got the material?'

I always feel like a rest cure when I come away from Laura's. Driving home today I wanted to take a detour and join a Retreat with a silent order of nuns.

When I got home, I was very pleased to find a note on the kitchen table to say that all four of our resident and semi-resident young people were eating out and then going to see a new Star Wars film.

So Bill and I had a very rare meal together, just the two of us. It started well. But then Bill told me afterwards while we were having a cup of coffee that whichever way you look at it, it's a bit odd that we have unrelated supernumeraries living in with us. He said the consensus at work is that it would be better if Baz and Sophie moved out, and we looked like a more conventional household.

I went to bed early, before any of them got back.

***

They were all in the kitchen this morning when I came downstairs, so I asked if they had enjoyed Star Wars, and they said they had, it was really good.

'What happens in this one?' I said, and I leant against the kitchen bench with a cup of tea in my hand while they thrashed it out.

'Well, it was about the rebellion against the Empire and getting the Jedi to use the Force to destroy the Death Star.'

'Wasn't it about the Jedi rebellion against the Force using the Death Star to destroy the Empire?'

'But isn't the Empire weak in the Force, that's why it's rebelling against the Jedi inside the Death Star?'

'No, the Force is strong in the rebels so they're using the Death Star to attack the Jedi outside the Empire.'

'Anyway,' said Sophie. 'They won in the end.'

'Oh good,' I said. 'That's all right then.'

After they all went out, I decided I was going to resist any proposal from above to evict Sophie and Baz and thereby achieve a more conventional household. But to do that, I would have to be very strong in the Force, because the life forms in the Election Campaign Landing Craft are very persuasive. They will present apparently reasonable arguments and make me feel like an idiot for clinging to the poor half-formed things that are my opinions. They will almost certainly explain to me that the current situation makes us vulnerable to attack by the Overlords of the Press, who might romp away with unconfirmed reports of what is happening under our roof, and chew up our life-style with their mouth parts. I will be warned that a reporter could catch Sophie or Baz off guard, and thrust a microphone at them and ask a leading question. An ill-considered reply might cause our mission to be swallowed whole by the Death Star, and terminated.

So I was sharpening my light sabre in the kitchen, and making sure it was charged up and buzzing loudly, when Susan from next door called round.

'I've come to pick your brains,' she said, which is an unfortunate turn of phrase for Susan because she has a carnivorous temperament.

'How can I help?' I said. I feel responsible for Susan's speeding ticket, so I'm trying to compensate by being very neighbourly at the moment.

She put some paperwork down on my kitchen table. 'What do you make of this? Apparently, I can either take points on my licence, or I can do a 'Speed Awareness Course'. What the hell's a Speed Awareness Course? Have you done one?'

I confessed to Susan that I had done one, and I explained that it's a course designed to show you how fast you're going so that you will slow down in the future. I said I couldn't remember much about it, other than I drove there at a normal speed, and then the course made me so aware of my speed that I drove home at six miles an hour.

She asked me if I would like to go with her, but I said I didn't think it was a plus-one kind of thing.

'I'm wondering if I should just take the points on my licence,' she said. 'I don't want to go on a course to be told off and rapped over the knuckles. Not at my time of life.'

I told her it wasn't like that. I said it's like being back at school in a geography lesson with a couple of bouncy teachers who are going to ignore how naughty you've been up to now, and be firm but fair. That is – as long as you're not disruptive, and you don't start letting yourself down and everybody else down. 'It's okay, really Susan,' I said. 'I'd go, if I were you.'

'Of course,' said Susan, 'you're not me. You don't actually have to go to this speed awareness thing, because you'd drunk too much wine that night and couldn't drive. That's why I had to go and get this speeding ticket in the first place.'

'I know,' I said. 'It was very unfortunate.'

'For me. Not so unfortunate for you.'

Susan can be very tiresome. I wanted to cut her to ribbons with my light sabre, and then send her fragments to the desolate ice-planet Hoth, where they would be crushed by the terrible jaws of the mighty cave-dwelling Squimm.

'It's going to get interesting over the next few weeks,' said Susan, changing tack. 'What with Bill going for bust in this leadership thing.'

'Yes,' I said, 'it is.'

'Don't worry,' she said. 'I won't say anything.'

'Say anything about what?'

'Oh, you know. This and that. There's been a few things over the years, hasn't there? And now this. Drunk as Lords over Christmas, and me racing through the night to stop your son-in-law battering your daughter's lover to death.'

'What! What? Susan! What did you just say? Where did you get that idea?'

'That's how it sounded to me the other night. Listening to them talking in the car. But don't worry,' she held up her hands. 'Mum's the word. Lips are sealed. We've been neighbours for years, and that must count for something. You can trust me not to say anything. If you like.' She stood up and collected her papers together. 'I mean it. Don't look so shocked.'

'Of course I'm shocked Susan! That sounded like a veiled threat.'

'No such thing! I'm quite offended. No such thing, Sally. Veiled threat? I'm just saying – all indiscretions are safe with me. That's all. Strange times we live in, eh?' she said, quite chatty now after dropping her bombshell. 'Speed Awareness. I ask you. What next? Turning Right Awareness? Changing Gear Awareness?' She shook her head at the absurdity of modern life. 'I'm off anyway. Let you get on with things. Tell you what though, Sally. I'm going to be very pleased to see the back of that pile of rubbish outside. Very pleased. But just when you're ready.'

'Yes, all right Susan. Point taken.'

'I'll have to get back and see to Derek.'

'How is Derek? I haven't seen him to say Happy New Year.'

'He's in bed.'

'Oh dear. Is he ill?'

'Yes,' she said. 'He's quite poorly. Stomach trouble.'

'Stomach trouble?'

'Yes. Came on just after Christmas. Too much rich food.'

'Oh. Has the doctor seen him? He might suggest Derek goes to hospital.'

'Hospital? Not if I have any say in it. Haven't you been watching the news? The Health Service is in a worse state than Derek. He doesn't want to be lying on a trolley in hospital gathering dust until someone can stop by long enough to take his pulse. Better off at home.'

'Well,' I said, 'I'm sorry to hear he's not well. Poor thing. I'll have to pop in and see him.'

'Will you?' she said. 'No rush, Sally. He's not feeling very chipper. Give him a few days.'

She left, and I went up to the bathroom to look across at Derek's greenhouse with the binoculars. The crop of rhubarb has all gone. Proves nothing, of course, but still...

Jen rang me around four this afternoon. She sounds happy. Sam is going up to stay a while, not with her, but with friends of his in her area. They will be meeting up to continue their new relationship, and to see where it might lead.

Jen is trying unsuccessfully not to get too excited. 'This could be it, Sally. After all this time. After all those years with what's-his-name, my husband. I don't want to be disloyal, you know I don't, but I never liked him. It's all right to admit to that now, isn't it? And Sam is so different. He can talk, he can listen, and he's not an idiot – I can't believe my luck! I'm so lucky that – that chap – my first husband, died in time for me to find someone I could be really happy with.'

'You should try and remember the poor man's name, Jen. It really isn't right to be calling him what's-his-name. It wasn't entirely his fault that the marriage didn't work.'

'No, you're right,' she said. 'It wasn't his fault we were incompatible. I should be more generous. I'm just so focused now on this new relationship. It's so exciting. I'm forgetting everything else. Anyway, getting back to er… . Well, never mind him. Tell me about you. How are things on the home front? Are you coping with this election thing? Everything okay?'

'Well,' I said, 'there's a few problems lining up, I've got— '

'Sally! Sorry – call waiting, ring you back.' I heard a little 'beep' on her phone, so I don't think she did that on purpose.

We had a nice evening meal. Baz made us one of his road kill casseroles. He said he thought more than one animal might have contributed. Chrissy tried to think of references to food in Romeo and Juliet. Sophie looked through the television listings and wondered why *The Bourne Identity* is always on. Dan said he had wondered the same thing. Baz said it's because you have to see it five times to know what the fuck's going on. Sophie said surely it's been identified by now.

But later I had a difficult conversation with Bill. He said we should look into finding alternative accommodation for Sophie and Baz. He said the arrangement we have now could so easily backfire at some point. He said it wasn't fair on his team to refuse to take their advice. They are working very hard for him, and he doesn't feel it's fair to compromise their efforts. They are the experts, they're on his side, and he thinks they're right.

I said hang on, Bill, and I asked him what alternative accommodation he thought might be suitable? Or even possible? He said, well obviously, they would have to go home to their parents. I said Sophie's parents live twenty miles north of us and Baz's parents live twenty miles south. Sophie would have to give up her job, and share her bedroom with her cousin. Baz would probably opt not to go back home, and I wasn't sure in that case where he would go. He's saving up for a Vespa scooter so he can get to work more easily, and he's strapped for cash.

Bill asked me whether all this was really our problem. I said I thought that was what he was in politics for. We looked at each other, and considered this.

'Hiya!'

'Sophie! I thought you'd gone to bed.'

'I was outside in Aspire with Baz. I'm going to bed now, but, Mrs Forth, do you remember ages ago, I said if someone kissed my hand I'd think I was really special?'

'Yes, I remember.'

'Baz kissed my hand. Just before. In Aspire.'

'Did he, Sophie?'

'Yes, he said I was really special.'

'Did he? That's lovely, Sophie.'

'I know.' She smiled at us both. 'I love living here,' she said, and went upstairs to bed.

Bill looked at me and said, 'Oh shit.'

***

So for the moment, nobody leaves. We are in this together. One for all, and all for one and all aboard. Although Bill has asked me not to take in any more lodgers. We might just about get away with two, but three really would look very peculiar. I said don't worry, there's only Baz and Sophie, and I'll suggest to Dan that Chrissy goes home most nights, even if we have to pay a taxi. 'Leave this to me,' I told Bill. 'I'm on it. I know what I have to do. Trust me.'

And so that's my job. I have to steady the ship through domestic waters, brace for potential squalls and discipline the younger crew members. I am also in charge of metaphors.

Bill is making regular appearances on television. It's odd watching him field questions on TV. I sometimes find myself thinking, 'God! Politicians! Why can't they just give a straight answer to a straight question?' And then I have to remind myself that I am married to this man on the telly. If Sophie is in the room while Bill is on television I can't hear a word he says, because she leaps up and chants, 'Go Forth! Go Forth!' The first time she did it I nearly jumped out of my skin.

Dan and Baz are preoccupied elsewhere at the moment, fortunately. Dan's relationship with Chrissy continues to blossom. They are seeing a lot of each other in every sense, I imagine. Chrissy is to take the role of Juliet in the Highfield Players production of R&J, opening soon. They sit for hours, each with a copy of the play in their hand, rehearsing her part.

Sophie thinks this is absurdly affected. She doesn't say anything, but she rolls her eyes upwards so efficiently that they can disappear inside her head for seconds at a time, and I find myself waiting for them to re-appear like twin sunrises from her lower lids. She is not planning to go to the performance of Romeo and Juliet. She says she must have heard the whole play by now anyway, and Shakespeare gives her a headache.

I will go, because Dan has worked hard on the stage design. The play is set not in Verona, but in a supermarket which they're calling Tescios. Juliet's family own the supermarket, and Romeo's family are the local farmers forced to sell their produce to the store for next to nothing. Chrissy says they wanted to bring the whole play up to date and give it real relevance.

I said yes, why not? Although I could probably have answered that question. Then I asked Dan where the famous balcony scene would take place. He said the balcony would be the mezzanine floor above the frozen foods counter, looking out across the store from the cafeteria. When Juliet appears on the balcony with a skinny latte to go, she says 'Romeo, Romeo, wherefore art thou Romeo?', unaware that he is filling up the fridge below with frozen peas. As interpretations of Shakespeare's work go, it's either genius or completely bonkers, and there is absolutely no way of knowing which.

Dan and Baz are very busy at work too, on an exciting new project. They are helping to create a maze for a wealthy client of the firm to get lost in. Apparently, the design is very clever. Once you are a few turns into the maze you could be wandering around in there for hours before you stumble on a way out. I said that was the general idea with mazes and they said yes, they knew that.

So, life is good for Dan at the moment: he has a girlfriend, a job that he enjoys, and an interest in Am Dram that plays well to his strengths. The only fly in the ointment for him is the fact that he is still living with his mum and dad, with no prospect of ever moving out. He's in the centre of that particular maze, and he could be wandering around looking for the exit for some considerable time.

I know it's frustrating for him, so I like to be fairly flexible and give him as much independence as I reasonably can. So when he said he wanted to redecorate his bedroom and turn it into an adult space because his Banana Man wallpaper was starting to feel a bit weird, I said, yes, fine, good idea. About time.

He said he was thinking of turning the room into the interior of the Death Star.

'I'm not sure about that, Dan,' I said.

'It'll be great,' he said.

***

Baz is very pleased with himself at the moment because he has caught one of Susan's moles. No doubt about it this time. He's keeping an eye on things to see if any more hills appear, and he has set another two traps. He says Susan is delighted and is looking into having the mole stuffed, because she wants it properly punished and put on display like a head on a spike. Baz says you can make good money catching moles and he sees this as potentially an additional income stream to add to his portfolio. He's hoping that another hill will appear next door, so he can hone his skills. He says once he gets his Vespa he'll be able to advertise and travel far and wide to rid frustrated gardeners of moles. He'll become rich, a mole mogul. Sophie thinks it's a great idea.

I thought I'd pop next door this afternoon and ask how Derek is. This might be a good time, now that Susan has been appeased by Baz's success in the tunnels under her lawn. I took a book with me that might interest Derek if he's feeling better, and went to knock on their front door.

Susan and Derek's house is a bit depressing. They don't really have a knack for interior decorating. Susan favours gloomy shades of plum and purple, and has managed to make her living room look like the interior of the Death Star without really trying. I don't know whether Derek likes it or just puts up with it, but he was looking rather glum sitting by the fire reading the paper when I went in.

I asked him how he was and he said he thought he was on the mend, but it had been a funny do. He looked as if he might elaborate but Susan told him I wouldn't want to know the details. So he changed the subject.

He said he'd just been reading about us in the paper.

'Oh really?' I said. 'That sounds interesting. Anything I ought to know about?'

'Yes, there was something,' he rummaged through the pile of papers next to his chair and pulled one out. 'Ah! Here it is. You might be interested to know,' he said, looking at me over his reading glasses, 'that you have built a makeshift refuge centre for young adults who can't live in harmony with their parents.'

'Oh,' I glanced at Susan. 'That's not strictly accurate.'

'No,' said Derek. 'I thought not.'

'We'll have to take that place down,' I said. 'I've been meaning to do it for ages. I promised Susan.'

'Don't take it down now though,' said Susan. 'Not now that this lad seems to be getting on top of our moles. He got one you know. Came to show me it yesterday. It's in the freezer. D'you want to see it?'

'Well...'

'I'll get it.' She disappeared into the kitchen.

'Did the paper say anything else, Derek? About the refuge?'

'No, not really. Just that it was an eyesore and probably a death trap.'

'Here it is,' said Susan, returning with a plastic freezer bag full of mole. She held it out for me and I took it between finger and thumb to inspect. 'Quite a good specimen,' she said, 'not like the last one.'

'No,' I agreed. 'This is a much healthier specimen.'

'Well, not that healthy,' said Susan. 'On account of it's dead. I'm going to have it stuffed, and then I'm going to have it mounted in a glass case. It should look quite good over there on the sideboard.'

'You can't be serious, Susan,' said Derek. 'It'll look like an aubergine.'

'I'm just keeping it in the freezer until I know if Baz can catch another one,' she said. 'I'd like a pair.'

'God help us,' said Derek. 'Two stuffed moles on the sideboard. Just what this house needs.'

There was a strange little interlude back home, just before dinner. I heard a knock on our front door and went to see who it was. A young man in a hoodie stood on the step. He spoke.

'My dad says I should ask you if I can move in to your refuse centre.'

'Lee,' I said, glancing around. 'Spew not with you tonight?'

'No. Dad and me have been arguing. He says I should come down here and live with you. I told him to piss off and said right I would come down and ask you. I was that mad.'

'Why were you arguing?'

'He says I should get off my arse and stop watching Sky telly and messing about on the internet.'

'Ah. I should tell you Lee, that the refuge doesn't have a telly, or the internet.'

'What?'

'No telly or internet in the refuge. Sorry.'

'Oh,' he considered this. 'I'll not bother then.'

'Sorry about that, Lee.'

'It's all right.' He turned to go, gave me a wave, put his hands deep in his pockets and started walking back up the hill.

By ten o'clock, I was hoping for a peaceful half hour or so before bed. The house was quiet. I didn't know where anybody was and I didn't care. I was flicking through the TV channels, looking for a therapeutic episode of *Allo Allo*, when I heard a key in the lock and Juliet and her Romeo came wafting through the kitchen and into the living room.

'Oh hello,' I said, rousing myself. 'Good rehearsal?'

'Yeah, good,' said Dan. 'Mum, Chrissy's staying with us for a while. Her dad's gone somewhere up north to visit Jen and she gets spooked in the house by herself, and the boiler's packed in at hers, so it's freezing cold. I said to stay here because you wouldn't mind.'

'Hope that's okay?' said Chrissy.

'Course it is,' said Dan.

'Hope that's okay, Mrs Forth?'

'Mum?' said Dan.

***

I was on the High Street today, and I went into Tesco's looking for HP sauce. I was searching along the aisles, when I heard an altercation. A young woman was blocking the aisle with her trolley. She was wearing a towelling dressing gown over her pyjamas, and she had her slippers on her feet. It was two o'clock in the afternoon, and she had a toddler with her.

An older lady, late seventies or early eighties maybe, smartly dressed in a cream coat and pink beret, had stopped to remonstrate with the young woman. I heard her say, 'Are you wearing your pyjamas?'

'Yeah,' said the young woman. 'And what's it to you?'

'I think that's disgraceful,' she said. 'And you've got a child with you.'

The young woman stopped and looked her up and down. She was going to take her on. 'Oh yeah?' she said. 'And why should I care what you think? You're probably demented.'

But the pink beret fought back. 'Demented? I think not. Ask this lady here, she'll tell you that you shouldn't be out shopping in your pyjamas.' She looked at me for confirmation.

I'd only come in for HP sauce.

'Well,' I said, realising I was in a tricky situation, being called upon to arbitrate between a frail old lady and a young woman on the defensive. It wouldn't be easy to please both parties, so I opted for a cautious, theoretical response. 'In an ideal world,' I said, 'I do think you should get dressed before you leave the house. I've been doing it for years myself, and I find it works really well.'

'Are you taking the piss?'

'See!' said pink beret to pyjama-woman, 'I knew she'd agree with me. And you've got your little girl to think of. What kind of example are you setting? Going out shopping in your pyjamas and dressing gown?'

'Leave my kid out of it, you miserable old cow. Who asked you anyway? Mind your own business.'

'But that's just it,' said the plucky beret. 'It is my business. You make it my business. I have to look at you walking around the shop. If you were wearing your pyjamas at home, that would just be your business, but out here, it's our business. Isn't it?' She turned to me again.

'You know,' I said conversationally to pyjama-woman, 'I hadn't thought of it in those terms before, but I think she might have something there.'

'You wouldn't like it if I came in here in my bra and pants, would you?' said pink beret. 'Nobody would, I'm telling you.'

'You're fucking mad,' said pyjama-woman. 'Both of you.' Her little girl began to whimper. 'You've made her cry now, by being so fucking stupid.' She began to push her way past us.

'Before you go,' I said, 'and this isn't meant as a criticism, but just out of curiosity because I'm interested – do you have night-time pyjamas and daytime pyjamas?'

'You cheeky sod! I've had enough of this,' she said. 'I'm getting the manager. I don't have to take this kind of crap from you. I'm making a complaint.'

'Now then, ladies.' A young man in a shirt and tie with a badge pinned to his top pocket appeared in the aisle, and when I looked around I noticed we had drawn a small group of interested onlookers. 'Can I help you?'

'These two old women have been harassing me. I want them thrown out.'

'I was merely pointing out,' said the elderly warrior, 'that I didn't think nightwear was appropriate for on the street at this time of day. And this lady agrees with me.'

'Actually ladies, Tesco has no problem with customers wearing nightwear in their stores.'

'Well, Tesco's might have no problem with it. But I do. And this lady does. So I don't see why I shouldn't express my opinion.' She was a gutsy old thing.

'You need to watch your mouth, you're upsetting my little girl.'

'Can I suggest, ladies, that you just agree to disagree and continue with your shopping now?'

'Tell these two to mind their own business,' the pyjamas insisted. 'I'm making a complaint.'

'I'm sorry, Mrs erm?' the store manager looked at me anxiously.

'Forth,' I said, 'Mrs Forth.'

'Oh!' he said. 'Bill Forth's wife?'

'Yes, that's right.'

'I'm very sorry, Mrs Forth, but I wonder if you would leave this young lady to do her shopping in peace now? Perhaps if you object to her pyjamas you could do your shopping a bit later, after she's gone?'

'Throw her out,' said the pyjamas. 'Posh bitch.'

'Well,' said the dauntless pink beret, 'my name, if you're interested young man, is Maureen Pugh, and I certainly don't feel like continuing with my shopping now. I'm going to shop somewhere else. And as for you,' she looked at her young opponent, 'hot water bottles are in the next aisle. Good day.'

And with a lot less style, I followed her out.

***

I have hit the headlines. But I didn't discover that until late this afternoon. The day began normally, or normally enough, when I had coffee with Judith. She said she had a proposal to put to me, and so I met her in Marks and Spencer's café which is where we hold all our summit meetings.

We got settled at our table, and assembled all our essential equipment and paper work, cups of coffee, flapjack, plates, spoons, serviettes etc. Then we got down to business, and Judith said, 'Here's the plan, and I think you'll like it. You and I should do a sponsored swim.'

I laughed, thinking this must be some sort of jape.

'I'm serious. I'm doing a sponsored swim to raise money for elephants. Remember I told you Persephone was giving up her job to follow her dream? Well, it has to do with caring for elephants. She's attached herself to an elephant refuge, and it's short of money. Seffy asked if I could think of ways to raise some cash to buy essentials for the elephants in the refuge. So I thought of a sponsored swim. I like swimming. I was going to ask you to sponsor me, then I thought, hang about, you could do the swim too. People love elephants, Sally. It would raise your profile a bit, and be good for business all round. What do you say?'

'Well,' I said, swallowing flapjack, 'one thing I might say is, what's the matter with these elephants? Why do they need a refuge?'

'What's the matter with them? I don't know exactly. They're distressed elephants. They need our help. Do you need to know more than that?'

'Well, if I'm going to immerse myself in water and get my hair wet on their behalf, then yes, I'd like to know what's wrong with them.'

'They're stressed.'

'Why?'

'Why? God, I don't know why, Sally. Persephone didn't say. She said they needed help, so that's good enough for me.'

'Well, I'd like to help, Judith, but I've forgotten how to swim.'

'Oh come on, Sally. It's not the Channel or anything. Just a hundred lengths of the local pool. And you never forget how to swim. It's like riding a bike.'

'It's nothing like riding a bike. It's much wetter. And even if I could remember how to swim, I'm not a serious swimmer. I only swim if I fall off an airbed.'

'You don't have to do a hundred lengths – just do as many as you can. Imagine the good press. Everyone loves elephants.'

'Let me think about it.'

'Well you haven't got long.'

'I can't do this at short notice. I'd need to train.'

'Train? Don't be daft. Just walk along the bottom at the shallow end and only swim if you're going to drown. It's a PR exercise. Seffy's elephant refuge gets a mention, the elephants get their essential supplies, and you look like you care.'

'Where is Seffy's elephant refuge?' I said. 'I don't know anything about it.'

'Somewhere hot. She did tell me. I've forgotten but I'll find out if you really want to know.'

'And what essential supplies do elephants need?'

'Well, food, obviously.'

'I thought they ate trees.'

'Are you up for this, or not?'

'Leave it with me,' I said.

I stopped at the Co-op on my way home, and that's when I saw the billboard.

MP Spouse Gran in Pyjama Spat!

Oh no.

I bought a paper.

> 'Sally Forth, the wife of local MP Bill Forth, was thrown out of Tesco's Metro store yesterday for molesting a shopper in pyjama wear. Lucy Shaw, who was shopping with her two year old daughter, said Mrs Forth made hurtful and sarcastic comments ...'

I went straight home. I would have to speak to Bill.

While I was unpacking my shopping and waiting for Bill to ring me back, Sophie came in with some shopping of her own.

'I've just been to the Co-op. For some eggs and Flash spray,' she said, 'and I saw the newspaper board.'

'Oh.'

'Are you the MP Spouse Gran?'

'I am, yes.'

'Mrs Forth, I can't believe you spat at someone in your pyjamas.'

'I didn't Sophie. I didn't do that.'

'I knew they'd got that wrong! I knew it! Fancy saying you spat at someone in your pyjamas when you did no such thing? It's outrageous, Mrs Forth.'

'I know, Sophie.'

'I'm going to tell everyone I know it's a pack of lies.'

'I did talk to someone in Tesco's who was wearing pyjamas. And there was a bit of a difference of opinion.'

'Well that's okay. People disagree about jim jams in shops don't they? I've seen women in shops in their pyjamas. I've never seen a man shopping in his 'jamas though. Have you?'

'No, come to think of it, I haven't.'

'Funny that, isn't it? Maybe they're worried about looking stupid?'

The phone rang, and someone called Felicity from the campaign team asked if she could come out tomorrow and have a chat with me about the unfortunate incident in Tesco's.

***

Felicity called around today and listened to my account of the unfortunate incident in Tesco's. I tried, in the telling, to make an amusing little tale of it, but Felicity wasn't in her job for fun. She smiled politely, and explained to me that they were considering whether they needed to take any steps towards damage limitation, or whether the best course of action in this instance would be to let things lie.

I said, I was surprised they were taking it so seriously, it was really a very minor incident.

She said she understood that absolutely, and if there was no further reporting of it they would be happy just to ignore it and move on rather than draw attention to it. But if the national newspapers picked it up and made something of it, there would have to be a plan, which would almost certainly involve me giving an interview of sorts. For now though, they just needed to know the facts, and they would monitor the situation closely.

'Oh,' I said. 'Is it likely that the national newspapers would be interested?'

'I think they'd be very interested,' she said. 'It would make a great little story.'

'So should I have something prepared, in case I'm asked about it?'

'That would be wise,' said Felicity, and she looked at me expectantly.

'Well,' I said. 'I think maybe the best thing to say would be that it wasn't really my argument. I was just on the side lines. The elderly lady in the shop started the argument, it was her fight, really.'

Felicity shook her head. 'But you wouldn't want it to look as if you were trying to push all the blame for the incident onto the old lady.'

'No?'

'No. You might say something like, there was a lively discussion among all the shoppers in the aisle at the supermarket, and although you personally wouldn't choose to shop in your pyjamas, you are very sympathetic to Ms Shaw's point of view, and you wish her well.'

'Oh,' I said, pleased at how reasonable I was.

'If someone asks why you spoke to Ms Shaw sarcastically, you might say you didn't think you had, and you're very sorry she got that impression, you certainly hadn't meant to be sarcastic – far from it. And obviously, you will be looking and sounding very sincere when you say it.'

'Right, yes.' Obviously I would. Very sincere.

'Does that sound like how it was to you? In the shop?'

'Well, broadly. Probably.'

But Felicity wanted more.

'Yes,' I said. 'That's how it was.'

'Good! Well, I won't take up any more of your time Mrs Forth, and as I said, with any luck this will be an end of it. We'll speak again if we need to take it any further.'

Dan and Felicity passed each other in the hall on her way out. 'Hello Dan,' said Felicity.

'Oh, hello,' he said, and stared after her as she left. He came back into the kitchen with me and asked, 'Who was that?'

'Felicity. She's on the campaign team. Came to talk to me about my altercation in Tesco's the other day. Apparently, I might have to do some sort of interview if the national newspapers decide to report it. God. That would be terrifying. I hope it doesn't come to that. You don't think it will, do you?'

'Really good-looking girl,' said Dan. 'Fantastic bum. Did you notice?'

Actually no, I hadn't noticed, but what I have noticed is the amount of noise and mess coming from Dan's bedroom as he evicts Banana Man and transitions to a Death Star module. The contents of Dan's room are stacked on the upstairs landing, and more is stacked in the hall downstairs ready to go to the tip. There is some curved shelving going up along two sides of his room, to achieve a lozenge effect, and the window is being reconfigured as a porthole. He is sawing up bits of wood in the back garden, and carrying them upstairs to his room with a pencil tucked behind his ear, like a pro.

He said, 'Don't go in my room until it's finished. I don't want you to see it until it's all done.'

'I'm not sure about that, Dan,' I said.

'It'll be fine,' he said. 'Trust me,' and he picked up two long planks of wood and took them upstairs.

Ella called. She said she wanted to know how we were coping with everything. She looked at the piles of stuff in the hall and asked me if someone was moving out.

'No,' I said. 'People move in here but they don't move out. Dan has a project on the go.'

'What on earth is he doing now?' she asked me.

'He's redecorating his bedroom.'

'Well, I hope he has the sense to stick to magnolia.'

There was suddenly a lot of noise from upstairs. Some loud hammering, a prolonged crash and a shout of 'Fuck!' None of which was consistent with sticking to magnolia.

I suggested we moved into the kitchen to have coffee.

'Don't you want to see what's happening up there?' said Ella.

'No,' I said. 'No, I don't.'

So we sat down at the kitchen table for a chat. I told Ella about the pyjama incident in Tesco's. She said in her day, anyone seen out shopping in their pyjamas would have been considered insane and would be on a ward with cot sides up before they could say the word 'Valium'. She said she had been to the dentist this morning, and that was another thing.

I asked if they were all in their pyjamas at the dentist's, and she said no, thank god, but they all call her by her first name, and when did that start to be all right?

'I went in to the reception area,' said Ella, 'to take a seat, and a young girl hailed me from the desk saying – 'Hello Ella! How are you today?' – I just looked at her and said – 'I beg your pardon? Are you talking to me?' – You know what I mean, don't you Sally?'

And I do know what she means, because I have a foot in both worlds, but I tried to explain. 'They think it's more friendly to be informal Ella, they think it's putting you at your ease, and helping you relax and feel comfortable, as if you're among friends.'

'Well I think it's a damned cheek,' said Ella. 'When I was a girl, if I'd called an older person by their first name I would have got a clip around the ear and be told to watch my manners. What's wrong with doing things properly?'

I opened a box of chocolates left over from Christmas and we had some with our coffee. It was consolation for Ella as she continued to mourn the good old days when children were clipped around the ear to teach them how to behave, and half the population were in mental hospitals with their cot sides up and the other half were doing things properly. She's fed up, because she has become an alien in her own back yard, and people she doesn't even know are insisting they're her pal.

When she left, I thought about doing things properly, and I rang Judith.

'Look Judith,' I said, 'I've been thinking about this sponsored swim for the elephant refuge, and I've decided I'll do it. But I'd like to know a bit more about it. What's the refuge called, for a start?'

'I haven't got the name in front of me Sally. It's a funny name, begins with a 'B'. I keep wanting to say Bosoms, but I'm not sure that's right.'

'So, where is it? I know you've told me it's somewhere hot, but can you narrow that down a bit?'

'It's definitely not China. I can tell you that for certain.'

I made Judith promise faithfully to ring me at the earliest opportunity with full details of the refuge in question, including photos, so that I can be properly briefed if I'm asked about it.

***

But Judith didn't ring me, and I forgot I was waiting for her call, and that's the reason everything has gone so badly wrong. There can't be anyone in the whole world now who hasn't seen my stupid interview on breakfast television.

I don't mind admitting that I have a renewed respect for politicians. Their ability to stay calm under bright lights and intense questioning is, in my opinion, superhuman. All those politicians I have sneered at on TV are now demi-gods in my eyes for being able to handle this kind of situation. I am in awe of how effortlessly they can keep calm, and not answer questions.

In the same situation, I did not perform well. I panicked, and I answered questions. Adrenalin flowed through my system like a hot wind over ice cream, and my ability to think straight melted clean away.

They had me on at 8.15 a.m. with Lucy Shaw, the pyjama lady from Tesco's. She sat opposite me on the curved sofa and, naturally, she was in her pyjamas.

'Lucy!' said Louise the presenter, 'you have become a champion of pyjama wear at all times of day, and being a true advocate, you have your pyjamas on for us now!'

'Well it's very early in the morning,' said the true advocate. 'I'm never out of my pyjamas at quarter past eight.'

'But when you were in the supermarket with Sally Forth, it was two o'clock in the afternoon. Shouldn't you have been out of your pyjamas by then, Lucy?'

'Not if I don't feel like it. I don't tell you what to wear, do I? You can wear what you like as far as I'm concerned. You could be sitting there in your bathing costume. I wouldn't mind.'

'So tell us, Lucy,' said our eager presenter, all engaging and cosy, 'what do you like about wearing your pyjamas all day?'

'Well it's comfortable, and it's up to you, isn't it, what you wear?'

And then Louise turned to me. 'Well, that's true, isn't it, Sally? Isn't it true that it's up to you what you wear?'

'Yes,' I said, decisively. 'And no. Some people find it a little disturbing to see people out in their pyjamas during the day. And I wonder whether we need to consider their feelings?' I was thinking of Maureen Pugh.

'What do you think, Lucy? Do we need to consider the feelings of people who might find daytime pyjama wear 'disturbing'?'

'Disturbing? Why should they be disturbed by pyjamas? That's weird.'

Again, the radiant smile turned in my direction. 'Are you disturbed by pyjamas Sally?'

I decided to move things sideways. I wanted to get myself out of any deep water associated with being disturbed by pyjamas before things became any more Freudian. But as it happened, and as everybody now knows, this turned out to be a big mistake.

'Actually Louise I was hoping, now that I'm here, I might be able to talk briefly about my charity work.'

'Charity work?' Louise glanced down at a paper on the coffee table in front of her, looking for, and not finding any mention of charity work. 'What charity work? Tell us a bit about your charity work, Sally.'

'Well,' I said, 'I'm doing a sponsored swim to raise money for an elephant refuge in, in a place abroad.'

'An elephant refuge? Oh dear,' said Louise. 'And why do the elephants need a refuge?'

'They're distressed elephants,' I said. 'Unfortunately.'

'That does sound unfortunate,' said Louise. 'And what is causing them distress?'

'All the usual things,' I said. 'All the usual things that distress elephants. Foot problems. Wasps.'

'Wasps?'

'And foot problems.'

'I wouldn't have thought an elephant would have been bothered by wasps.'

'And junk food. Junk food is a problem.'

'Junk food?'

'Yes. Junk food is a massive problem today. And not just for elephants.'

'I can see this is a project very close to your heart, Sally,' said Louise.

'It is, yes. It's very close to my heart,' I said, trying to smile.

'How interesting! So tell us, where is the elephants' refuge?'

'Where? Well, it's definitely not in China, I can tell you that for certain.'

'I see, so we have to guess!' Louise gave me a dazzling smile. 'Africa maybe? India?'

'Yes,' I said, knowledgeably. 'I was going to suggest Africa.'

She nodded. 'And the name of this refuge...?'

'...begins with a 'B'.'

'That sounds mysterious?'

'Not really, no. Lots of places begin with 'B'. Brighton begins with a 'B'. And of course, Brecon Beacons has two Bs. So – not particularly mysterious.'

'Ah! So the refuge is in the Brecon Beacons?'

'Is it?' This took me by surprise. 'I didn't know there were elephants in the Brecon Beacons.'

'Aren't there?'

'Are there?'

'I thought you said there were?'

'There might be. It's a long time since I've been to the Brecon Beacons.'

'Jesus,' said Lucy Shaw, somewhere to my left.

'I think we've got our wires crossed a bit here,' said Louise. 'Can you give us the name of the refuge Sally? Our listeners might want to look it up.'

'Yes of course. As I said, it begins with a 'B'. I think it's Bosoms.'

'Bosoms? I see. So, Sally, tell us a bit about Bosoms?'

'Well...' The lights were very hot and bright, and I was aware that this was going terribly wrong. 'There are a number of elephants taking refuge in Bosoms, and, er...' I heard supressed laughter coming from somewhere, but I couldn't see beyond the lights.

'Have you visited Bosoms yourself, Sally, to see the elephants?'

'Em, as I said, elephants are very close to my heart, so obviously, I want to see them taking refuge in Bosoms, and so, er... Yes.'

Louise bashed on, enjoying herself far too much to stop, 'So, have you brought any photographs to show us, Sally?'

'Actually Louise,' I said, my mind now a quaking void, 'I don't think I have any photographes of Bosoms to pass around. But could I just say one last thing about pyjamas? And then maybe Lucy could come back in?'

'Pyjamas? Of course! Go ahead Sally.'

'I think pyjamas are really uncomfortable.' It was the best I could do.

'Do you prefer a nightie in bed, Sally?'

'No,' I said. 'I don't wear anything in bed.'

I heard laughter, and I could just make out someone standing behind the camera gesturing cutting his own throat.

I got a quick call from Felicity as I was leaving the building. She said she had seen the interview and was she just ringing to say, don't do any more. She said interviews could be very tricky and she'd noticed me falling into a few traps. She was kind enough not to say elephant traps. I said I wasn't planning to do any more interviews, and she said good. That's good.

When I got home, I sat with my head in my hands on the kitchen table and groaned aloud.

Dan came in and said, 'Hey Mum! That was hysterical! You've already got loads of hits on YouTube.'

Well, I've knocked that Flood Gran clean out of the water. She can sink or swim as far as our local Press are concerned. Nobody cares about her or her insurance policies any more, because I am the gran of the moment.

MP Spouse Gran Reveals All! says the billboard outside the Co-op. And that's me.

I asked Bill last night whether he thought I'd blown everything with the Breakfast TV interview.

He said no, he didn't think so. He said the team had watched the interview and decided that I had come across as unprepared and a bit bonkers, but they didn't think it would be especially damaging because fortunately, no animal or human was harmed during the course of the interview, except me. I had limited the damage to myself, and had managed to hold only myself up to ridicule.

So. That was good to know. Well done me.

Bill says he will have to deal with some quips about my nightwear, or lack of it. He has already been asked if there was any truth in the rumour that he had been too mean to buy me a pair of pyjamas at Christmas.

He said if anyone says anything to me when I'm out and about, I should smile and wave, but don't rise to any bait because it will bite back. I said don't worry, I'm done with answering questions. A wave and a smile is all I have for anyone now. Good, he said. That's fine then.

***

I was in school today. In a maths lesson with Lee. I didn't think there was much chance he would have seen or heard about my TV interview, but I couldn't be sure because he can be surprisingly well informed.

'Miss,' he said when he saw me, 'I heard on the telly you don't wear no pyjamas in bed.'

I was calm and unruffled, and said wisely, 'You shouldn't believe everything you hear on TV, Lee.'

'But it was you said it. On the telly the other morning. I heard you.'

'Well, what of it Lee? It's not very interesting news. Let's think about your maths.'

'My dad thought it was interesting. He don't wear no pyjamas neither. He wears boxer shorts.'

'Well, thanks for that, Lee,' I said. 'Now then,' I pointed to his maths exercise book, 'let's make a start on some of these. What's three times nought?'

'Nought,' he said. 'Do you want to know what I wear in bed?'

'No thank you, Lee. So three times nought is…?'

'Nought. Only, I know what you wear in bed, so I thought— '

'Nought?' I said. 'How can three times nought be nought? You've still got your three, surely?'

'It's nought. I'm surprised you don't get cold in bed with no pyjamas on.'

'I'm warm enough thank you, Lee. Now let's move on. Nought? It can't be nought.'

'It is. It's nought. You could just wear the trouser part, on cold nights. If you wanted.'

'I'll bear that in mind. How can three times nought be nought? It's got to be three. Think about it.'

'I am thinking about it. It's nought. Or you could just wear the top part instead of the trouser part. But then your bum would get cold if it stuck out of the duvet.'

'I'm grateful for your concern, Lee, but let's keep my bum out of this if you don't mind. Concentrate for me please – three, multiplied by nothing, is…?'

'Like I said – nothing. You could try a nightie. Some women wear nighties.'

The maths teacher was doing his rounds, so I motioned him over to our table and said, 'Mr Parks, Lee is having a bit of a problem with three times nought. I've told him it's three, but he's insisting it's nought. Can you help us out here?'

Mr Parks is a maths teacher and sometimes the subtleties of a social situation can escape him.

'Lee's absolutely right,' he said. 'And you're wrong. Three times nought is nought. How could it possibly be otherwise? Well done, Lee. Crack on.'

Lee looked at me with cheerful concern. 'You're not very good at maths, are you Miss? You're good on the telly though. My dad says you're the funniest thing since Morecambe and Wise.'

Chapter 9 – February

In the days since my TV interview, I have had forty-eight pairs of pyjamas sent to me through the post. One package simply addressed, 'To the Butt Naked Wife of Bill Forth'. Amazing, isn't it? Forty-eight pairs. Some had a note inside them. One said, 'I find these really comfortable, but your need is greater than mine.' Another pair were decorated with pink elephants, and came with a note, 'Saw these and thought of you.' In a slightly creepy variation on the same theme, one enclosed a photograph and said, 'Wear these and think of me.'

A local radio phone-in programme ran a little discussion on what people wear in bed, and I was contacted and asked if I would like to make a comment. But I told them I had said all I intended to say on the subject and really, I didn't have anything new to add. Interest seems to have died down now, and I'm hoping the whole thing has blown over.

Judith rang me, and asked me why on earth I hadn't rung her to get more details about the elephant refuge before going on TV?

I said, 'What good would that have done, Judith? You didn't know anything about the elephant refuge.'

She said, 'You'll have to do the swim now, otherwise people will think you just made the whole distressed elephants thing up.'

I said, 'I have every intention of doing the swim. I've said I'll do it, and I'll do it. Even though I am considerably more distressed than any of the sodding elephants.'

***

Only a few more days to go until the leadership election. I'm aiming to keep a low profile. I find that works best.

I'm concentrating on the problem of what to do with forty-eight pairs of ladies' pyjamas, all surplus to requirements. I tried to think of somewhere which might be struggling to decently clothe forty-eight women, all on the point of turning in for bed, but I drew a blank. I scanned the internet for any requests for help in this area, searching for posts along the lines of 'Please! We are forty-eight ladies with not a pair of pyjamas between us. CAN YOU HELP?' But no luck.

Eventually Sophie said she could take them off my hands and use them at work in the care home where, on occasions, a spare pair of clean pyjamas is worth more than rubies.

Had a bizarre conversation with Susan over the fence this afternoon. I was sorting out a pile of recycling when –

'Sally!' she called over in that urgent, confiding tone she uses for her significant utterances. 'Sally, your lad Baz has caught another mole. I've got the pair now. Now then. I'm looking for a taxidermist, and I wondered if you knew of any?'

I wanted to be helpful, because Susan has eased her stance on Aspire. I wanted to be able to say, actually Susan, I can recommend Timothy's of Pimlico, they see to all my taxidermy needs.

'Sorry, Susan,' I said, 'I don't know if we have a local taxidermist.'

'Maybe if I ask at the doctors' surgery?'

'The surgery? You could try, I suppose. It's not really their line though, is it? At least, you'd hope not. Why don't you just google taxidermists and see what comes up? I think that's the best way.'

'Yes I've done that. But I was hoping for a personal recommendation.'

'Can't help you there Susan, I'm afraid.'

'I'll try the surgery,' she said. 'They were very interested in Derek's stomach.'

'Okay,' I said, 'good plan.' No further progress was possible because I had no idea what she was talking about. 'Let me know how you get on.'

And I went back to the recycling.

***

I've only heard from Jen once since my humiliation on national television. She sent me a text saying, Saw your interview. Hilarious!! Absolutely priceless! What were you thinking?! Such a laugh. Speak soon.

It wasn't the sort of comforting, never-mind-it'll-all-come-out-in-the-wash-don't-worry-about-it response I could have hoped for. Rather cavalier, I thought, after all my concern for her recent predicaments. I decided to give Jen a ring, and ask how she was, in the hope that this might prompt her to ask how I was. That's how things are supposed to work.

'I'm good!' Jen said. 'Great! I'm really good. Sam's here at the moment. Staying a while. Great guy! Yeah. Lovely guy. All good here. Did you want something?'

'I just wanted to ask, how's things? That's all really. Just wondered how you were.'

'Yeah, great. I'm really great. Listen, Sally,' she said, 'what are you up to, at the moment?'

'I did the recycling yesterday. I humiliated myself on national TV last week. What do you mean, what am I up to?'

'I mean, what are you up to? What are you doing, for you? What plans have you got, just for you? What's, you know, floating your boat at the moment? I meant to ask you at Christmas, but I forgot.'

'Well,' I said, 'we've got this election on the go. I've got to think about how to recover from being an idiot on the telly. I'm not at a loose end, exactly.'

'Yes, but, you know, what about you? After the election, what are you going to get into?'

'God, Jen, I don't know. A hot bath, probably.'

'You need to think about it,' she said. 'You're too young just to be somebody's wife.'

So I did think about it, while I was making a lasagne for dinner. What am I into? What floats my boat? I was staring out of the window, thinking, when Baz knocked politely on the kitchen door. He came in, and as always, he unlaced his boots on the door mat.

'I've been talking to Mrs Dingbat next door,' he said. 'She's looking for a taxidermist to stuff those moles. I've told her I'll do it. I've been thinking about it anyway, adding taxidermy to my skills set. I've told her to keep them in the freezer until I've looked it up on YouTube.'

'YouTube?' I said. 'Taxidermy?'

'Yeah yeah,' he said, 'it's easy. You can learn how to do it on YouTube. It's a piece of cake. Or it's a piece of meat. I reckon I could be quite good at it. Obviously, you have to do it so that things look normal, you know, naturally shaped. You can't have a mole looking like a ripe banana. But basically, it's just stuffing stuff. What I'm thinking is that if I can do gardening, catch moles and then stuff the buggers, I'll have more to offer my clients. Once I get the Vespa.'

I nodded.

'Of course, I'd learn to stuff other stuff. I'm not just going to just stuff moles. But it would be a good place to start.'

I told him I admired his can-do attitude, and then he said, 'Can I do it here, in the utility room? I'll need a bright light and a bit of bench space.'

'Er, I don't think so Baz. Seriously. I don't think that's a good idea. We can't have entrails draped around the dishwasher. It wouldn't be hygienic. It would make too much mess.'

'No, no. No mess. I'd just bring the skins in here, there'd hardly be any mess at all. You'd make more mess carving a chicken. But it's up to you, of course. I can find somewhere else to do it.' He went into the utility room to assess its suitability for conversion to a taxidermy studio. 'This would be fantastic though, bright light, plenty of bench space. Here's Sophie now,' he said, looking out of the window. 'She's talking to a bunch of men with cameras and microphones. I think she's being interviewed by someone.'

'No,' I said.

'Yes, she is. She's being interviewed. She's chatting away there. Looks quite relaxed. Don't worry, she's handling it.'

'Oh God,' I said. 'What's she saying?' I went to look. 'Oh no.'

'She's really letting rip out there,' he said, watching her as he leant against the bench top with his arms folded, smiling fondly, full of admiration. 'She's giving it both barrels. Not mincing her words, I reckon. What a girl. She's a corker. Look at that. Waving her arms and everything.'

'Baz,' I said. 'Go out there and tell her dinner's ready. Tell her to come in.'

'She's finished now. Here she comes, she's coming in. What a star.'

The kitchen door flew open. 'Hiya! Guess what? I'm going to be on the telly! Tonight!'

I sent Bill a text to warn him. Bill, Sophie was interviewed coming into the house. Local TV crew I think. Likely to be shown this evening. God knows what she's said. She was ambushed and I wasn't quick enough. Sorry Bill. Maybe it will be ok? Xx

It was an anxious wait until the local evening news on TV. Sophie went out to buy popcorn, Dan rang Chrissy and suggested she left work early, Baz sent a message to all his phone contacts telling them to watch. Bill was not going to be home until late, but he and his team were in the brace position.

I summoned up the courage to ask Sophie what she had said, thinking it might be better to be prepared. Depending on what response she gave, I might decide not to watch at all.

'What did they ask you about, Sophie?' I said, holding on to the edge of the kitchen table for support.

She was so excited she was barely coherent. 'Lots of stuff,' she said. 'Stuff about sleeping arrangements and other stuff. I'm so excited! I've always wanted to be on the telly! I'm just worried my hair won't look all right. I should have had it tied back. I always have it tied back at work but it came loose on the bus. I kept sort of shaking my head a bit so it wouldn't flop forward.'

'Sleeping arrangements?' My blood ran a little cold.

'Yeah,' she said. 'Sleeping arrangements. But it was a bit windy and my hair kept flopping forwards. I didn't want to put my hand in front of my face, you know? It might look as if I'm hiding something or something? So I just kept shaking my head a bit to keep my hair back. Do you think that'll look okay?'

I rang Laura to warn her.

'Did Sophie tell you what she's said?' Laura asked me.

'I can't get much sense out of her. She's worried about how her hair is going to look.'

'Oh god yes. It's very windy isn't it? I bet her hair was all over the place.'

'She said they asked her about the sleeping arrangements here.'

'Sleeping arrangements? They'll be looking for great headlines. **MP in Three-in-a-Bed Orgy Romps!** That's what they want.'

'Oh god.'

'Don't worry, Mum. Sophie will put them straight.'

'Oh god.'

'Anyway. I'll go and put the telly on. Don't want to miss it. Catch you later.'

I put the phone down, and went into the lounge. The television was on, everyone was assembled, the local news was starting, and there was a little introductory piece about the price of housing and how all the generations are having to bunk up together, and one such household being that of... Sophie was beside herself with excitement: 'It's me! I'm on next! Shut up everybody! Quiet! Look! That's me!'

And there she was on the television screen, our very own Sophie walking along the road towards our house, frowning slightly at the man approaching her with a microphone.

'Sophie Sullivan, am I right in thinking you're living with the Forths at the moment? And if so, would you mind if we asked you a few questions for our viewers? We're interested to hear your views about the accommodation problems in our area.'

'Are you off the telly?'

'That's right. Sophie, do you consider yourself to be lucky to live with Bill and Sally Forth?'

'Yeah. Dead lucky.' Sophie looked straight into the camera lens, and said solemnly, 'I consider myself dead lucky to be living with the Forths.'

'Good, er...' The interviewer waved slightly to attract her attention away from the lens of the camera. 'Sophie, some people have said that it's odd that so many young people are living with the Forths. What would you say to them?'

'Well there's just me and Baz, and Dan of course, and Chrissy at the moment, and before me there was someone called Gentle Rain, which is a crap name if you ask me. So not that many, really.'

'There have been unconfirmed reports of licentious behaviour at the Forth household, can you deny that outright?'

'Mrs Forth said if anyone asked I should just say 'hello', or 'lovely day', or 'awful day'.'

'Sophie, there are rumours circulating about parties at the Forth household which Mr and Mrs Forth themselves may be involved with, parties with freely available drugs and sex on offer. Is this your experience?'

'What? Sex? At the Forth's? Drugs and sex?' Sophie laughed in astonishment, and had to steady herself against the gate post. 'Drugs and sex? Mr and Mrs Forth?' She wiped an incredulous tear from her eye. 'Mr and Mrs Forth don't have sex.'

'Oh. So, are you categorically denying these rumours?'

'Look,' said Sophie, 'I probably shouldn't be telling you this but,' she motioned the interviewer closer, 'don't say anything, but I'm in the bedroom next to Mr and Mrs Forth, and I don't think they have sex any more. They're too busy. They talk about stuff, but then I think they go to sleep. I know, 'cos I hear them snoring. They're lovely really, but I don't think they – you know – do anything. They talk about elections instead.'

'Ah. And er, drugs? Are there drugs on the premises?'

'Drugs? Well, I've got some paracetamol. Mrs Forth wants us all to take multivitamins, but Dan says we don't need to if we eat broccoli.'

'Right, well.' The interviewer gave a little cough to cover some slight embarrassment. 'It seems some of these rumours aren't accurate. So, there are no wild parties at the Forth residence, in your experience?'

'We've just had one party, at Christmas. Just a family do. That was quite a good party, but nobody got drunk at that. Oh – except Mrs Forth. She got drunk. But she wasn't bad. She was able to walk about still, and she wasn't sick or anything. You'd hardly notice apart from some of the things she was saying, and her dress was a bit wet where she spilled her wine. You know,' she became reflective, 'Mrs Forth was my favourite teacher at school. She tried to teach me English for five years. And that's a long time to bang on about the apostrophe.'

'Really? Five years? Okay, so Sophie, would you mind telling us what accommodation you have with the Forths? Do you have your own room?'

'Yes, I've got my own room. I don't have to share. There's a washbasin in the corner.' Sophie turned, and again she spoke straight at the camera lens with gravitas. 'I'm absolutely thrilled to have my own room with the Forths. It has a washbasin and everything. It is a dream come true.'

'Right, er... Finally, Sophie, can you sum up for us – why do you like living with the Forths?'

'Hmm,' she thought about it. 'Because, I can get to work and back easily, and Baz is in the room upstairs from me, and most days we all have dinner together in the evenings and have a laugh. It's good to have a laugh over your dinner, don't you think?'

'Thank you Sophie.'

'Oh!' she said, putting her hand on the interviewer's arm. 'I've just remembered.' She rummaged in her bag. 'Look at this!' And she pulled out a *Mr Forth First!* T-shirt. 'I got these made.' She held it up close for the camera, and for a second or two it was all we could see on the screen. Then it was whipped away to reveal Sophie's beaming face. 'What do you think of that? Do you want one?' she asked the interviewer. 'Seeing as I've done this interview?'

'Yes, thanks Sophie,' said the interviewer. 'I'll take one. Thank you.'

'Great,' she said. 'That'll be five pounds.'

And we were transferred back to the news room.

Dan switched the sound off when the interview finished. Sophie looked around at us all. 'Was that okay?' she said. 'Did I do all right?'

'You did really well, Sophie,' said Dan.

Bill texted, about an hour after the interview was aired. He said, She might actually save the day. Shame about our sex life.

***

So, how did that happen? I appeared on television and managed to make a complete idiot of myself, then Sophie appears on TV, ambushed, totally unprepared, no prior briefing, and comes out covered in glory. I crept around for days after my television appearance hoping no-one would recognise me, and Sophie is flouncing around in her 'Mr Forth First!' T-shirt, being applauded on the streets and in the media.

Those T-shirts are selling like hot cakes. And Sophie's appearance has spawned others; one says on the front, 'It's good to have a laugh over your dinner.' And on the back it says, 'Don't you think?' Another doing the rounds says on the front, 'Have sex or talk about elections?' and on the back it says, 'Tough call.'

There is a little item on the BBC website today, 'Bill Forth's biggest fan? The Sophie Interview.' And of course, the billboard outside the Co-op has gone into meltdown – **MP Lodger Sophie A Sensation!**

Nothing for it but to grin and bear it. It has given a boost to Bill's campaign in a quirky sort of way, although I feel that certain aspects of my reputation may have been sacrificed. All in a good cause, I suppose, and my colours are nailed to this mast.

The latest thing now is that our local paper is doing a little feature on Sophie, they want to talk to her about being a young person leaving school and looking for jobs and accommodation in our area. They plan to do the interview here, and take a photo of Sophie at work.

In the meantime, I have to do my sponsored swim. One hundred lengths? Really, I don't think that's going to be possible. Judith swims regularly, but I only swim on holiday to cool off, and I shoot out of the pool vertically like a penguin as soon as someone shouts, 'Does anyone fancy a nice cold glass of white?'

But it had to be done, so I found my costume and went down to the baths this morning. Judith was warming up when I got there, and she suggested I do the same. I said no, I didn't know how many lengths I had in me, but I wasn't going to waste any of them on a warm-up. She swam to the side and said I should have done some training, really. I reminded her that she'd said I didn't need to train, I could just walk. She denied having said that, and told me I'd have to swim.

'Okay,' I said, 'let's get this over with.'

Someone from the baths was counting our lengths officially, and would give us some sort of certificate when we finished to verify our performance. She blew a whistle and Judith launched herself into the pool like a torpedo. I launched myself into the pool like an arthritic tortoise, and asked if they could turn the heat up a bit.

Judith went up and down that pool until I began to think she was fathered by a fish. God Almighty, the woman must have gills. I stopped for a breather every time I got to the deep end to have a chat with the officiator, Paula. She told me all about her husband's hernia while we watched Judith power up and down and I got my breath back, and was ready to strike out for the shallow end again.

Paula gave me some advice after my fifteenth length, and said I would manage better if I swam more horizontally through the water. She said I was swimming in a very cramped, upright position, cutting through the water like a submarine periscope and doing breast stroke with my upper arms clamped to my sides. She said it was an unusual technique, closer to a sea horse than anything else she could think of. She said I must be doing some very efficient paddling with my feet, and she was surprised I stayed afloat. I agreed, and said my technique was lousy and to get any forward momentum my feet had to spin round like propellers.

Anyway, by the time Judith finished I had done thirty-two lengths, and I pronounced myself finished too. Judith said, 'What about your sponsorship money?' And I said, 'Bugger the sponsorship money – that's your lot.' So we both agreed to call it a day.

When I got home I had an odd phone call from the doctors' surgery. The practice manager spoke to me and said she understood I had been telling people that their surgery offered a taxidermy service, and she wondered where I had got that information from? She said they'd like to nip that rumour in the bud because it didn't fit well with their mission statement. No sooner had I sorted that out, than the reporter from the Echo arrived, and we sat down and waited for Sophie to get changed after work and come downstairs.

I took the opportunity to ask the young reporter about the paper's fascination with grandmas. She didn't know what I was talking about at first, so I had to explain. Eventually she said she thought it might have something to do with people's expectations of older women, but she would ask her boss. I asked if her boss was a grandma but she looked puzzled, so I don't think I got my point across.

Sophie came downstairs, and I was going to leave them both to it, but the reporter asked me if I would like to stay. It was interesting to listen in. I could see the angle the reporter was going for. Sophie was a young, impassioned carer, desperate to hold down her job, plucked off the street and saved from destitution by a rich householder with a bit of a conscience and more rooms in her house than she knew what to do with. But Sophie didn't always fit the stereotype.

'Sophie, were you incredibly relieved when Mrs Forth told you you could come and live here and continue with your work at the care home? I expect it was an answer to your prayers?'

'Well, I knew I would be able to twist her arm. She was my English teacher and she always believed me when I said I would bring my coursework in the next day. Even though I hardly ever did. And if I said, "Honestly Miss, I haven't copied any of my coursework off the internet", she would never say, "You're lying". So I thought she probably would let me stay if I told her I couldn't go back home.'

'Oh,' the reporter glanced at me before writing something down.

Sophie watched as the reporter wrote, and said, 'Write down that I really love it here, because that's the most important thing.'

'Do you think you will ever be able to afford a place of your own in this area, Sophie?'

'No, not a house or a flat or anything. But Baz says boats are cheaper. Maybe I'll be able to live on a boat. I'd like to live on a boat but at the moment the river is in the wrong place for me. Baz's friend Chaz lives on a boat. I think we'll probably all live on boats eventually, and just float around until we get old.'

After the interview and the arrangement for the photo at the care home, the reporter asked me rather archly about my 'charity work' and the sponsored swim. She was a little taken aback when I told her I'd just finished my sponsored swim; maybe she thought I'd made the whole thing up. 'How far did you swim?' she asked me.

'Well, I was supposed to swim a hundred lengths of the pool, but bloody hell, I didn't get anywhere near that.'

'How many did you do?'

'Thirty-two,' I said. 'But I put a lot of effort in, and no-one need know.'

***

Well, no-one need have known. But this morning, down at the Co-op: **'MP Spouse Gran's Sponsored Swim Shame!'**

I bought a paper and glanced at the article, then got straight on the phone and asked for the reporter who did the interview yesterday, and they put me on hold. While I was waiting, I had a better idea. I got the car, and parked on a double yellow line outside the Co-op. I was only there long enough to jump out, open the boot, and grapple with the billboard. A passer-by gave me a hand, and we dumped it in the boot of my car. There will be other billboards, but at least I'd got one of them.

I thanked the kind lady who helped me. She said it was the least she could do, she still watched my TV interview on You Tube every time she needed a good laugh.

I sat in the car for a few minutes to calm down once I got home, and then I looked to see what Lois Lane had said about me in her article. The heading for the piece was 'Homes Ahoy!' There was a photo on the front page of Sophie at work in the care

255

home. She was in her uniform, and she had her arm around a very thin, elderly lady sitting next to her, who was wearing a *Mr Forth First!* T-shirt. The shirt was folded and pleated awkwardly across the lady's narrow and ancient bosom, so the only letters remaining in view spelled improbably, 'Moist!'

The offending text came right at the end of the interview with Sophie. It read:

> 'Before I left the Forth household I asked Mrs Sally Forth about the progress of the charity work she tried to talk about on Breakfast TV last week. She told me she had just done her sponsored swim, to raise money for the mystery elephant refuge. She said she swam less than half the prescribed distance, but she wasn't going to confess, because no-one need know. Oops, Mrs Forth, hope we haven't dropped you in it!'

I was furious. I had done my best in that pool, swimming up and down, wheezing and grunting like a set of sodden bagpipes for much longer than was good for me. And as a result I'm accused of doing something shameful. I'm glad that billboard is in the boot of my car, and I have no intention of giving it back. Or maybe I could use a permanent marker to write my own headline, and post it somewhere prominent. **Avenging Gran In Billboard Heist!** That should do it.

***

My mood spilled over into my session with Lee at school this morning.

'Hiya Miss!' he said when he saw me, and he was so cheerful I sensed trouble and was immediately on the defensive.

'Listen Lee, I don't want to hear any remarks today about my pyjamas, or my ability to swim, or any other aspect of my personal life which you may have heard mentioned on TV, or in the newspapers. I don't want to know what you think, and

I don't want to know what your dad thinks. At all. Do you understand?'

'Yes.'

'Yes?'

'Yes Miss.'

'Good. Because if we can understand each other, we'll get on just fine this morning, but if we can't, there will be serious trouble. I mean it Lee. Okay?'

'Okay.'

'I'm just not in the mood for any stupid remarks. Right?'

'Right.'

'Good.'

'My dad says you probably just need a good rogering.'

I'd had quite enough of Lee by the time I left school at lunchtime. Home felt like a refuge for distressed women, despite an evolving Death Star in an upstairs bedroom, and the prospect of taxidermy-lite taking place downstairs in the utility room.

And now it's the night before the count. The leadership election is nearly over and we should have the result by four o'clock tomorrow. I wanted a quiet evening, with my feet up and a glass of wine and something soothing and uncontroversial on television. Bill, when he got home, wanted the same. We sat together on the sofa and watched a programme about wildebeest. We watched them racing in panicky herds across the savannah, and Bill said it reminded him of the division lobby of the House of Commons.

After the wildebeest, Bill and I went early to bed, because tomorrow is going to be a long, long day. Sophie made us each cocoa as we were preparing to go to bed, and we set off upstairs carrying our mugs like good children. Once safely in our room, we sat on the bed to drink the cocoa and talk to each other, before settling down. It was an interesting talk. Bill gave me some insights into his career as a politician which he has never mentioned before.

They were prompted by a text from Jen. *Exciting eh? Are you nervous? Someone said on the box last night Bill might win!!*

I texted back to say, *Yes, very exciting. Very nervous. Not long to wait now.*

I showed this exchange on my phone to Bill. 'Good news?'

'No. Not really.'

'Do you think there's any possibility of winning this?'

'No chance,' he said.

'Strange to hear you say that when you're so upbeat on television.'

He smiled. 'Well I can hardly be seen to sink my own ship. Someone else can sink it, but I can't. I was never going to win this.'

'Why did you agree to stand?'

'Oh, all sorts of reasons. It's not always about winning. Sometimes it's about making a good job of losing.'

'But you have a team working on your campaign. Fiona, and the others. They must think you could win? Otherwise what are they working for?'

'They're working towards me losing by a respectably slim margin. I was never a front runner. If I do better than expected they can take the credit. They're very young, they're just cutting their teeth on my campaign. They don't tell me I'll lose, obviously, but that's what they expect. They've worked hard. I'm sorry I won't be able to give them a win, but they'll go on to better things, and promote a winner next time. And that's all right. That's how it should be. It's pretty obvious who the winner will be tomorrow.'

'You mean, because she's a woman? The papers are saying it's time a woman got the job.'

'Well, not just that. She's got a lot going for her. She's very attractive, she's energetic, she's very clever, she can crack a good joke. She's relaxed, she doesn't have that head-girl-earnestness that can hobble women in politics. She can take a risk and be lucky. And she has a lot more hair on her head than me. She has more hair on her head than her closest rival, and he has an impressive head of hair. And of course he looks like a toothpaste advert, which is a huge advantage in public life. He's always tucking his hair behind his ears, have you noticed? I think he does that to draw attention to it. He knows hair attracts votes.'

'I never know when you're being serious.'

'I'm very serious. I read somewhere that there's a positive correlation between the number of hairs on your head and the number of votes cast for you in a by-election. I don't have enough hair on my head to get the top job. Apart from Winston Churchill, there's only been two PMs since 1945 who had no hair, Clement Attlee and Alex Douglas Hume, and he only lasted a year. And then of course, my face isn't right.'

'What's wrong with your face?'

'Nothing's wrong with it as such, it's just not a winner's face. I can't win at this level with this face. At this level, I have the face of a stalwart loser. I would have done better with this face in politics just after the war in the 1940s. Faces weren't so important then. But I would have been up against Churchill. He didn't have hair, but he didn't need it in 1951, he'd just saved the country from annihilation.'

'What about policies? I thought politics was all about policies?'

'That's a common mistake a lot of people make. Even experienced politicians can fall into that trap. Policies are important of course, it's useful to have a few policies to wave about. But it's also about personality and engagement, and warmth, and who likes you and who doesn't, and what kind of gut feeling people get when they look at you. And what persona the Press choose to give you. And what photographs of you do the rounds. I could have a problem there because my smile isn't right.'

'Your smile? What's wrong with your smile?'

'It's potentially demonic. If I put a foot wrong in office, the papers would give me red eyes and a couple of horns and a little forky tail, and I'd be Lucifer himself. Look at me – when I smile I'd make such a good anti-Christ.' He grinned. 'See?' He pointed to his mouth. 'This canine tooth doesn't help. Fiona suggested I have the point filed off. Also of course, there's my voice.'

'Your voice?'

'Yes, I can sound hesitant when I'm being interviewed. As if I'm hedging my bets, as if I'm trying to work out what not to say. Actually – it's true – I am trying to work out what not to say, but it shouldn't tell in my voice. It makes me sound as if I'm covering something up, when actually I just don't want to make myself a hostage to fortune. So I have to be very careful, because when I'm trying to sound less hesitant I can sound annoyed. And that's a disaster.'

'Anything else?'

'I could do with being about four inches taller. In fact, if I had an extra six inches, that might even cancel out my face. Difficult to say for sure because it's not a straightforward calculation. But in politics, the taller you are, the less your face matters. Unless you're hideously ugly, of course, in which case being very tall would probably be a disadvantage. And interestingly it's the other way around for the voice. The taller you are, the more your voice matters. If you're six foot eight tall, people will pay close attention to your voice, and judge it. More so than if you're five foot four.'

I shook my head. 'How do you know all this?'

'More than twenty years in politics? It's bound to teach you something.'

'So, what do you have going for you?'

'Ah! I do have something going for me. I'm not particularly memorable, so people can't remember whether I was associated with any measures in the past they didn't like. They don't remember that it was me who pissed them off. I'm more taint-proof than my good-looking, glossy-haired rivals. Of course, equally, people might not remember me well enough to give me any credit, when credit's due. But in this game, the punishment you get for being wrong is greater than the credit you get for being right. It's more important not to be wrong, than to be right. If you're right about something people say, 'Well, looking back, it was obvious that was the right decision to make.' Which means you're not so clever for being the only one to make it. But if you're wrong, people say you should have known you were wrong, and you were an idiot, and you'll always be an idiot and always be wrong. They won't forgive you.'

'Would you say you enjoyed politics, Bill? Honestly?'

'Honestly? I love it. It's fascinating. Even when it's dull. I'm fine about tomorrow. I'm not expecting to win.'

'I think that's a shame. You have a lot to offer, and you'd do a good job.'

'Well I'd try my best, obviously. But there are no guarantees of turning good intentions into good outcomes.'

'I'm not so convinced you won't win.'

'I won't. But it won't get me down. Considering I don't look right or sound right and I'm not hairy enough or tall enough, I've done extremely well in politics. Up to now. We should be celebrating. I just needed the whole package to make this last jump, and I don't have it.' He shrugged. 'Too bad.'

'So – what if the two front runners drop dead overnight?'

'What, both of them? Wiped out overnight? Wonder Woman and the Handsome Hairball? Oh well, in that case I'd walk it. I'd romp home. I'd have world domination in my grasp. I'd be the Boss.' And he smiled a satisfied, demonic smile, and toasted me with his cocoa cup.

He's asleep now, and he looks quite harmless.

***

Rather touchingly, everyone was here today, they were all at home for the count. Ella came round, and Laura. Dan, Chrissy, Sophie and Baz had all arranged for time off work, and were all here after lunch. It became a party, long before the result came in. I wasn't sure about opening the champagne at lunchtime, but events were gathering momentum and there was no stopping them. The television was on, of course, although there was so much noise I didn't hear much of it. There was a taxi coming for me at two, so that I could be there with Bill for the announcement.

Sophie and Ella wanted to know what I planned to wear. I tried a few things on, and they picked something out for me. They told me that my chosen outfit made me look too formal and stuffy, and they were both so much in agreement, I took their word for it. So I left wearing something comfortable, fortunately, because there was so much about the rest of the day that wasn't.

I arrived shortly after ten to three, and the room was packed with people. There was a lot of noise. It was very warm; all the lights were contributing to the heat. Everyone found a seat close to four o'clock and I sat next to Bill at the front. Before the announcement at nearly ten past four, all the candidates were in the spotlight. But once the result was announced Bill was totally eclipsed, very definitely an also-ran of no further significance. All the focus was on the winner, and she received it well. She was gracious in victory and made a sincere and genuinely funny little acceptance speech. She was generous in thanks for her support team, and considerate in not boring us with talk of new dawns. She got it just right.

I wanted to leave the party an hour or so after the result was announced, but Bill said no. He said the winner had deserved her win, and it had to be properly celebrated. He didn't want to be seen sneaking away early with his tail between his legs. I saw his point, so I circulated a little and struck up a few conversations here and there. I spoke briefly with another woman who was, like me, standing by herself, scanning the room and holding a glass of fizz.

Once we had swapped introductions and had both acknowledged the winner's victory and given her due credit, my new friend Amanda asked me what I did. I said I used to be a teacher. 'Oh,' said Amanda, 'Gosh. So what are you now?'

I was stumped. I tried to think what I was. Eventually I said, 'Now? I'm just a person.'

We laughed at my comically lame response, and I moved on, because Amanda started to glance around the room, hoping to engage with someone who had more to offer than just being a person. I tried to think of something else to have ready for the next time I was asked what I did, because I guessed this was going to be a recurring theme in the room.

Seconds later I was talking to someone else. A man this time; he was looking around the room after sending a message on his phone. We made eye contact as I walked past. He slipped his phone into his pocket and held up his glass. 'Warm fizz.' He pulled a face. 'I hate warm fizz.'

I moved towards him and saw his face fall slightly when he realised that I had regarded his remark as an invitation. He was worried in case he got stuck with me.

'So!' I said brightly. 'Quite a night!'

'Well, if you say so.' He looked around the room, apparently close to despair.

'Ah,' I said. 'You seem a bit world-weary. Have you seen all this before?'

'Many times,' he said. 'Too many times.' He turned his attention to me with an effort. 'So, what do you do?'

'I'm Sally, Bill Forth's wife,' I said. I made it sound like a career choice.

'Oh. Yes of course.' He looked out at the room again and his gaze rested briefly on Bill over by the bar. Then he turned back to me, 'Bill Forth's wife. So – is that enough for you?'

Again, I was stumped for a reply, and was toying with telling him to piss off when his phone rang. He gave me a brief nod and retired to the fringes of the room to answer it. I set off again around the room.

I was squeezing past a knot of people all engaged in conversation when a man on the edge of the group moved suddenly and bumped into me with his elbow. He turned around. 'So sorry,' he said, 'didn't see you there.'

'That's all right,' I said. 'Quite a crowd in here.'

'Yes indeed,' he said. He wanted to turn back to the group, but having just pranged me in the arm with his elbow he realised he might have to spend some time talking to me. He held his hand out, 'Tom Forge,' he said. We shook hands.

'Hi Tom,' I said, 'I'm Sally. Sally— '

'Marvellous,' he said. I sensed that he wanted to telescope our conversation into as short a time as possible. 'Hi Sally. So what do you— '

But then She swept by, The Golden One. She was doing a circuit of the room with some of her entourage, to shake hands and spread good will and generally shower us all with gold dust. She stopped to speak to me. 'Sally!' She knew my name. 'Really good of you to stay for the bash. Thank you, I know you're very busy.' She put her hand on my arm. 'Thanks, Sally.' She used my name again. 'What a jamboree politics is.' She gestured towards the room behind her. 'Give them a couple of months and they'll all hate me.' She laughed, and leaned towards me. 'We must get together for a chat. I hear a lot about you, and your teaching work. I'm in awe. Soon – let's get together soon.' And she moved on.

Tom Forge took a renewed interest in me. 'What did you say you did?'

'I'm a lion tamer.'

His eyebrows shot up. 'Good lord,' he said.

And that was much better.

It was ten thirty when Bill and I got into the taxi, and nearly eleven when we got home. On the way back I told Bill I'd had some difficulty explaining to people what I did. He said there was no reason why I should have to explain to anyone what I did, and then he fell asleep. He had a power nap while I looked out of the window, and thought about things. I thought about who I am and what I do. And if it is enough.

I was glad everyone (except Ella – Dan had taken her home at eight o'clock) was still around when we got home, and hadn't left. They were determined to party. Sophie was emotional when we first got back, but soon regained her composure. Dan and Bill slapped each other on the back and said bracing, manly things to each other, and Laura gave Bill a hug and said she loved him and she was glad it was over.

We drank toasts, and laughed, and Baz told some jokes and Bill rang Ella and spoke to her for a little while. Sophie sang, 'I Will Survive' and we all joined in. There was a flurry of excitement a little later when Baz presented Sophie with a ring which he had made himself. It was made from a band of plaited hair, which was gathered into what we thought at first was a pearl, but Baz explained it was a remodelled tooth. Baz said the hair was his own, and so Sophie assumed the tooth was his too. She was so impressed that Baz had been prepared to knock a tooth out of his own head to declare his love for her, that he didn't immediately confess it was a dog's tooth. By the time Baz did own up, we had drunk too much fizz to be disappointed by his lack of commitment.

It was after one o'clock when we went to bed.

***

Jen texted the next morning and said I expect things will get back to normal soon?

And I replied Not if I can help it.

Because I'm not sure now whether normal is enough. I woke up this morning feeling dissatisfied and wanting change. It was a difficult feeling to describe, even to myself, but if I had to summarise it I would say

MP SPOUSE GRAN
SEEKS
NEW LIFE

Acknowledgements

Very many thanks to Kevin and Hetha Duffy at Bluemoose Books for giving me this chance. Bluemoose is a bold, energetic and passionate independent press, and I was lucky to catch their eye.

Thank you to Lin Webb, my editor, for making the edit enjoyable, painless and interesting. Lin's advice has been invaluable, and in addition, she has taught me everything I know about penguin eggs. Many thanks, Lin.

Thanks too, to Lulu Allison, for the illustration on the cover. (I know we worried about her, Lulu, but she's been sitting there a while now, so I think she must be quite comfortable.)

Grateful thanks to Trix Jones, for her helpful and positive feedback over many careful readings of the book.

And thank you to my husband Keith, for his unwavering and unstinting help, support, encouragement and belief, without which there really would be no book. Every single time I thought I'd deleted everything, you managed to find it. XX